The Anam Cara

April D. Berry

To my husband and soulmate, whom I'd find in any lifetime.

Dreams are constructed from the residue of yesterday.
SIGMUND FREUD

Preface

Welcome to the innermost recesses of my dreams. Please keep in mind the story that awaits is full of seemingly impossible and improbable happenings, but what if?

Also, this book is not suitable for those under 18 years of age. As with all my books, there are explicit consensual adult scenes.

I hope you enjoy.

CW: Loss of Parents, Kidnapping, Explicit Sex Scenes, Explicit Language

Chapter 1

The sound of the clock ticking rapped in my eardrums. I was already irritated that I had to retake BIO. What did that have to do with Computer Science anyway? Not that I was sure I wanted to stick to that major, but it was the most recent one I moved to. This professor was tougher than the last. We barely had any class discussions and the reading he assigned was a lot considering all the other courses I had to worry about it. Here I was, probably about to fail the final, again. *Stop it, Viv. You studied.* No sense in worrying until there was something to worry about.

I stopped watching the clock tick on the wall of the small auditorium-style classroom and looked back at the paper, my dark curls hanging over the desk. I drew in a deep breath then read the next question, hoping I made it through this time.

After I handed my exam to the professor, bookbag in arm, I left the class and headed to my ragged sedan. Mom and Dad gave me their old car once I went to college so I could get around easily. They got an upgrade and left me with the "well loved" beast. At least it ran and for a sedan, gas wasn't terrible. I climbed in and headed home, wishing the air conditioner worked better. May in Georgia was sweltering.

Thoughts of the test nagged at me the whole ride home. The rest of my exams were pretty solid, but I wasn't sure about the BIO exam. I was already on thin ice with Mom and Dad since I failed it last year, and this was the first opportunity I had to add it to my courses. They paid for the insurance on my car and gas, but said if I failed another course, I'd have to get a part-time job. I wasn't sure how that would help the situation since I already felt like I was drowning.

I had coasted through college this far, but honestly wasn't sure what my plans were afterwards and couldn't settle on a major. That was a totally different fight. They made it seem like I should be surer of my life by now. But I wasn't even old enough to drink, not legally anyway. Nothing felt right.

Although, I did enjoy learning about programming. Finding work behind the screen of a computer seemed up my alley since I wasn't the most outgoing person. I could be chatty with people I'd grown to know but that always took time. But my skills were likely not going to land me any engineering jobs. How was I supposed to know what I wanted to do with my life at 20 years old? I didn't even commit to plans for the weekend yet.

I pulled into the driveway of our cookie cutter house in our large HOA-ran neighborhood. Everyone's home was two stories with brick on the front and white siding on the back and sides. The yards all looked exactly the same and the grass was perfectly full and green thanks to the weekly lawn treatments everyone paid for. But some did have black doors while others had white.

I walked in through the garage noticing my parent's car wasn't there. It wasn't completely out of the ordinary for them, but they were usually home early on Tuesdays. They were both professors of anthropology at a different college, so their schedules varied greatly day to day. They also traveled a great deal for research. They went to the United Kingdom and visited England and Scotland just last year. I had hoped to go, but I had registered for a make-up class for BIO. But the class was canceled at the last minute, and it was too late for me to go along. Probably for the best. They never took me on work trips, but I had always wanted to visit the UK. I was drawn to it as a child and used to love reading books about it then became fascinated with television shows and fictional books set in the UK. Now I was finally taking the course again and crossing my fingers I didn't fail a second time.

There was some leftover spaghetti in the fridge, so I warmed it and ate in the large and excessively white kitchen, clearing my plate before refilling my water and heading to the living room. I snuggled into the plush grey couch and pulled the soft blanket from the back of it over me as I flipped through the channels. Studying for the exam kept me up late, so my eyes were heavy as I browsed for something to watch. I landed on a familiar show and rested my head on the arm of the couch. Even if I fell asleep, they would wake me when they got home.

I didn't feel as if I had been asleep very long when I heard someone banging on the door. Leaning up, I felt disoriented from the short nap and grabbed around for my phone after pulling the dark curls stuck to the side of my face away. Realizing that I must have left it in the kitchen, I grabbed the remote and clicked the info button for the time. It was just past six p.m.

"Mom, Dad? Are you home?" I asked. There was no movement in the house, but there was another bang on the door. They sometimes needed help with groceries, but they always came in the garage and banged on the interior door for me. The bangs were coming from the front door. I sat still hoping it was a salesman that would take the hint and leave.

Bang, Bang, Bang.

Curious, I rose from the couch and walked to the dining room to peek out to the driveway. A police cruiser? Why were the police here? My mind started replaying all the recent parties I had attended at school. And I did have the car parked in a yellow zone a few days ago, but it was only for five minutes. *Surely, they wouldn't come arrest me for that?*

My heart pounded in my chest as they rapped on the door again. *Be cool, Viv.* It's probably the wrong house, or at best a misunderstanding. No sense in worrying until there was something to worry about.

As another round of bangs echoed through the house, I grabbed the knob and slowly opened the door, my arms immediately crossing over my abundant chest.

"May I help you, officer?"

"Miss, are you related to Henry and Elaine Acworth?" the officer asked.

"Yes," I answered as I nodded slowly.

"Miss," he said as he pointed to his badge, "I'm Officer Jones. May I come inside so we can sit?"

"Um, I'm not sure I feel comfortable with that. Am I in some kind of trouble?"

"Miss, why don't we step inside, and I can explain."

I grabbed the door and closed the space, still poking my head out.

"I really don't feel comfortable with this, sir. So, if I am not in trouble is it okay if I ask you to leave?"

The officer pulled off his hat and stepped back off the small cement landing in the front of the door and onto the sidewalk.

"I understand Miss, and you are not in any kind of trouble. But I'm afraid I have some bad news." The edges of his lips turned down and his bushy eyebrows pinched together over his dark brown eyes.

I crossed my arms again as thoughts swirled in my head. My lips began to tingle, and a tightness formed in my chest. I couldn't pull in a good breath. I glanced over at the mirror in the entryway, my blue eyes popping more than normal as redness filled the whites of my eyes.

"I, I can't breathe. I think I'm having a heart attack. I can't feel my lips," I said in slurs as I tried to get my lips to function.

The officer dropped his hat to the ground and rushed to me as my knees buckled beneath me, grabbing the soft curves of my waist awkwardly. We landed in a crumpled pile on the threshold of the doorway. My mind was still swirling and while things around me sounded distorted, I could tell he was radioing for help. I looked down at my hands that had also gone numb. He pulled his legs from beneath me but sat with me until the ambulance arrived.

Time seemed to pass slowly as my mind became fuzzy but when the ambulance arrived, I was loaded onto a gurney and whisked to the hospital. I lay on the gurney with an oxygen mask over most of my face glancing at the space around me. I had never been in an ambulance. But only one person sat with me, not multiple like you saw on television. There were trays lining the walls and it was bright.

The man sitting with me asked me to move my fingers and toes, flashed lights in my eyes, and repeatedly checked my pulse. My limbs were all numb and my jaw was tight. I couldn't feel my lips at all by now and the tightness in my chest was clamping like a vice grip around me. The fact that the officer never told me what he came to say was only making it worse.

"Miss, can you tell me your name?"

"Bi--Bib," was all I could get out. *So now my name was Bibian?* Wonderful.

"Miss, can you try to breathe regularly? Do you have any conditions you are aware of? Has this happened before?"

The questions came fast but I couldn't make out intelligible words. Luckily, we arrived at the hospital, and I was passed along where nurses and doctors started working and not asking questions.

Hours later, my breathing returned to normal, and all

major conditions were ruled out. No heart attack, no stroke, no blood clots, and no aneurysm. They admitted me to be monitored but the doctor that came by once I was settled into my room said it was likely an anxiety attack.

The doctor was still making notes on his tablet when the door opened and the officer from earlier appeared around the curtain.

"Doctor, may I have a word with her now?" he asked.

The slender, black-haired doctor gave me a tight-lipped smile then nodded to the officer.

"Vivian, I'll be at the nurse's station, and you can hit the button next to your shoulder should you need anything," the doctor said before leaving the room.

I looked up at the round clock hanging on the wall near the nurse's whiteboard. The time was past ten. I looked around the room as the officer stood patiently.

"My parents aren't here," I said plainly.

The officer nodded and looked down at his feet. I looked out the window and let it wash over me that my life would never be the same.

Chapter 2

I had been fortunate to stay unnoticed so long, crouched and peeking from around stacked bags of grain. I couldn't help but watch him. Beads of sweat rolled over his broad shoulders and down his chiseled back. His disheveled, dirty blonde hair was slicked down from the steady stream of sweat and met the top of his shoulders. Every muscle, the obvious ones along with the tiny ones you didn't notice unless they're working, were flexing with each stroke he made. The act of shoveling hay wasn't anything special, but him doing it was nearly sinful to the eye.

The light of day began to fade so I turned to slink away into the barn since I didn't have a lantern with me, but my long skirts caught on something and pulled shovels and pitchforks down in a loud clanking spectacle. He turned toward me to investigate the noise.

My heart slammed in my chest, and I stood petrified as he slowly began moving in my direction. With the light fading, I couldn't make out all the details of his face as he approached but I could see full lips within a full beard and a strong brow. He had a large, rounded chest and his long, lean abdomen flexed as he moved toward me. He reached his arm out and I quietly blew out the breath I had been holding. He was remarkably close, but I still couldn't see his eyes. But I could see a wicked smile turn up his full lips which made me flush all over. Still holding his hand out to me, he said my name, then...

I bolted straight up in my bed, laboring to catch my breath.

Another dream of my mystery man.

The house was quiet and all I could hear were a few nocturnal animals roaming around, hooting outside, and my radio faintly playing The Cranberries. I turned to the clock. It was just three in the morning. The witching hour. Or was that two? That didn't matter, still too early to get up for work, but I needed to jot this down.

I clumsily felt around for my journal and a pen and began documenting every detail. His face was clearer than ever this time, but still no actual memorable picture of the man. *Why does it always feel so real?*

One of these days I would love to get a clear look at his face.

\\\\\\

I had drifted back to sleep after I recorded the dream. I woke again, but this time to a noisy alarm beeping loudly near my head. Ugh...I would be a zombie at work today. I fumbled around and finally found the snooze button after knocking something to the floor with a thud. Before I could even stretch my body or push my long mess of hair out of my face, my door flew open, and my wild hippie aunt stood there with a bat in her hand.

"Viv, I heard a noise, what happened?" she blurted out, waving the weapon over her shoulder.

"Um, maybe the ghost of Christmas past came for you and ran off at the sight of the bat," I grumbled sarcastically. "How did you get in here so fast?"

Aunt Rose walked over, picked my journal up off the floor, and passed it to me.

"Another mystery man dream? What was it this time, dear? Spill!" She jumped onto the bed and swung her bird-legs together like a schoolgirl waiting on the latest gossip. It would have been cuter if she wasn't in her late sixties and wearing a raggedy old bath robe that was so worn it was hard to tell if it was originally its current shade of beige or used to be dove white.

"Nothing fancy to tell Auntie," I sighed, "just some faceless man bailing hay." She grabbed my hand with her small frail one, long skinny fingers around mine, and gave a warm smile that made me forget I was irritated by her early intrusion.

"I think it's good you journal them," she exclaimed while patting my hand. "I think they mean something, but I just don't know what, yet." She sprang up from the bed, her thin but elegant stature slowly exiting back the way she came, carrying her bat with her.

I stretched my body and exhaled a deep, tired breath before I threw my white fluffy duvet cover back and tucked my feet into my slippers. My aunt's home was one of great childhood memories and warmth, but I hadn't gotten used to the cold hardwood floors in my bedroom just yet. Or saying it was my home now.

Aunt Rose was already pouring coffee for us as I walked into the kitchen, so I grabbed a mug and we both sat at the breakfast nook overlooking the backyard. It was a beautiful sunny morning but the condensation on the windows told me the air outside was cool. It was late November in Georgia, and that could mean seventy-degree nights or thirty-degree nights.

"It froze last night you know," Aunt Rose started in on me as I sat down. "I had to go down and cover the plants and bring what I could inside. You would have helped I'm sure, had you been here." She sipped her coffee as she looked out the window. Her yard and porch were the envy of the town. She certainly had a green thumb. She spent so much time and money on her plants and flowers, she'd never let them see a touch of frost.

I could tell from her tone she didn't approve of my late return to the house. It had only been a few months since I'd moved here, at her request. We hadn't quite figured out our roles or how to play them.

"I would have. I'm sorry," I said lightly while letting out a defeated breath, "but I was at the shop sorting through a new lot brought in and just lost track of time."

She put her mug down, then took my mug from me and placed it on the table. She grasped both hands and looked me square in the eye.

"Viv, you can't keep doing this," she pleaded. "You need to make friends. Go out. Be young while you still can! It's been nearly a year and you can't just work and have fantasy man dreams and die."

I glared at her a little for the not-so-pep-talk.

"It's only been six months, Auntie, and the first was mostly me on the phone dealing with the estate after we got the funerals taken care of." I reminded her. "You asked me to come help you around the house and work in the shop and that's what I've done. You didn't lose both parents in one swoop, so please don't tell me how to live."

She let go of my hands and I saw her thin lip quiver gently. The warmth she had moments ago grew cold, turning down the lines on her face with tears welling up in her crystal blue eyes, making them shimmer.

"You're right, I didn't lose my parents in one swoop," she snapped, "but I did lose my sister and one of my oldest friends." She stood graciously and tilted her chin up to knock the tears back into her head. "I have to go get dressed. I'll see you later at the shop."

As she walked away, I could hear each creaky step as she

made her way to her bedroom. Now we both felt terrible and all she was trying to do was help.

I waited for her to leave before I went up to get dressed myself. While walking in front of my full-length mirror I stopped briefly and took in the drowsy sight of myself. I had my dad's brown, wavy hair. But it was thick and even the best of flat irons couldn't straighten it. I kept it long so I could pull it up and not have to fool with it. Just comb it wet and go or toss it into a messy bun. My mother had kept her hair short, and she would wake up early to style it every day. No thank you; I appreciate sleep more than my appearance. I imagined I'd look like a dark-stained cotton ball with mine short anyway. Of course, Mom's hair was thinner and not as wavy as mine, more like Aunt Rose's. But Aunt Rose kept hers long and left it natural as her greys grew in.

I had many of Mom's features, like the blue eyes with defined dark brows and the high cheekbones, but also many of Dad's like his straight nose and almost squared jawline.

Glancing at the clock I realized I needed to hustle. I tossed on my skinny jeans, my fuzzy boots, and found a pink plaid tunic that was thick and warm, but thin enough I could wear my jacket over it. One more look in the mirror to tousle my brown curls into submission and look presentable.

Had my curves gotten bigger? I'd never been thin, and my chest was a nuisance. But since moving in with Aunt Rose, I had eaten a lot of fast food and take out. I needed to be mindful of that before I had to buy new clothes. I looked back at my face in the mirror and the image of my parents staring back started to haunt me. God, I missed them. I took a deep breath, shook it off, then grabbed a hair tie from the counter and headed out.

Aunt Rose liked to be at the shop well before opening time, but she didn't mind that I went in later as most customers didn't come until at least lunchtime. Luckily, it was a short walk to the square from her, well *our* house, so I took the time to clear my mind.

I had been raised in a suburb that boasted a small-town feel, but that was just a farce to attract new families into the once rural area that became riddled with new neighborhoods anytime a developer found a patch of grass or trees to clear off.

I didn't leave much behind when the accident happened and staying in college wasn't an option. I could barely remember what day it was, much less imagine keeping to my class schedule. I'd only been alone at my childhood house for a week when Aunt Rose invited me to move in with her and help her out. She said it would be a great weight off her shoulders as she was getting older and sicklier, and it was hard to keep up the house and tend to the antique shop alone. When I realized there was little way for me to make payments on the house, especially while I waited on the insurance money, it seemed the best course of action to sell it and live with Aunt Rose until I figured out when, or if, I was going back to college. Or maybe until I figured out what to do with my life. I was never sure college was right for me. How can someone not old enough to buy alcohol make such a decision?

My grades were decent, but I changed majors three times in the two years I attended, and the accident happened right before enrollment for fall semester, so I just let it go. Good thing my parents weren't here to see that total waste of money. They were loving but driven and expected the same from me. Aunt Rose was always so fun and carefree. I felt guilty that I'd wanted to spend so much time with her growing up once the time with my parents was cut short. And I had felt guilty ever since the accident for leaving school because it would have made them all so proud for me to graduate, find a great paying job, and settle down.

I sold the house with the help of Auntie's friend and was able to pay off the mortgage, all credit balances and the car, and had plenty left for myself between the sale and the insurance payout. The one thing I can say for my parents is they were organized and took care of their debts. Still, it was overwhelming to be the adult at twenty years old, responsible for the settling of your own parent's things.

Aunt Rose had been a blessing and let me grieve on my own time. At least until today. I wish I hadn't reacted so harshly because deep down I knew she was right. Maybe it was time for me to start living again, at least to try to get out of my funk, but...*how*? I had some friends over the years, but no one close, and the introvert in me was okay with that. I had spent summers and lots of weekends with Aunt Rose when Mom and Dad were away on business trips. I always loved the sounds, the smells, the feel of the town and her house.

Aunt Rose had an older house near the town square, one of the oldest in the county. It had a very southern charm feel to it and most certainly had lots of life in it. It had a large white front porch spanning across the whole front of the house, which was a faded shade of white, complete with a porch swing on one side and it always had huge seasonal planters scattered on the corners and by the door. It was a two-story house but wasn't huge. It was quaint, cozy, and lived in. There was an overhang above the porch that I would climb onto from my bedroom window when I was younger. As with most older homes, there was a cellar below the house but as a child I was petrified to even open the door to go down. As an adult, that fear hadn't changed much. Aunt Rose was an older country woman, so it probably just had canned fruits and veggies from her garden and maybe some baking supplies since the kitchen didn't have a pantry.

There were some kids around when I was younger and we got along fine, but I only hung out with or talked to them when I was in town. I think they let me play just to be polite, although we did spend a lot of time at Aunt Rose's because she always had the best snacks and kept icy pops in the freezer in the summer for us. Now most of the kids I had known here were grown and gone. Some were still in college, and some had gotten married and moved out to the faux rural areas that you could find all over the state. So, me re-entering society would require making new friends and I hadn't done that in so long. Plus, who would want to deal with such a damaged girl?

My thoughts and reminiscing were interrupted by the sweet smell of dough and sugary confections mixed with strong coffee. The local donut shop was just ahead so I decided donuts and coffee could make a nice peace offering for Aunt Rose.

I stepped into Dawson's Donuts and immediately was greeted by Mr. Dawson. Then I stood and waited my turn as I looked over one of the small menus by the door.

There were two people ahead of me in the small, but quaint, establishment. I could hear Mrs. Dawson in the back humming away as she prepped dough and checked the fryers. I was looking down at the menu still when suddenly a sturdy figure plowed into me. *Shit!*

It took me a moment, but when I gathered my wits after the impact, I was staring into the chest of someone. My gaze traveled north to see a beautiful man looking as sheepish as I felt.

He immediately began apologizing and fumbling to recover the shape of the box he held and tried to knock powdered sugar off my black leather jacket. I wish I could say I was stunned by the box of donuts plunged into me, but I was more so trying to gather myself as I took in the sight of this tall and broad-shouldered man. Something was so familiar about him. Maybe he grew up here and I just didn't recognize him as an adult?

He had soft and beautiful blue eyes with specks of green in them set under a prominent brow bone. His hair was a bit shaggy, but in a stylish way, and was a lovely dark golden color. His full beard surrounded full rosy lips that turned into a bright smile, once the commotion was over.

He reached for my hand and started to apologize again, and I was hit with a shot of electricity as our skin connected. He fumbled his words then pulled his hand away.

I shook it off. "It's really okay, I shouldn't have been standing right in front of the door," I said, trying to reassure him the incident wasn't that serious. "I must need more coffee."

His voice was smooth and low. "Can I at least pay for your coffee?" he offered.

"Maybe another time." I felt like an idiot. This insanely handsome man was trying to buy me coffee and I declined.

He smiled and finally exited with his donuts. Once he was gone, my head was still spinning at the thought of him when I realized the other three people had been staring at us the whole time.

Mr. Dawson finally broke the silence. "What'll ya have, Dan?" The gentleman in front of me gave a small order for a coffee and one donut and already had exact change ready. I stepped up and smiled like a child who had been busted with their hand in the cookie jar.

"So, you met Jake I see." Mr. Dawson winked. "I don't imagine he's been by the antique shop. What can I get ya, dear?"

His wife yelled at him to mind his business, so I chuckled a bit and asked for two coffees and a dozen mixed.

"Jake hasn't been in town long, either ya know," the jolly but nosy man informed me. "I'm not surprised the two of you haven't run into each other. Good kid. Anywho, here ya are, that's $15.90, dear."

I handed him a twenty and while I waited on change, I asked about this Jake person. "So, did Jake move here with his family then if he just got to town?"

The rotund man gave a huge smirk and said, "If you're asking if he's here with a wife, the answer is no. His dad's lived here for years but his parents were divorced at a young age. He was only here a couple weeks during the summers and some holidays but normally they weren't here for that, off somewhere exotic. He's been here several months working for his dad. I think he has an apartment outside of the square. A man of his age doesn't want to move home ya see?"

I felt my cheeks get pink at the idea that someone near my age shouldn't be living with a family member. I grabbed my items, smiled, and gingerly walked out to be certain I didn't run into anyone on the way out.

I walked down the sidewalk of the square in front of the various shops and restaurants and up to the door of Yesterday's Treasures then gently tapped the door with my foot. My hands were full, and I didn't want to spill the sacrificial coffee to get back into Auntie's good graces. She came to the door and a wide smile spread across her face.

"What's this?" she asked, nodding to the goodies. I walked past her then put the donuts behind the counter and handed her a coffee.

"This is me saying I'm sorry. You were right and I shouldn't have snapped at you."

Her weathered blue eyes became misty again but this time with the upward wrinkles of a grin.

"I just want the best for you, Viv. You've been through a lot and you're so young. You still have a lot of life ahead of you but only if you get out and live it."

She reached out and gave me a hug, but a real hug that transfers love and warmth into the depths of your soul. One that only a mother, or the best auntie, can give. After a few moments, we both took a deep breath and let out a good sigh, followed by a chuckle, before letting go.

"A lady came by earlier with a new lot, but you've been so meticulous with the new items I left it all over there for you," Aunt Rose said as she nodded to the back where I'd come to enjoy sorting and pricing items as we got them in.

I grabbed my coffee and headed that way. She followed me with the donuts and napkins, so I took a napkin and grabbed a donut. I hadn't eaten yet and it was nearly eleven. I glanced over the lot since I had a donut in my hand and mentioned the odd interaction I had with Jake.

"Ah yes, he's a handsome young man. If I were twenty or thirty years younger, I would take him for a spin."

A bit of coffee came out of my nose and blood rushed to my cheeks. Aunt Rose grinned and gave a knowing nod.

"Yes, he was good looking, but couldn't get away from me fast enough," I finally got out after my choking fit.

What I didn't mention is that when he grabbed my hand, it felt like a bolt of electricity had run through my arm and throughout every nerve-ending in my body. I was remembering that moment and trying to figure out the familiarity I'd felt when I realized Aunt Rose was trying to get my attention.

"Honey, are you okay? You totally spaced out."

I told her I was fine, only tired from waking in the middle of the night. I promised her I would come home at a decent time tonight. I did need a good night's sleep.

The new lot we received today had mostly decent home items that didn't require much refurbishing but there was an old album that had some pictures and old letters. Things that would take time to sort through. I set it off to the side to go back to later and started pricing the other items.

Before I knew it, it was a few minutes past closing time.

Aunt Rose had left some time ago, but I hadn't realized it had been that long. I stretched my arms over my head with a groan, stiff after sitting so long with no customers. It had been a slow day so there was little for me to do to close up. I made sure to grab the trash and turn the main lights off before locking up. I tossed the trash in the shared dumpster in the side ally and began my short walk home.

As I walked past the neighborhood bar, someone came rushing out of the door and crashed into me. *How did this happen twice in one day?*

I stumbled a few steps but quickly got my bearings. As I did, I looked over and sucked in a short breath at the sight in front of me. It was Jake again, looking even more handsome than this morning if that were possible.

We both laughed a little this time and he again apologized vehemently. He offered to take me into the bar for a drink to make up for it.

"Well while that sounds nice, I won't be twenty-one for another few weeks."

He smiled and said, "That's ok, I'm just twenty-three. The only reason I go in there is they have good food, and the owners are good friends with my dad."

I smiled and turned to walk.

Jake cleared his throat and walked with me. "Sorry again for running into you...*again.*"

"If I didn't know better, I'd think you were trying to run into me." We both laughed nervously. "So, what brought you to town?" *How lame.* I had to say something else quickly to recover. "It's Jake, right? I'm Vivian Acworth but everyone just calls me Viv."

He grinned and confirmed his name was Jake. He jutted

his chin out with a curious look. "Wait, you're named after the town?"

I laughed and told him we had family ties but none of my direct ancestors founded the city.

"Oh, I see. I've been working for my dad. He owns Adams' Law Firm. I believe he thought it would encourage me to go back to law school."

"You were in law school? What happened?"

He sighed with a slight grin. "I did pre-law in undergrad but loved the investigation aspect, so I decided to be a detective. But dad offered me a much better salary to do his office's investigations."

"How do you like it, working for your dad?" I asked.

"Well, I thought the money was good, so I took it. Plus, we were never that close because I lived with Mom, so I thought maybe this was a chance to build that relationship ya know?" He ran a hand through his hair with a tight smile, making me think the relationship still wasn't what he had hoped. "But I stay busy during the day while he's at the office or at court and don't see him as much as I thought. It's not all bad. Definitely not as dangerous as being a police detective. What about you, how did you end up here? I don't remember seeing you before."

We slowly walked together in the direction I needed to go. I hadn't had to explain to anyone how I came to be here since the accident, and I barely knew Jake, so I didn't want to break down in front of him.

I was trying to gather a reasonable but vague response when he took my hand. That stopped me dead in my tracks. The electricity from his touch shot up my arm into my chest. *Why did that keep happening?*

I was barely breathing when he used his other hand to tip

my face up towards him.

"You don't seem to want to talk about this, and that's ok." His face was serious but inviting. "But may I ask you something?"

While I was relieved that he let me off the hook about how I came to be here, I was reeling at the electric charge flowing through me. Unable to speak, I simply nodded.

"Could I take you to dinner sometime?" he asked me, and I let out a small sigh.

"Yes," I nodded, happy I could get out words. "That sounds good." I winced at my own response. "Maybe this weekend sometime?"

He let my hand go to pull his wallet out and handed me a business card. I mentioned I worked at Yesterday's Treasures.

"Great, why don't I meet you there Friday night and we can go grab a bite then?" he asked.

I was trying not to smile like an idiot when I replied, "Sounds good."

Looking around, I noticed we had ended up in front of my house. I awkwardly looked down when he reached out his hand and grabbed mine again. It was soft but firm and, again, every nerve in my body was firing all at once. He stepped closer and I my heart raced as my mouth watered. Jake leaned down and kissed me on the cheek, longer than a peck but still very innocent and sweet. But when his lips touched my skin, I felt the nerves firing like fireworks being shot off. Warmth accumulated between my thighs as his beard tickled my face. I inhaled his scent as he lingered close. It was manly but citrusy at the same time. I took a breath to calm myself and softly pulled my hand from his. When I looked up, he looked as shaken as I felt.

Taking a deep breath, he stepped back a little.

"I assume this is your house we are standing in front of?"

"Yes, this is me. Thanks for the ki-I mean walk home. I guess I'll see you Friday night."

I turned toward the front steps and didn't look back as I fumbled with my house key. I could feel his stare boring holes in the back of my head. I finally got the door open to find my aunt had been staring out the window. She smirked at me, turned off the lamp, and walked upstairs. It was only a quarter past nine and there was no way I could sleep now.

Chapter 3

I went upstairs and decided to take a nice long shower to relax. As I waited for the water to heat up, which took a bit since the house and pipes were so old, I stared into the mirror and inspected myself. I leaned into the mirror checking for puffiness under my eyes, any signs of lines, and then did a teeth check hoping it was all clear since I had just been talking with that incredibly attractive man. The sparks felt to be there from both of us but looking into the mirror I couldn't imagine why.

I was pretty basic at best. Not ugly, just not anything special. And you could tell by looking at me I needed a good night's sleep. My eyes were tired, and my skin was pale from hiding out here or at the shop all the past months. He, on the other hand, was exceptionally good-looking. Definitely well rested and very fit. And he must get a decent amount of time outdoors because he wasn't very fair skinned, but not overly weathered. I looked so long in the mirror I began questioning why he even asked me out.

Luckily, steam started filling up the bathroom and the mirror became a fogged-up wall, so I took a deep breath and stepped into the shower. The hot water trickling over me felt good and I took time to enjoy the warmth and calming sensation.

As I closed my eyes, I had flashes of the day's encounters with Jake. I tried to shake it off and opened my eyes, but there he was again and again every time I closed my eyes. Why had I reacted that way when he touched me? It's not like I've never been touched by a man, but this was different. Instead of a small swarm of butterflies in my stomach, he made every fiber of my being jolt with some other worldly flash of energy that came in waves over and over every time he touched me. Even to be near him and hear his deep, soothing voice made my heart race and either sped up my breathing or stopped it altogether.

I was still lost in thought when the water began to go cold. Deciding I definitely needed to snap out of it and get some rest, I hurried to wash and quickly turned off the water and grabbed my towel. I finished up at the sink then headed to my room to get dressed in some warm pajamas.

It was past ten now, but I knew sleep wouldn't come easy tonight. I climbed into bed and grabbed my journal off the nightstand and began turning the pages. Months' worth of dreams with the same man. There was never a clear picture of his face, but I knew it was the same man each time. And stranger than that, many of the locations were the same. Looking through the scribbled pages, I realized there were four different settings and always me and him, whoever he was.

I saw a therapist briefly after the accident and the dreams had started by then. The therapist suggested I keep a sleep journal, not just to document my dreams, but to track my actual sleep. With any trauma, sleep could become an issue, but she wanted to be sure it was improving. And of course, she used the dreams to explain some underlying thoughts I was trying to work out on my own.

I would admit, therapy helped with the initial shock of it all, but eventually we weren't really dealing with the grief anymore so much as my life in general. Even though I quit going, I felt the journal was helpful. It was the only thing I had real control over, even though I couldn't make sense of the dreams.

Months had gone by now with these vivid dreams happening at least several times a week. In some we were only acquainted, even though I certainly was attracted to him, while in others we were an actual couple. But it was only ever bits and pieces. Snapshots of us together.

The more I flipped through the pages of my journal, the more I realized I'd felt today's feelings with Jake before, in these dreams. I stopped turning the pages. How did this Jake person remind me of my mystery dream man? That was a tad unsettling, but perhaps I was longing for some comfort from someone besides my aunt and my dreams were filling that void until I met someone. Was Jake that person?

This was all silly. I just met this man. *One walk does not equal swoon, Viv.*

I slammed the journal shut and put it on the table. Then I reached further to turn my radio that doubled as a phone charger onto my eighties playlist and switched off the lamp. Maybe the sound of The Cure would provide enough of a distraction to help me drift off to sleep.

Chapter 4

I was sitting at my vanity in my sleep gown, carefully combing my wavy hair. As I combed, I inspected my face, looking for lines or signs of aging. There was quiet music in the distance, but I couldn't make it out well. I saw through the shutters that it was getting late as the sun was going down.

I decided to light the candles before it became too dark to find the flint. I didn't want to have to stumble through the room and open my door with just my sleep gown on. The sun went down quickly but I had lit just enough candles that I could see where I was walking. It was warm so there was no need to light the fire, it would just make the room insufferable. In fact, it was so warm that I went to pop open the shutters to let some air into the room before I laid down.

As I pushed them open, I saw the faint outline of a man sneaking around the dirt road below. I knew it was him. My heart was racing. Would he be seen? Did he dare come here for me?

I stepped away from the window and tiptoed to the large wooden door, trying to not make the wooden floors creak beneath me. I was already becoming flushed at the thought of him here, in my room, this time of night in my current state. If either of us were caught, well, we both would have repercussions.

I looked around quickly to find a more appropriate cover other than just my sleep gown and remembered my winter sleep robe in my wardrobe. I quickly put it on and tightened the belt to hold it closed. Just as I was doing so, I heard the light tapping on the door.

I gingerly rushed over and cracked the door. While it was dark, I knew it was him. I opened the door enough for him to push inside then made sure to slip the bolt shut. As I turned around, I saw him there, close. I then realized I hadn't lit nearly enough candles to light the room and couldn't make out his face. But that didn't matter. What mattered is he was with me.

He paused briefly, watching me and while I couldn't see his face, I could see his breathing was heavy from the motion of his shoulders and chest. Then suddenly, he quickly but quietly came to me and grabbed me hard around the waist with one arm and grabbed the back of my head with the other. Before I could say anything, he drew me into him and kissed me hard. His strong lips parted mine and he entered my mouth. My knees felt weak, but I reached my arms around him to pull him even closer and kissed him back hard. After several moments, though, I pulled away and began to say something when he put a finger to my lips and instructed me to not speak. I wanted so badly to say we couldn't, to profess my love, to tell him to stop, to tell him to keep going, to tell him to leave, to tell him we could run away. But words couldn't pass my lips as his hands began to loosen the belt on my robe and find my breasts over the thin fabric of the gown underneath. My skin tingled at his touch, and I was at his mercy as his hands softly grazed my nipples.

He moved the robe off my shoulders and pushed it slowly off my arms. I stood there shaking knowing with just the right angle of candlelight he would be able to see through my gown completely. His hands continued to run lightly over the fabric, then he started to slide the top of the gown off my shoulders and...

The alarm felt like it was yelling at me this time. I let out my breath and rolled over and flung my arm out to try to hit the snooze button to silence the alarm quickly. I lay there still catching my breath as my heart pounded in my chest. *It was him again.* We had been there before but not alone in the bedroom at night.

The room seemed so familiar, but I hadn't ever been there except for my dreams. It seemed like some sort of old place. Maybe Colonial Williamsburg where they have everything setup like you were in that time period still? But I had only read about that and seen pictures of it, I had never been there.

I found my journal and logged what all I could get out. As I wrote I noticed my pulse began to race. Once I finished the entry, I put the journal back in the drawer on the nightstand and took a deep breath and turned my radio off. After a few deep breaths and a good stretch, I put on my slippers and headed down for coffee. I could smell something amazing as soon as I opened my door.

Aunt Rose was up, already dressed, and had made me breakfast.

"Good morning, dear," she practically sang out. "You look well rested! I'm glad you took my advice and have been coming home earlier this week." She grabbed my shoulders for a quick squeeze then kept buzzing around the kitchen.

It had been a few days since the two chance encounters with Jake and tonight was the night. He had asked me to dinner on Friday. *How was it already Friday?*

"It's been nice, you were right," I sighed out with honesty. "I feel more human now that I got some rest. I can't believe you cooked all this!" She had a feast prepared.

"Well, I know you have your dinner date later and you don't want to act famished so you can start your day with a big meal and then be sure to snack all day!" Leave it to an older southern woman to think it's inappropriate to eat in front of a man. I never took Aunt Rose as so old school.

I smiled and ate my food. It was nice to have a real breakfast. My parents were always leaving for work early, so I usually just had cereal or pop tarts. When a southern woman cooks for you, it just tastes better than most food. Almost as though you can taste the love.

"Why are you up and dressed so early, Auntie?" I asked while shoveling food in my mouth.

"I have an appointment this morning. Just my annual physical. Gotta make sure all this fabulousness stays in good working order," she said as she stretched her arms across the length of her body. "Can you open the shop today?"

"Sure, totally," I mumbled out with a mouthful of pancakes.

I gobbled up the delicious breakfast quickly then hurried to get dressed and out the door.

Aunt Rose dropped me off since she was driving to her appointment anyway. When I moved in with her, I brought my car and we started sharing it. I could walk to the shop from the house, and she was older, so it seemed right to let her use it. She was letting me live with her after all. I opened the shop and went back to working on a few items needing to be refurbished. A few patrons came in and browsed and made small talk but didn't make purchases.

I had started to put some of the new items on the display when a middle-aged man wearing a dress coat and a hat entered.

I greeted him. "Hi there, let me know if I can help with anything."

He came straight over and removed his hat. He then asked urgently, "Do you have any gemstones?"

I nodded and pointed as I started to walk to the area where we kept what little we had. "We don't get many, but what we have would be over here."

He looked through the shelf and shook his head. "I am looking for a large, light red or pink stone," he said without looking up at me. "It won't be cut, just a raw gemstone."

I nodded and thought for a minute. "I'm sorry, I don't recall one like that. But I can always ask my aunt when she returns. She's the owner so maybe she can point us in the right direction. Do you have a card or want to leave your info with me, and I can call you when I find out something?"

He straightened up. "That won't be necessary. No need to mention it to her. Good day to you." He put his hat back on then tipped it to me and quickly left.

Strange. But working in an antique shop taught me that strange things and people happen. I shrugged it off and went back to placing new items out on the displays. Aunt Rose finally came in and she barely looked at me.

"Hey, is everything ok?" I asked as she put her coat on the rack and forced a smile through tight lips.

"Oh, honey yes, everything is fine. I just got shook up." She shook her head and smiled to dismiss anything bad. "The doc wants me to have another mammogram. The one I just had was inconclusive, so I gotta go back. I'm sure it's nothing." She walked to me and put one arm around my shoulders. "I shouldn't worry, and neither should you!" She was right. *No sense in worrying until there was something to worry about.*

"Auntie, those things happen. I wouldn't worry about it. What do you think about the display?"

We quickly moved onto work, and she was constantly reminding me to eat so I didn't seem ravenous on my date. She stayed much later than normal when it finally occurred to me, she was waiting on him to show up.

At half past seven, Jake came to the shop. Aunt Rose jumped up and walked over dramatically to greet him. He shook her hand and introduced himself. I walked over and said it would be just a bit before I could close up.

"Nonsense, I will close up, you kids go get a table while you still can! It's Friday night, date night," Aunt Rose said, tossing her arms up like I had gone mad. I smiled at Jake before asking Aunt Rose to go to the back with me for a second.

"Auntie you haven't closed in months. It's dark and late."

She was shaking her head at me before I even finished then said, "Exactly! It's already dark and late so half an hour isn't going to change anything. Plus, I have the car, so I won't be walking in the dark. It's fine, you go, enjoy that man!" She grabbed my shoulders and planted a good smooch on my cheek. As she pushed me toward the front of the shop, I grabbed my bag from the counter. "You two kids have fun; I will see *you* in the morning," she said as she practically kicked us both out while giving me a wicked grin.

It was bustling on the square despite the cool temps. I figured we would have to wait outside for a while anywhere we went. I didn't know where we were going but Jake reached his arm out for me to grab it, so I obliged.

We were both bundled up with coats and gloves now, but that didn't stop the waves of electricity from flowing through me. I tried to act natural and was happy for the chill in the air that I could blame my shivers on. We exchanged some niceties on the walk around about our days then we stopped in front of Vincent's, the only Italian restaurant on the square.

"Do you like Italian?" he asked.

"I love it, but that line looks like it'll be a bit of a wait!"

He smirked a little and told me to wait where I was. He

came back in just a minute, if that, and reached his hand out to me to come in.

I took his hand, we walked inside, and immediately were following the maître d' up a flight of stairs to the party room area. I trailed behind a little nervous and curious at the same time and couldn't help but appreciate the view ahead of me. He had on a grey wool peacoat that hugged him enough to show his broad shoulders and back that ran down into his trim waist. And his jeans weren't skintight but also didn't leave much for the imagination.

There were a couple rooms bustling with corporate events according to the signs outside the rooms. We walked past both, then down a short hall. I had never been upstairs here before, but I imagined the hall was leading to the kitchen. Instead, the maître d' opened the door and nodded for us to enter.

I walked in and there were only four round red booths in a large room, in their own little cozy corners, giving plenty of privacy while seated. The back of the booths had stained glass going up the back to the ceiling keeping each booth semi-private. It was dimly lit and besides the traditional Italian music playing in the background, it was quiet. Much quieter than downstairs or the party rooms.

I went to the table we were directed to and sat down once we took our coats off. It was a circular booth, so I scooted in, not quite to the middle, to allow us to face each other, and some space between us. I was still trying to calm myself from the arm holding and the whole mysterious walk up and through the restaurant.

A server promptly came over and placed a napkin in my lap and handed me a large one-page menu then handed one to Jake as well, no napkin in the lap for him, though. He then offered a tasting of the house wines, but Jake quickly declined and asked for a large pitcher of water along with anything I'd like. I nodded in agreement to the water. The server then asked if any appetizers could be ordered and went over the specials before stepping away.

It had been a long time since I had eaten out, much less at a place as nice as this. And it was even more intriguing in this room than the main dining area that I had sat in as a child with my parents or Aunt Rose.

The menu we received only had a few options listed. Jake looked over and asked if I knew what I wanted. I wasn't sure, I hadn't snacked all day as Aunt Rose tried to push on me and I was famished. Everything sounded delightful.

"I'm not sure, do you come here often? What's good?"

He chuckled and said, "Honestly, I haven't eaten here since I was a child, but we just assisted Mr. Ricci with a very nice settlement so I called in a favor when you agreed to have dinner with me."

I felt blood rush to my cheeks, so I put the menu up to my face to try to hide it. The server came back with the water and some bread.

"If I may, can we both have the special this evening?" Jake asked the server. He looked to me as if making sure I was ok with this bold assumption, but I honestly was too nervous to decide on my meal, so I smiled in reassurance that it was a good idea.

Once the server collected the menus and hustled away, Jake took a deep breath and let it out slowly. He was looking intently but warmly at me, "So, Vivian, I must admit, I'm a little nervous. You're awfully quiet." I was sipping water when he made this declaration, so I took my time to finish and set the glass down.

I shrugged trying to be nonchalant, "I'm not sure why you would be nervous, you asked me, remember?" A big smile stretched across his face, and he leaned slightly closer. I must have straightened up quickly because he grabbed my hand, gently, and told me to relax.

"I just haven't been on a date in a long time," he started, still smiling. "But for some reason we kept running into each other, so I figured fate was nudging us. Do you believe in that sort of thing?" he asked.

I honestly had never really given much thought to it. It was a scary thing, fate. If I believed in it, did that mean I believed it was my parent's time to die?

I pulled in a deep breath then slowly let it out before answering. "I'm not sure I do. But-I'm not complaining about running into you more than once. Besides that, what made you ask me out and go through so much trouble for this?" I asked, motioning to the opulent room we sat in together.

He leaned back to his original seating space and thought for a moment. "Well, I do believe in fate," he answered with a raised eyebrow. "I also believe I know a beautiful woman when I see one. I brought you here," he said motioning to the room we were in, "because it's quiet enough we can talk without yelling and enjoy each other's company. Here is a better question, though, why did you accept?"

I took another sip from my water, partly to buy time for a decent response and partly to cool myself off. Each time he looked at me, spoke to me, it was as if I was in a dream. His deep and soothing voice washed over me like warm ocean water every time he spoke. He was strikingly handsome, successful, maybe even more than he let on, and seemed very gentlemanly. I still couldn't figure out what exactly made him ask me here.

"Well, a girl's gotta eat," I finally said, shrugging and grinning to lighten the tension that was growing between us.

We both let out a small laugh but then I finally answered him, "Fate may be a strong word, but it did seem odd to me that we kept running into each other. Plus, you seemed like you probably aren't a serial killer." We both laughed again and suddenly our first course was being placed in front of us.

As we savored the Caesar salads, we both were a little quiet, but I kept catching him watching me. As the Chicken Francese was brought out, one of us occasionally asked how the other was enjoying it and made comments about the server, seeming as though he floated in and out like a ghost, so quick and quiet. I kept cracking small jokes to dispense the tension I was feeling, but his constant gaze was making it difficult.

The server returned after we finished the main course and asked if we wanted dessert. I was going to say no as I was stuffed, and Aunt Rose's warning was playing in my mind. But Jake spoke up before I could and asked for cheesecake and Death by Chocolate. He looked over at me as the server walked away, his grin putting me over the edge. His deep blue eyes turned glossy and were fixed on me as he slightly leaned toward me. I was out of witty quips, so I looked around the room we were sitting in together still feeling his intensity. I wasn't used to someone who looked like him looking at me.

Once the server returned with dessert and poured coffee into our cups, he exited quickly again. Not a long enough interruption to quell the heat at the table. *Chill, Viv, act natural.*

I was carefully adding cream to my coffee and when I looked up Jake was holding a piece of the chocolate cake out to me on a fork. He motioned for me to take the bite, so I leaned in as elegantly as possible and grabbed the bite of cake from the fork. It was so delicious I made a face and a little mmm sound.

He took a bite and exclaimed in a low rumble, "I see why they call it Death by Chocolate." He scooped up a forkful of the cheesecake and again held it out for me and nodded to it, so I took the bite and tried to be less obvious this time. It was rich and delicious, but nothing compared to the face Jake made as he took a bite, head cocked to the side, eyes gently closed, and a slight lick of his full bottom lip. I wasn't sure if I was more jealous of his lip or the tongue licking it.

I felt myself staring, so I picked up my coffee to take a sip as an excuse to avert my eyes. But I could feel him watching me still and was getting flustered, suddenly thinking of him doing more than just sitting across from me. *Vivian, snap out of it.*

Finally, I spoke up as casually as I could muster. "So, tell me, do you plan to stay here and continue to work with your dad's firm?"

He took a sip of coffee and placed the cup on the table but still held the handle, never breaking his gaze, but his eyes were warm as they held steady on me.

"I'm not sure. Sometimes I think he's right, I should go back to college," he said as he let some tension out of his shoulders. "But sometimes I just feel content to do what I'm doing. I imagine if I don't do the former, he will tire of me, and I may have to seek employment elsewhere. And in small towns like this, the Sheriff's detectives don't often need replacing. But for now, I just live day to day. What about you?" he asked pointedly. "Are you in school or taking time off? The nearest university is a bit of a drive from here for daily commuting."

I ran my finger around the rim of my mug and suddenly felt my jaw clenching. I hadn't said any of this out loud to anyone. At first, I was trying to find a way to get out of this conversation, but I briefly moved my eyes back to him and something came over me as I looked into his attentive and caring eyes. His smile was slight, but soft. My jaw loosened and my shoulders slowly fell down from their usual fixed location above my collarbone. Before I knew it, I was spilling everything.

It all just came pouring out like a dam had broken. But he sat, leaned toward me, and watched me tell my story, listening intently. I started with how I lost my parents earlier in the year in a terrible car accident. It was a hit and run and neither the other car nor driver was ever identified which made it difficult to gain closure. I explained I sold my childhood home, moved in with Aunt Rose, and how surreal that experience was. Then I told him I left college and honestly wasn't sure if I was ever going back but felt horribly guilty for quitting. That the only company I have had for months was Aunt Rose and the few patrons we get in the shop frequently that know me now.

After I finally got it all out, I took a deep breath then looked down. I was horrified with myself when I realized I had just given him a synopsis of the worst year of my life. Unsure of what to do next I finally began blabbering, "I'm sorry, I can't believe I just unloaded all of that on you. I guess I just needed to get that out."

I forced myself to look up at him and he didn't look ready to run but I wasn't sure what was going through his mind, so I continued nervously speaking, "I haven't told anyone the whole story, not that way anyway. I did see a therapist for a short time, but I didn't exactly have to recount what happened and that was short lived. Aunt Rose knows it all of course, but I haven't said all of that out loud even to her."

I was looking back down at my lap, embarrassed I just treated him as a therapist. The tension had started building in my shoulders again, when suddenly he was right next to me. He grabbed my hand and the jolt forced me to look up at him. His head was tilted with eyebrows drawn together.

"Wow, that's a lot to handle. I don't know what to say except, I'm sorry. And thank you for sharing it with me."

"I didn't mean to unload all of that. So, thanks for being so understanding." I was trying to keep eye contact, but my gaze kept falling to his mouth. I felt myself lick my lips and noticed a grin stretch slowly across his face.

"Vivian, this may be bad timing, but I'd very much like to

kiss you. May I?"

My heart sped up as I slowly nodded, trying to not seem overly eager. He gently turned my face to his and leaned in. His smell was intoxicating, not overpowering but fresh and crisp. He guided me the rest of the way to him with fingers under my chin. His lips were soft to the touch, but his kiss was strong and slow. He tasted like coffee and subtle hints of cheesecake. He had my face in both of his big, strong hands but it was all so gentle. It felt like time stopped and my whole body was rushing with excitement. For a moment I forgot where we were, and a small moan came out.

He finally pulled away, but just barely, while he still held my face between his hands and his hooded eyes looking back into mine. We continued to stare into each other's eyes in that same position until the server came back with the check. He left it there and walked away but we both could feel him just around the corner. This interruption broke up our moment but did nothing to slow my heart rate.

Jake let out a small, irritated growl but then stood up. He reached out to help me up. We both put our coats on, he quickly took my hand again, and left the money on the table. Neither of us put gloves on and the skin-to-skin contact sent waves of electricity coursing through my hand, clear into my chest through my arm.

I was still flustered from the kiss and intense staring game but was able to keep my composure walking down the stairs and back out onto the still busy square. When we stepped outside, the huge clock in the middle of the square began chiming. It was already eleven. We could see our breath, but I certainly didn't feel the cold. I couldn't believe so much time had passed already. It seemed like forever and just a moment at the same time.

"I should get you home. I didn't realize the time," he stated as he turned us toward my house. I wasn't ready to leave him, but I didn't want to seem needy, so I walked with him. He held my hand tightly as we walked briskly, occasionally running his thumb across my hand. Each stroke reignited the surge of electricity of his skin on my skin. I kept thinking I should say something to break the silence, but I was finding it difficult to breathe normally with him so close.

It wasn't long before we arrived at my house, and he walked me up to the porch. He still had my hand, so I gently pulled him to the porch-swing side since I figured Aunt Rose was sitting in the parlor waiting for us. She wouldn't be able to easily see us there and the porch light wasn't on, we only had the soft glow from the streetlamps. We didn't sit, though. He turned to face me and grabbed my other hand. He finally looked up; eyes filled with the same primal hunger he had at the restaurant.

"Vivian, I had a really great time with you," his voice was low and smooth, "I hope I can see you again, soon."

He leaned in, still holding my hands in his and once again placed his soft, full lips against mine with his beard tickling my face. As I melted into his kiss, our hands slowly released, and I found myself wrapping my hands around his broad and warm neck. Suddenly I felt his large, cool hands reach into my jacket but around my waist to my back, pulling me closer, sending all new bolts of electricity through my core. If it weren't for his coat being so thick, we would have been against each other there on the front porch. The kiss became more intense, and the electricity was turning into sheer heat all throughout me, especially in my lower abdomen and between my legs. My breathing was more abnormal than labored. I began to feel his strong hands traveling to my upper back and up around my sides, right by my breasts but then suddenly he pulled away.

"I'm sorry, I got carried away. I better get going," he said between deep breaths, still just inches from my face. "But can I see you tomorrow?"

I was still catching my breath and trying to keep my balance because my legs felt as if they were going to betray me.

"Yes," I gasped. "You better."

I watched him slowly walk down the steps, half watching the steps and half watching me until he finally made it down. He kept watching me, slowly walking backwards as I walked into the front door. If the door wasn't mostly glass, I would have stayed leaning against it to absorb all that had happened in the last few hours. As it were, I locked the deadbolt behind me and started to tiptoe toward the stairs, so he didn't see me acting like a teen girl in a cheesy movie. *Oh, how I felt like one, though.*

As I was about to step onto the staircase, a hand suddenly reached out and grabbed me. I nearly jumped out of my skin with a short yelp. But when I looked over it was Aunt Rose.

"My goodness! Are you trying to give me a heart attack? What are you doing in the dark?" I half whispered, half shouted at her.

She was in her robe but had a mug in one hand.

"I had just come down for a cup of decaf and saw you walking up, why are you so jumpy?" She made a wincing face. "Was it bad?"

She looked genuinely concerned so I grabbed her hand reassuringly and told her with a huge grin, "No, complete opposite of bad."

She excitedly wiggled and then led me to the kitchen. "Grab a cup then sit, you need to spill!"

Chapter 5

I was feeling exhilarated, I had just left the stage where I was singing. The club was bustling with at least a hundred people. Swanky black and white décor was strung about leading to the large stage with the grand piano and band full of brass instruments blasting out the upbeat swing music. Just below the stage was a large wooden dance floor full of couples moving to the music. Behind the dance floor and on the edge of the large room was a cluster of large round tables with full dinner settings, water goblets, and wine glasses. Servers dressed in white hustled around bringing out beautifully catered finger foods and pricey wine and champagne. From behind the stage, you could just barely make out the narrow hall that leads to the staircase up to the main restaurant.

I let go of the velvet curtain I was peeking around and turned to go to my dressing room down the long, narrow hall. As I went to open the door, I felt an arm reach around my waist. I knew it well and smiled with excitement.

I turned and could barely see in the poorly lit hallway, but it was him. His dirty blonde hair was slicked back perfectly, and he reeked of smoke and sweat but I didn't mind since I probably did, too. I reached up with my gloved hands and grabbed his broad shoulders and pulled him down to me. As we began to kiss, I felt his hand reach behind me, and he opened the door to the room.

It was dark without the vanity lights on but a small lamp near the door was on, so we walked in, still intertwined without stumbling.

"Your performance was amazing," he whispered between kisses, his warm breath prickling the hair on my neck.

"Well, your playing was equally amazing, sir," I said, grinning through kisses.

I pushed his tux jacket off his large shoulders and arms then began unbuttoning his shirt as he was reaching for my dress zipper. My body slammed against the wall and the straps on my dress began to fall with the back of my dress open.

"I have waited all night for this," he said softly in my ear, his mouth nuzzling against my neck.

I yanked off his dress shirt so that he was down to his white under-tank and pants. He gently pulled the straps of my dress t off my arms and gently slid the garment down to the floor and leaned down with it, sending goosebumps across my skin.

My body had become ready quickly, the heat radiating off me and moisture gathering. He slowly kissed his way up the length of my body, caressing my legs, then my backside while teasingly running his fingers under the trim on my panties, then working his way up to the back of the corset, still allowing the skin of his cheeks and mouth to run up and over the front of my bosom. I could feel the ties loosen then one hand ran from behind my back to grab a handful of my breast while the other was slowly undoing the strings on the back of the corset.

We were kissing hard now, and the corset was getting looser and looser as his free hand continued to slowly unlace. It was about to fall off and we both pulled apart for a moment and gazed at each other in the dark. Even though it was dark, something was becoming clearer, and then...

BEEP, BEEP, BEEP, BEEP, BEEP...I slammed my arm down onto the nightstand and managed to knock the clock off before I could get it to stop beeping. I clumsily fell to the floor and reached around aimlessly with one eye barely open to grab the loud torture device and turn it off. I finally found the off button.

I sat on the cold floor for a moment leaning against the bed still holding the clock. My heart was still pounding, and my chest was heaving quickly. I took a deep breath and slowly let it out before I put the clock back on the table. I stood up and put my slippers on but sat back down on the bed. I reached into the nightstand and pulled out my sleep journal. *I had to get that entry in.*

As I wrote I kept shaking my head. I know it was just a dream and my mind was likely just inserting things from my real life, but at the end it was eerily like looking into Jake's eyes in the dark of night. And that voice. When the deepness was in his voice this time, it was familiar. It sounded like him. *But why? How?* I wrote, "Jake??" at the end of the entry before my mind wandered to him.

We had been on several dates since that night at Vincent's, but he had been working on something big at the firm. That tied up a lot of his time, but he made it a point to still take me to dinner a few times and he regularly came to the shop. We even caught a few quick lunches.

It was almost my birthday and he said he had big plans, so he had to be sure to wrap up what he was working on. I didn't mind because sometimes being with him was so intense it was overwhelming.

We hadn't had much more than some short but hot and heavy make out sessions so I couldn't even wrap my head around anything much past that. His touch alone sparked every nerve ending in my body. When he had his strong arms around me and soft lips on mine, I could hardly remember to breathe as the sheer currents of electricity continuously flowed through me from head to toe. I of course had thought about more, but even the idea of it made my legs feel weak and my head spin. *Snap out of it, Viv.*

I had to stop daydreaming, I needed to get ready to go to the shop. I inhaled deeply to shake it off before I put my journal away and went downstairs for coffee.

"Good morning, dear," Aunt Rose greeted me. I nodded at her and grabbed some coffee from the pot and sat down.

"Honey, remember a couple weeks ago when I had to get a repeat mammogram done?" I nodded my head in agreement but up to that point I had forgotten all about it.

"Well, that day I did have another mammogram, but I also had an ultrasound at the doctor's request to be safe." I sat up straighter as she continued.

"They are referring me to a lung doctor. The strange thing they saw ended up being behind my breast tissue and they believe it to be a nodule on my lungs." She could see the tension building in my jaw and put her hands up and waved them down quickly to downplay what she was telling me.

"I gotta go to the hospital for a procedure to remove it and will be there for a few days. They think it's all going to be fine, and they will send it to be tested but don't think it's malignant," she said as perky as she could to make it sound good. "So, I don't want you to worry!"

I sat for a moment with my mouth hanging open. Unable to say anything as my heart raced, I finally stood and threw my arms around her tight. My thoughts were all over the place and I began shaking, trying hard to not cry.

"Breathe dear, just take a breath," she said as she gently pushed me far enough back that she could look at me.

"Auntie," I said frantically, "what do I need to do? Can I stay with you there? Do we need to prepare somehow? Tell me what to do."

She still was holding me by the shoulders and said calmly,

"You just need to be sure to keep the shop open, let the faucets drip here if it gets in the twenties overnight, and be sure to spend some time with that hot man of yours." She winked and grinned. "And maybe give me a ride to the hospital and back."

I couldn't believe she was so calm. "Auntie, I can't let you stay at the hospital alone. Surely, we can just put a sign up at the shop. And Jake will understand if I need to be with you."

She chuckled at me and led me back to the table to sit. I took a deep breath then grabbed my coffee.

"Tell me what you want, Auntie, and I'll do it." She asked that I just keep the shop up and running and not mention this to customers until she got the results back.

"They would just worry," she told me with a warm smile. "Oh, and will you be sure the plants are watered? You don't need to cover any that are in the ground now. They'll be fine. But the ones I brought inside need water."

"When is the procedure so I can take you to the hospital? I can make sure you have your bag packed with all your things, too."

She scrunched her face. "Well, they asked if I could go in Thursday and likely be discharged Monday morning early."

Jake had something planned this weekend for my birthday.

But this was Aunt Rose. There will be other weekends.

"That's fine, you told them yes, I hope. You need this taken care of *now*."

She nodded but I could see the apology on her face as her lips turned down and her brows furrowed. We both were still sitting so I leaned in and squeezed her hard. Finally, Aunt Rose broke free and stood up.

"I am going to the shop and will get as much in order as I can in the next few days for you. Don't rush in, dear." She leaned down and kissed my cheek then grabbed her keys and bag and headed out.

I sat there for a few minutes watching my coffee get cold. She was all the family I had left. *She had to be ok. Stop, Viv.* No sense in worrying until there was something to worry about.

Chapter 6

I was sitting at the counter, and I heard the bells jingle, but I was so distracted thinking about the news Aunt Rose shared earlier I didn't look up. But when I heard a familiar and comforting voice it snapped me out of my trance.

I sat up a bit and Jake came over with his big, warm smile and soft eyes. When I looked up at him, I had a flash of the dream from last night. I was frozen as my brain struggled to process it.

"Vivian, are you ok? You look shook up," he said with brows pinched together as he placed a hand on my arm. I was excited to see him, and his touch disrupted the momentary freeze.

I forced a smile to ease him then asked, "Can you go for coffee with me for a few?"

He nodded his head with a confused smile, so I went to tell Aunt Rose I would be back in just a bit and grabbed my coat.

We went by the little shop around the corner that had a sign that just read "COFFEE SHOP" even though everyone called it Joe's. There weren't many people inside, so we ordered our coffees and sat down at a small table near the back away from the cold doorway.

Once we were settled, he finally asked with concern in his voice, "You seem weird, are you okay?"

I clasped my hands together on the table and took a deep breath. "Well, I have some bad news. I can't do the birthday thing this weekend."

His head tilted as a frown formed on his lips. He grabbed my hands across the table. "Why, is there something bothering you?" He asked as he searched desperately in my eyes for an answer.

I explained the issue with Aunt Rose. That she didn't want anyone else to know until she knew it was all fine but that it required a hospital stay and they scheduled her this weekend.

"Well okay, I mean she has to get it done," he said very matter-of-factly. "So maybe we can just move our plans around here for now. You still have to celebrate your twenty-first birthday, so we'll figure something out," he said as he pulled my hand to his face and kissed my fingers. I felt a strange combination of calm from his reassurance and excitement from his lips on my skin.

"I'm glad you showed up when you did, Jake," I told him as the tension melted out of my body. *How did he so easily set me at ease?*

He drank his coffee fast and then reached his hand out. "Come on, you can bring your coffee, but let's take a little walk and get some air. You seem like you could use it."

Even though it was literally freezing outside now, I immediately jumped up at the idea and grabbed my coffee in one hand and his with the other. We strolled casually around the park. He asked me about the plans for the procedure and offered to help get her to the hospital and back.

"It'll be early Thursday, she has to be there before the crack of dawn, or five a.m. as some people call it," I said sarcastically. "I can only stay with her until she is moved to the surgical floor, but they couldn't tell her how long that is.

"I require sleep, or I may bite someone, so I planned to go home once they take her back and nap if I have time before I go open the shop. That's an hour."

He laughed a bit under his breath. He had told me before he was an early riser. I am not.

"Well, I'll bring you some lunch Thursday and Friday and we can do dinner in the evenings." He held my hand, running his thumb across mine as we slowly walked back. "Since the shop closes early on Saturday maybe we can plan the rest of the weekend together?"

We hadn't spent that much time together in so few days since we met. A whole weekend. The longest we'd been together at a time is several hours. And while it was always amazing, it was intense. Something about him disrupted my soul, even if it was in a good way. I had imagined being truly alone with him many times, even though it made me incredibly nervous. And also, incredibly hot and bothered.

"That sounds good," I said as calmly as I could, but the thought alone had made me forget what we had been talking about before he said that, at least for a few minutes.

We made it back to the shop and I went to open the door, but he quickly pushed it with one hand and grabbed me, pulling me close with the other for a quick but toe-curling kiss as my curls blew across both of our faces from the cool wind that kicked up. I swayed a little and he caught me, grinning at his accomplishment of almost knocking me off my feet. He opened the door for me and raised a hand to wave at Aunt Rose and told us bye. The grin he had as he walked away would stay with me a while.

"I wish you would do that in front of the store more often, maybe it'll attract some attention," Aunt Rose said smugly. I just grinned as I blushed and put my things down and then went about sorting some new items we got in.

Aunt Rose had walked to the back of the store when I heard another customer come in, so I offered to go up and take care of them. When I walked up and could see around the shelves, I saw it was the same gentleman from a few weeks ago asking about the gemstone.

I walked over and smiled. "Good afternoon, sir. So happy to see you back in. What can I do for you today?" He walked over to the same shelf as before and looked around at the gemstones we had.

He shook his head. "No stone still–like the one I described before? What about at the counter?"

I motioned for him to look for himself to see that we didn't have any displays at the counter. "I would have remembered if I saw it after you had asked before. If it's a precious gemstone, have you thought of the pawn shop maybe? We don't often get those types of things."

He looked me over as if sizing me up. "Your Aunt doesn't have such a thing, perhaps?" he asked.

I shrugged and was about to say I really didn't know when Aunt Rose came walking up.

"Do I have such things as what, sir?" She stood with a suspicious look on her face, arms crossed.

"I beg your pardon ma'am. Just a little trinket. Thank you for your time." He tipped his hat to us and left quickly.

"What did he say he was looking for, dear?" Aunt Rose asked.

"Well, he was here a few weeks back and asked about a gemstone," I said, trying to recall everything. "He said maybe pink or light red, pretty sizable. Now that I think of it, he never mentioned any particular kind. We didn't have one then and don't still, but today he asked if you had one before you came up. Really odd man."

Aunt Rose stood still looking suspicious and very tense.

"Odd indeed." She paused briefly, staring out after the man. "Oh well, we don't have one so there ya have it." She shimmied back to her place in the back again.

That whole thing was odd to me, but again, it's an antique store and nobody ever accused Aunt Rose of being normal. Although, she seemed bothered. But she had a lot on her mind and his behavior was curious if nothing else. I'm sure it was nothing.

///
//////////////////////

The next few days were boring, but we planned it that way. I didn't see Jake much because I wanted to spend some time with Aunt Rose and be sure she had great dinners since she would be stuck at the hospital for a few days.

Jake did swing by the shop every day and even brought Aunt Rose lunch. His big plans for the weekend for us were foiled but he said he still had some fun stuff in store.

It was finally Wednesday, and Aunt Rose and I drove together in the car so we could have a late dinner together and then go home since the following day was her surgery, and she couldn't have anything by mouth after midnight.

I was doing my best to keep Aunt Rose in good spirits and to distract myself as well, but I was getting more and more nervous. With the hospital's strict visiting hours, I would only get a brief chance to see her in the mornings before I head to the shop. She of course insisted that I didn't need to come to see her there, but I had to if I could.

That night we went for Pho and had lots of appetizers. The soup was delicious, warm, and filling. Perfect for a cold night and a last meal before being stuck with hospital food for days. It was one of her favorite restaurants. We took our time, enjoyed the food, and sat talking for a while.

"Oh dear, they're going to get mad and kick us out soon," Aunt Rose exclaimed finally. "It's well past ten and it's a weeknight!" We both grabbed our coats and stood, and I swiped up the check before she could grab it, making a victorious face at her.

"I am treating, you always do everything," I said, then dramatically walked over to the counter to pay and she finally caught up behind me. I made sure to leave a substantial tip since we were there well past closing time.

We went to the car, and she cranked it up and sat for a few minutes to warm up. We both were rubbing our hands together for warmth and laughing. It was late and we were tired, and I think we both were a little nervous about the morning even though she would never say so. Once the laughter subsided, Aunt Rose cleared her throat and ran her hand through her long grey hair. She was smiling but I knew it was forced. She always put on a brave face. I put my hand over hers and she smiled through tight lips at me before she finally put on her seatbelt, so I did the same. Then she put it in gear to drive home.

Before I showered, I went to her room first and made sure her bag was packed with her nightgowns, plenty of underwear, her toiletries, and clothes to come home in. I also made sure the new phone charger we got for her to take was there and a good book for when she was bored. All she had to do in the morning was get dressed and I would grab the bag and take it down to the car. We had a good long hug and she finally kicked me out of her room saying she needed her beauty sleep. I felt like she was leaving town or something. I wanted to be sure she had everything she needed.

I went to the bathroom and took a very quick shower after wrapping my head up. There was no reason to wash and deal with the wavy mess tonight and it was too cold to sleep with it wet. I certainly couldn't turn the dryer on while Aunt Rose was trying to sleep for her big day. *God, I sounded like a mother.* Like her mother. But it was Aunt Rose. Practically a mother to me.

I went to lay down but just tossed and turned. My nerves were on edge, and I couldn't quiet my brain enough to sleep. It was only exacerbated by the fact I kept thinking how tired I would be tomorrow. *How would I be able to run the shop this way?* I also kept thinking about Jake. He popped into the shop briefly, but I wanted to spend time with Aunt Rose this week before she was admitted. It was my idea, but I still was longing for his touch. When I was with him everything always seemed better, or at least he distracted me from my worries.

I glanced at the clock over and over, watching my possible sleep time continue to shrink. Background noise could help. I leaned over to turn my radio on, nineties alternative tonight. I was born at the wrong time, I loved seventies, eighties, and nineties music so much more than the current tunes. I shimmied in the bed to get comfortable again and closed my eyes, immersed by the sounds of Incubus, Pearl Jam, and Oasis. I let the music fill my mind and tried to silence the anxious noise. At some point, my body and mind finally gave way and I drifted off to sleep.

Chapter 7

My bedchamber was aglow from the warm fire. I was melting into the bed, and layers of blankets covered me. The flames danced in the fireplace, creating shadows throughout the room, but the tapestry hanging from the bed kept the light from my face. I was warm and cozy, and it made my eyes heavy.

I heard a creaking sound and cracked my eyes back open, leaning up just enough to look at the door. When I saw he had entered, I sat upright, revealing my sleep gown now that the blankets had fallen onto my lap.

He had soot and dirt all over him and smelled of the earth. He took long strides over to the bed and knelt beside it, next to me. The tapestry was casting a shadow on his face, but I saw his big hand reach out to me with something in it.

The light of the fire hit the object in his large, dirty hand. It was a gemstone.

It was a fantastic hue of light red, almost pink like nearly ripe raspberries, and when the light from the fire hit, the facets sparkled and shined. It more than filled his large palm.

I stared at it for a moment then looked in his direction and asked, "What's this?"

His deep, sultry voice answered, "A gift…for my love, my life, my soul."

Instead of reaching for the gemstone, I reached for his neck and pulled him to me into the bed. An intensity was building between us, within me, in the room.

He slowly and delicately kissed me. I was shaking from nervous excitement as a flood of emotion coursed through me. His weight was over the length of my body, but the blankets were between us still. I needed to feel him against me, now. I rolled us both over so I could pull the blankets from beneath me and feel his firm body between my legs when...

I rolled over and slammed the alarm clock. *Oh God, it was four thirty a.m.*

Jumping quickly from bed I stumbled around my room to get dressed. As I slipped my shoes on by the door, I could smell coffee wafting up the stairs. I ran down, and Aunt Rose was in the kitchen, dressed and smiling.

"I made a to-go cup of coffee for you." She smiled and handed the cup over. She was dressed, her long hair braided and pulled over the front of her shoulder, her face entirely too bright for this time of morning.

I gave her a big hug and without saying anything grabbed her bag and the keys and ran to the car. I turned the heat on hoping to warm it up some before she came out, but she wasn't far behind me. Luckily, the hospital was nearby.

"I'll drop you at the front and then go park the car. Just sign in and I will be right there." She chuckled as she could see I was flustered. It was bad enough she had to go, I must have hit the snooze button more than once and felt rushed to get her there on time.

"Don't worry dear, they tell you to come so early just to be safe." She patted my hand. "We will still sit there for a long time before they take me to pre-op."

She was right, but even so, I hated to be late.

I dropped her at the front when we arrived, and I watched her walk through both sets of automatic doors before pulling around to park.

It was quiet inside, but bright with a light and steady beeping of medical equipment and a small number of nurses and other staff were walking here and there. I found the waiting area, so I sat down next to Aunt Rose, grabbing her hand. Only two other people were there, and they also appeared to be together. Once I sat, the adrenaline seeped out of me quickly.

"So, what are your plans for the weekend with that hot man?"

I took a big gulp of coffee, wishing to replace the adrenaline since Aunt Rose felt like talking. I was surprised I got us to the hospital in one piece this early in the morning.

After one more long sip, I shrugged, "He hasn't said specifically, just that we can have dinner every night and we will spend most of the weekend together since we close early Saturday."

That's all I could get out in a cohesive sentence for her so far. She grabbed my hand and gave it a little squeeze. I squeezed back and looked over at her, blowing out a deep breath through puffed cheeks.

"Everything is going to be fine, dear; I promise," she said with a reassuring smile. "And they have your info to notify you when I am done today." She patted my hand then let go to adjust her braid. "Once I am awake and, in my room, I can text you."

I still wasn't okay with her being alone and made a last-ditch effort to convince her to close the shop.

"Are you sure you don't want me to close the shop and just put a sign up? I know people would understand. I have the inventory listed on the website and I can even make an update there."

She looked puzzled.

"Website, what do you mean, our little social media pages?" I had briefly mentioned setting up the website but maybe she didn't get what I was talking about then.

"I set up a website for the shop so we could show inventory, make updates, that sort of thing," I tried to explain without confusing her. "I haven't set it up to sell directly from the site yet, but I'm hopeful I can do that soon." She smiled and grabbed my hand again.

"Whatever you think is best, I don't know much about that kind of thing, but I suppose that's the time we live in now." She held my hand and shifted in her seat.

"I hate that I'll be here for your birthday. We should plan something for when I am home. Whatever you want to do," she said, her frustration coming out and the other people in the waiting room looked our way. We chuckled quietly at each other then I started to try to think of something fun we could do together. *What could Aunt Rose do to celebrate that wouldn't cause too much exertion?*

Lost in my thoughts, I leaned my head back and closed my eyes when it hit me...*I had a dream, and it didn't go in the journal.*

I jerked my head up and my eyes popped open. I didn't want to forget the details, so I began to explain it to Aunt Rose. As I told her out loud, it occurred to me that the odd man who came to the shop twice now had asked for something like what the man was showing me in the dream.

I was still tired, so I was just babbling, "I wonder what that stands for. I know it has to be some sort of symbolism but how odd that my brain pulled that." *So weird.*

It certainly was just my subconscious pulling from recent events, but it felt strange, nonetheless. And it was a different bedroom than the one that seemed to be in Williamsburg, even older based on the fixtures of the room, the huge fireplace, and the clothing the man had on. Almost like an old castle.

I finally took a breath between words and looked at Aunt Rose. She looked as if she was going to say something when her name was called. She smiled and stood so I stood up as well and walked over with her.

"We'll have to take her from here. Will you be staying, or do we have your contact info," the nurse asked?

"I am going but you have my info down. She said you'll notify me when she is done, is that correct?" The nurse nodded and smiled. "Or I can stay? How big of a deal is it if the shop is closed today?" I asked. Aunt Rose sat in the wheelchair they had brought for her, so I put her bag in her lap and leaned down for a hug.

"I love you, Viv, very much. Everything will be fine. You go, you'll hear from us soon."

I squeezed her tight, trying to fight back tears. "I love you, Auntie." I leaned up and watched as the nurse rolled her away. Once she was out of sight, I grabbed my coffee and left the hospital.

It was only half past six when I got home so I decided to lay back down for a bit before I had to open the shop. I didn't even take my shoes off and plopped down on the bed. I reached over to set the alarm and remembered I needed to write down that dream, so I grabbed my journal and a pen.

I was replaying it in my head, as much as I could remember now, and writing. It all felt so familiar and real. I could feel his weight, smell the soot and dirt, but more importantly, the feeling. The deep-down-in-my-bones intense and overwhelming feeling of desire, but also...*love*.

I had felt the desire so many times before, but this was different. This was more than lust. This was all-encompassing. I definitely wanted this man in my bed, but I wanted him in all other ways as well.

That dream was one of the shortest with the smallest amount of detail, but somehow it felt bigger, or maybe more important than any of the others. I closed my eyes to be sure I recalled everything. As my mind replayed the dream, I was overcome by intense waves of so many different emotions at once, joy, excitement, lust, but most prominent, love. Tears formed in my eyes, and my breath became unsteady as the emotions consumed me.

I opened my eyes and took a few cleansing breaths, put the journal down, and lay in my bed. I took another deep breath to calm myself, but the feelings didn't subside. The tears had slowed, but some still squeezed out of the corners of my eyes. *Shake it off, Viv.* Aunt Rose will be fine, and I just needed some rest.

I settled down into the bed and took a few more deep breaths to calm myself. I was so exhausted and overwhelmed that eventually my eyes could no longer stay open.

Chapter 8

The alarm came quickly, I felt as if I had just fallen asleep. I slowly rolled over enough to stop the beeping, my head and eyes not moving as fast as my body making me slightly dizzy. The house was quiet and still. It's just a few days. I can do this.

I slowly leaned up and allowed time for my eyes to adjust before getting completely out of bed. I stopped in front of the mirror to be sure I was presentable. I had my hair up this morning, and it was wild and coming out of the hair-tie from laying down. I took the hair-tie out and did my best to tame it before I put it in a loose bun. Luckily, I had the car, so I didn't have to shove a warm hat over my head today. When I was satisfied enough with my appearance, I grabbed more coffee and headed to the shop.

We never got much traffic in the shop this early, so I logged into the website and began checking analytics. Someone had searched for keywords, "gemstones," "stones," "gems," as well as, "rhodochrosite." I had never heard of the last one, so I jotted it down to research later. *What was that guy's obsession with a gemstone and what did it have to do with my aunt?* It had to be him; he's been in here twice and now he's checking our site.

I was pulled from my thoughts by the jingle of the door. Jake came strolling over with his handsome grin and handed me a coffee and a little bag from Dawson's, but I was more interested in the hands that delivered them. I wanted them on *me*.

"I wanted to come check in and be sure you had something to eat," he said as he came around the side of the counter, "and I figured coffee would be welcome." He tucked a stray curl behind my ear before he slid that hand around the back of my neck and pulled me to him, planting his soft lips on mine. It was hard to tell what I craved more, his touch or the electric reaction of his touch. *No, it was definitely his touch.*

When he pulled away, he had a grin across his face that sent my mind wandering about the places those lips could be. He briefly looked down, almost as if he could read my mind and it made him blush. He looked down at the paper I had written the strange word on and asked what I was looking at.

I nearly told him his plump, moist lips, but snapped out of it before my words betrayed me. "Oh, I was checking our website, and someone was looking for this stuff." Still finding it difficult to look away from his mouth, I decided to change the subject. "So, are you still feeding me this evening?"

He stepped closer again, pulling me right up against him with those strong hands on my back, so our lips were mere inches apart. "Wild horses couldn't keep me away." *Smooth as butter.*

Our lips met again, and he took in a deep breath as they did as if he was breathing me in. I found it hard to breathe at all. He pulled back gently, still grinning down at me, and ran his thumb over my bottom lip which made me realize I was biting it. His face looked as if he had successfully completed some naughty task, or maybe like me, he was thinking of participating in some. He made a low sound, like a mix between a chuckle and a small growl that sent a flush of heat to my core. *Geez, Viv, it's a public place in broad daylight!*

I cleared my throat and his grin turned to a smile. He slowly released his arms from my body. He walked to the door before turning to give me a small wave, and I saw him biting his own bottom lip before he walked out. *Oh, Dear God.*

Once I gained my composure and remembered where

I was, I stood and walked around the shop, taking time to straighten up the displays and check for loose trash. I walked to the front and looked out around the square through the huge floor to ceiling windows, realized then that all the other shops had decorated for Christmas, and we hadn't. A shiver went up my spine...this was the first winter holiday season without my parents. My face felt warm as the blood rushed up and pressure behind my eyes was growing strong. *Ugh, shake it off.*

I was all over the place today between dropping Aunt Rose off, the dream, and encounters with Jake always leave me emotionally floundering. I had processed a while ago that my parents wouldn't be there for my twenty-first birthday but somehow the holidays escaped me. But I still had Aunt Rose and now Jake. I'd come so far; I didn't want to dwell on this sadness. I patted myself under the chin, hoping to quell the tears and snap out of it. Back to business, decorations.

I was sure Aunt Rose already had decorations somewhere, so I went to the back room and glanced around but didn't see anything labeled as decorations. Although, there were some boxes and I probably needed to go through them. Who knows how long they've been up there unopened?

Before I could get started sorting through them, I heard the jingle of the door. I walked back to the main area of the shop and greeted the ladies that had come in. We chatted for a while and they picked up several items, so I offered to take them to the counter so that they didn't have to carry them around. I put their items down on the counter as I continued listening to their conversation, occasionally chiming in.

Once they finished browsing, they came to the counter, and I moved the mouse to wake up the computer. I saw the search with the gemstone and looked down to realize my piece of paper was gone. I looked around, shuffling some things and even checked the floor around the counter but it wasn't there. It probably just blew off from the door opening and closing. I was sure I'd find it when I cleaned up. To be sure I didn't forget, I grabbed another piece of paper and wrote down "rhodochrosite" once more, putting it in my pocket before I closed the window so I could pull up the register.

After the ladies checked out, a steady stream of customers was in throughout the day. It was a nice distraction, but I had been checking my phone all day in between customers. Finally, it rang as I was ringing up a customer.

"I have to take this, so sorry," I told her, holding a finger up.

"Hello this is Vivian Acworth." The man on the other end introduced himself as Dr. Johnson, explained the surgery went well, and Aunt Rose was in recovery and a nurse would notify me when she was moved to her room. Thanking him as I hung up, I took a deep breath and straightened up to keep from bursting into tears. Relief was washing over me and the nerves I had built up all week so desperately wanted to be released from my eyes, but there was a customer. I took another deep breath, shook myself, literally, and turned back to the customer. After apologizing, I thanked her for waiting and then completed her transaction. She was truly kind, gave a reassuring smile, and said she hoped it was good news.

"Yes ma'am, it was. Thank you. And thanks for coming in today," I managed to get out, shakily but still without tears.

After she left it was empty but the sidewalks outside were full. I didn't want to break down in case someone came in. I kept staring at the phone, tapping my fingers on the counter, and shaking my foot uncontrollably waiting for a call or text from Aunt Rose. My nerves were making me so fidgety that my loose bun started to fall so I finally just let it down. I was getting impatient.

I needed a distraction but didn't want to start sorting through old boxes in case she called. I pulled the paper from my pocket and googled the mystery rock. Lots of different pictures and references came up. I scrolled around a bit reading the details listed in each reference, many remarkably similar, but one stood out to me somehow, so I clicked it.

It was a blog entry, some new age or holistic reference but I read the entry about the gemstone. It was often red or pink and difficult to mine without damaging the stone, so it was rare to find one with little to no flaws suitable for jewelry. It was quite beautiful, even in its raw form but there were images of sparkly stones that appeared to be pink diamonds, and some looked more like rocks. But the physical description isn't what caught my eye, it's what the blog said. The blogger first referenced the basic physical attributes of the stone and where it can be found. But as I read on, it was getting more into the new age and holistic side of it.

The blogger had listed so-called "abilities" of the gemstone, one being it was believed to attract a soulmate. *Interesting.* Or perhaps someone to teach you a life lesson. *Ominous.* I never really took stock in any of that stuff, although I knew someone in college who read Tarot cards and it was fun, but definitely nothing I would ever take seriously.

It went on to say the gemstone encouraged self-love and could help heal traumatic experiences. It could even help you find the courage to find your path in life and lose your fear of rejection.

I leaned back a little and tried to process this. So much of what this stone supposedly could do were things I desperately needed. But honestly, *mystical gemstones?* I mean what's next, Prince Charming has it and if I find him my life will be all better? *I wish.*

Still, I kept reading, and as I scrolled down to see the rest of the entry, I stopped abruptly, took my hand off my mouse, and gasped at one of the pictures. *I had seen that stone before.*

Not just that kind, but *the stone* in the picture. I

straightened up in my chair.

It was the one from my dream.

I closed my eyes and could see the large, dirty hand reaching out to me with the stone held inside. My eyes shot open, and I looked at it again and it was identical. This was crazy. I'm not a trained jeweler and I couldn't be sure it was the same, it couldn't be the same. But still, something in my gut told me it was.

My shaky hand clicked the mouse over the picture and the description at the bottom indicated it was a stock photo. I blew up the picture and could see a sign in the back. The name of the stone was at the top of the sign and there was some smaller print below. I tried to blow it up, but it pixelated so badly I couldn't read it. We had a magnifying glass we used for small details on items we were refurbishing so I ran to the back to find it.

Once I found the magnifying glass, I went back to the computer and put it up to the screen. Under "Rhodochrosite" it listed fourteen cm, Origin Devon, UK, then below that the date 6/1/14-6/2/14, and below that it listed London Exhibit.

My head started spinning and my lips and fingers were tingling. *My parents were in London last summer.* It was their twenty-fifth anniversary trip. They had asked if I wanted to go but I had a summer makeup class, BIO. By the time my class was canceled it was too late to add me to the itinerary. I remember something had been shipped home while they were gone but I didn't know what it was. They had said it was easier to ship it home than try to bring it on the flight. And now someone was looking at my aunt's shop for this gemstone which coincidentally also appeared in a vivid dream I just had.

I leaned my head down and took some deep breaths until the tingling went away. I leaned back up and looked back at the screen. When we sold the house, we went through everything. We would have found this. *No, they didn't bring this home.* These are all wild coincidences. I just got worked up because of the surgery for Aunt Rose and I'm exhausted. It was all nonsense anyway. I closed the blog and pulled the register back up.

I had still been gathering my wits when my phone dinged from a text. It was Aunt Rose. *Oh, thank God.*

She let me know her throat was raspy from the intubation tube so she couldn't talk yet, but she felt fine, just tired. She was in her room and would try to call or text later, but she was going to rest. I let out a huge, audible sigh of relief.

Then the phone rang. It was a nurse notifying me Aunt Rose was in her room and gave me the room number. She gave me a brief update on how the surgery went and how she was doing in recovery. She then reiterated that Aunt Rose was doing fine, with extra warmth in her voice, before ending the call.

I had fought back tears all day, but when I hung up the phone, they poured out of me. My shoulders shook as I tried to reign them in, but that seemed to only make it worse. Between the weird gemstone stuff, Aunt Rose, the dream, Jake, and sheer exhaustion, I couldn't hold it together any longer.

There were several hours before the shop was closing so someone could walk in anytime. *Pull it together, Viv.* I reached into our mini fridge under the counter and grabbed a cold bottle of water. After sipping the cold liquid, I started to feel better. The cold water helped the tears subside and cool my face. I pulled some tissue from the box on the counter and wiped my face off and blew my nose since nobody was there but me.

Once I could breathe almost normally again, I stood up and decided since there were no customers, I needed a distraction, not on the internet. I finished off my water then decided to go pull down some boxes from the back and see if I could find decorations.

None of them were labeled and some decorations were in

several boxes but were mixed in with old junk and photo albums, so I took some time to move all the junk to one box, the albums to a pile, and the decorations to the rest of the boxes before I started putting them up.

I didn't even realize the time when I heard the door jingle. Still sitting on the floor, I peeked around the back-room door and saw Jake. I had been fine for a while now, busy with the mess I undertook in the boxes. But when I saw him, I felt my lip quiver and my breath started to feel choked. The pressure was building behind my eyes again and tears were fighting to come out. The blood was rushing to my face, and I felt my eyes filling and it took everything I had not to blink. For some reason, seeing him made it okay to let the roller coaster of emotions soar through me.

He saw me and his huge smile quickly turned to concern and confusion. He turned back and locked the door and pulled the open sign plug. He then rushed to me and knelt, his huge frame engulfing me there on the floor. When he did, the floodgates opened. I was trying so hard to not cry that my body was shaking as I held my breath. I felt silly for having such a visceral reaction when I knew for now, Aunt Rose was fine. The fear should have been gone. But she still was stuck in a hospital, and we didn't have any answers, just that she made it through surgery.

He began stroking my head and whispered, "Just let it out." I finally gave in and dug my face deep into his chest, grabbing a fistful of his shirt and let the tears and whimpers flow. He held me and kept petting my head. His closeness was soothing and helped me calm. I decided to focus on the fact that Aunt Rose was fine and in good medical hands. No sense in worrying until there was something to worry about.

A few minutes passed and I was still breathing irregularly but the tears had slowed. Jake pulled back a little without letting me go as I managed a few deep breaths. I didn't want him to look at me all puffy and red, but he lifted my face up with one of his hands. Another wild cry hiccup escaped, and I was going to look down again from embarrassment, but he leaned in and kissed me deep and hard, his tongue searching every recess of my mouth. My breaths were still jumpy, but the tears had stopped, and I gave into the kiss and the moment. I quickly forgot about the tears and was instead filled with waves of electricity. I melted into the kiss and into him. I clenched his shirt tighter in my hands, but it wasn't from sadness or exhaustion, it was to pull him closer.

We were interrupted by my phone, and I became very aware that we were in the shop on the floor. We pulled away at the same time and he helped me up before I walked to the counter and looked at my phone. I tried to act natural, but my legs were like jelly, and it wasn't because I had been sitting on the floor.

Aunt Rose was just checking in. She had been up for a short walk and went to the restroom but was very tired from all of it and was about to go to sleep. She loved me and hoped I had a good night. I glanced at Jake quickly, feeling some of the tension releasing from my shoulders at the sight of him near me. I texted her back that I was glad she was doing so well, and I would see her in the morning. Then finished with, "I love you."

I looked up again and Jake was watching me, his brows pinched together and his lips tight. Just looking at him and knowing he was here with me, for me, was making me feel better. I was still worried but somehow him being with me made it easier to manage.

I needed a change of scenery, so I smiled and grabbed his hand. "You promised me dinner." I grabbed my coat and keys, turned off the lights, then locked up on the way out.

We went to the burger joint next door, so we weren't far from the car, plus they had the best fries in town. I wasn't starving with the day I had but I could always go for some fries.

The restaurant was retro and had huge red booths with bar lighting over the tables making them cozy and semi-private. It was buzzing with its typical classic rock music. Currently one of Aunt Rose's favorites, Fleetwood Mac, was loud enough to hear but not so loud you couldn't hear your date. And there was chatter from other patrons, but you couldn't make out their conversations. The server came over and took our drink orders, but I was ready to order my fries, so Jake went ahead and ordered a burger and fries for him. He also ordered a chocolate shake but when she brought it, he pushed it across the table to me.

"Seems like you could use this today." I wasn't going to argue that point. We sat waiting for the food and he kept smiling at me from across the table, but his eyes seemed tight, and his hands were clasped together tightly on the table. I took a few sips from the shake and was hoping he would say something, but he just kept watching me and smiling. I couldn't take it anymore.

"Are you going to speak? You're making me nervous," I blurted out.

He chuckled and his hands seemed to loosen. "I was just letting you enjoy your shake. Seems like you had a rough day. By the way, what's the word on your aunt?"

I told him the doctor said it went well and so far, the rest of the day had gone as expected.

"I need to get up early tomorrow so I can go see her before I head to the shop. I can be there at eight and stay until nine thirty so I can get back in time." I let out a tired sigh. "She is insisting the shop is open normal hours."

Our server came back and put our plates down and put some ketchup on the table with a smile, and then quickly took off again.

"So, if Aunt Rose is okay, why the tears earlier?" I held a

finger up as I chewed the fries I had just shoveled in.

"Well, I dunno," I said, still mumbling as I swallowed the last bit of fries in my mouth. "I guess my nerves finally gave way." I took a deep breath and blew it through puffed cheeks. "I had been trying so hard all week to hold it together and just make sure she was calm and happy. I guess I needed to get it out. And it came out of my eyeballs."

He choked on his burger as he chuckled but gave me a thumbs up as he took a big sip of his drink.

"So, did you otherwise have a good day at the shop?" he asked finally. I wanted to tell him about the gemstone, and almost did. But it all was so far-fetched and crazy I couldn't bring myself to, so I went basic.

"It was a pretty normal day, decent amount of business for a Thursday but the evening was slow." He nodded and kept eating. I may have still been feeling tension from the week or my day, but I started sensing that something was off. He seemed more quiet than normal, though he wasn't usually extremely talkative. But I noticed it several times during the meal, like he was holding back or figuring something up in his mind but then never said it. And once our food was brought out, he wasn't doing his normal staring. He always stares, regardless of whether I catch him. Maybe it was just my crazy day making me irritable.

I waited a moment to see if he would offer up anything but when he didn't, I prodded. "So enough about me and my crazy day, how was your day? Everything okay?"

He stopped eating and the edges of mouth turned up as he licked his lips. "It is now."

Maybe he just had a bad day at work and didn't want to bring me down since I was already in such a fragile state. I smiled back and finished my fries, shaking off the odd feeling.

When we finished the server came back, asked if we needed anything else, and left the check for us. He put some cash down with it at the end of the table. I grabbed my coat, and he grabbed my hand once I put it back on.

He walked me to the car and once I unlocked it, he opened the door for me and I leaned against the car, grabbing at the bottom of his coat. I had such a weird day, I just wanted to end it on a good note.

"Do you want a ride to your house or anything?" I asked him as I gazed up into those blue eyes.

He grinned and let out a cross between a sigh and a growl. "You need to be up early tomorrow and so do I." He was holding the door with one hand but put the other up next to my head on the car, leaning close. His warm breath danced across my lips and chin. "I think if I get in the car, one of us won't be going home."

I felt blood rush to my face and down deep into my abdomen all at the same time. "Well, would that be so terrible?" I couldn't believe I just let that pass my lips, but I did, and the idea sent a rush of wetness to my core.

He stepped in remarkably close and grabbed my hands in his and looked down into my eyes deeply, clenching his jaw.

"Vivian, I would be lying if I said I didn't want to but just trust me, tonight isn't the night."

Wow, I read that wrong. Heat rose in my cheeks, and I pulled my hands from his, adjusting my jacket.

I fumbled with my keys and went to quickly turn to get into the car, but he grabbed my arm, swinging me back and pulling me so close that our lips were almost touching. I felt my cheeks still flushed but now it was a mixture of embarrassment and anger. If he didn't want me then why did he grab me again.

I made a move to pull my arm from his grasp, but he just tightened his grip.

"Vivian, listen to me." He squeezed every time I tried to wiggle loose. His voice was low and gravelly. "When I said I wanted to go I meant it, but I just can't, not right now. Please don't be upset."

Before I could say anything or pull away, he pulled me in hard and kissed me so deep I was seeing stars. My legs were about to betray me, but he was holding me so firmly I don't know that I would've fallen if they did. I gave in and swirled my tongue around his as he attacked my mouth. After a minute he pulled away slowly and I couldn't help but let out a small gasp.

"Go see your aunt in the morning and I'll come see you before lunch, I promise." I nodded before I climbed into the car, and he shut the door. I could see in the mirror that he stood and watched me drive off.

Even though he had a good reason and tried to reassure me by kissing the sense out of me, I was horribly embarrassed. I normally wouldn't have ever suggested that. I never had been so forward with any man, but it seemed like Jake and I were on the same page. Maybe I was right when something seemed off. Oh well, regardless of why, I still had to go home with my tail between my legs.

It was quiet and dark when I got home except for the light over the stove, and I could see the soft glow upstairs from the nightlight we kept in the bathroom. I went ahead and made coffee to be brewed for the morning, made sure the house was locked up, then went upstairs to shower before bed.

It was still fairly early, and I was alone, so I took my time in the shower and planned to dry my hair since it would warm me up. The furnace worked well downstairs but since the house was over 100 years old and drafty, my bedroom was cold.

After the day and night that I had, I was exhausted but mentally my mind was still racing. Aunt Rose was at the hospital alone, post-surgery, and she was fine, but it was still a big deal. Then the gemstone thing that made no sense and too much sense all at the same time. And of course, the coup de gras, me throwing myself at Jake and being shut down. *What a day.* I just wanted it to be over. I finished drying my hair most of the way then headed to my room.

My journal was there on the nightstand, so I grabbed it. As I climbed into bed, I turned my lamp on and pulled the covers up after making sure I set the alarm for tomorrow and turned my radio on low.

I flipped through the pages of the journal and skimmed over the entries. There were a few that referenced that old room with the poster bed and a fireplace and no lights, just candles. But none with a gemstone. I started to think the only reason the gemstone even popped in was because that man kept asking. That didn't explain it looking identical to the one I found later that same day online, but maybe I was remembering wrong. It just didn't make sense and wasn't anywhere else in my journal. *My mind was playing tricks on me.*

I needed to get some sleep. I wanted to be sure to go visit Aunt Rose in the morning and even though my mind wasn't completely quiet, my body was about to force the issue. My eyelids were struggling to stay open. I put the journal in the drawer, turned the lamp off, then lay down and pulled the covers up the rest of the way to let the sound of The Smashing Pumpkins send me to the Sandman.

Chapter 9

My alarm went off and I rolled over to hit the snooze button. I took a big stretch and sat up. I actually slept through the night. I didn't recall any dreams, either. What a relief. I had enough confusion to last me a while.

Rolling out of bed, I slid my feet into my slippers before heading down for coffee. Since Aunt Rose wasn't home, I decided to take the coffee back upstairs with me so I could finish it while I got dressed. Since I was going to the hospital, I put on my Chucks; I didn't want to be clodhopping on the tile floor. I grabbed a hat in case it was frigid then pulled on my jacket, checking to make sure my gloves were still in the pocket.

The clock now showed a quarter until eight, so I ran downstairs and made a to-go cup of coffee and headed to the hospital. I made it over in no time and found a parking spot quickly, so I grabbed my coffee and headed in to find the floor Aunt Rose was on.

It smelled like rubbing alcohol and old coffee as I passed the nurse's station. Low and steady beeping was all I heard besides the sound of a nurse typing furiously at a computer in the hallway. I eventually found Aunt Rose's room and tapped on the door that was already cracked open. I slowly walked in, and she was there leaned up in the hospital bed with the typical white and blue hospital-issued gown, pillows stuffed behind her with a tray in front of her, her hair loosely pulled into a ponytail at the nape of her neck. She looked tired, but well.

"Viv, I am so glad to see you! Come here to me," Aunt

Rose exclaimed with her arms outreached to me. I put my things down on the table next to the bed and leaned in for a big hug, trying to not squeeze too tight since I wasn't sure where the incisions were.

"You can speak today. How are you feeling?" She took a sip of her hospital coffee from the tray and winced.

"I would be much better if I had some decent food and beverages. I think this coffee was brewed three days ago." We both laughed but I grabbed my coffee and offered it to her. She eagerly took it and took a sip. "Ah, much better. So, tell me, how was the shop yesterday? How was your dinner date? Anything to report?"

I didn't want to rehash it all, so I just said the shop was fine, I had some nerves waiting to hear about her, then dinner was ok. She could sense I left something out and gave me a knowing look, so I reluctantly told her how I threw myself at him and was shut down.

"Well honey, I am sure he had his reasons. Who knows, maybe he is trying to be chivalrous?" I told her I wasn't sure but either way, I was embarrassed.

I was ready to change the subject, so I settled into the chair next to her bed. "Oh, remember that man that had come by asking about a gemstone? Well, you may think I'm nuts, but I had a dream, do you remember I was telling you about it before surgery?"

I stopped and looked at her to be sure she was following, and she gave me a small nod, so I continued, "Well, I checked our site yesterday, and someone was doing a search there for the same stone, had to be the same guy. But he searched for the name of the gemstone, so I researched it and it was so wild. I ran across this blog, probably some new age lady just winging content," I said as I waved my hand up dismissively, "but it caught my eye regardless."

74

She leaned up a bit. "What caught your eye, dear?"

"Well, I don't know how to explain it, it doesn't really even make sense to me. But one of the keywords that came up was soulmate, so I clicked it. Apparently, whatever this gemstone is, it 'supposedly' attracts your soulmate but can also help you find your path in life, overcome trauma, even let go of fear. It was just strange, like I needed to read *that* particular site." Even as I said it all it sounded ridiculous. I shook my head. "I know it's all nonsense, but I dunno how to explain it, the timing was just...weird. Do you think I'm crazy yet?" I expected a laugh, but she sat there with her brow furrowed and wrung her hands nervously.

"Honey, you're not crazy. And I hope you don't think I am after I tell you something." I was confused but nodded to her to go ahead.

"Well, remember when your parents went to London last year?"

I nodded slowly and shrugged.

"Well, they got a gemstone. Actually, I guess were given one. They wanted me to get it appraised so once they got home, we took it to a friend of mine. It turned out to be exceedingly rare and incredibly old, centuries old. And it was worth a lot of money."

I wasn't sure why she was telling me this and I'm sure my face gave away my confusion.

"Your parents wanted you to have it, they said the person who gave it to them said it *must* go to you." She paused briefly. "But I think they felt fearful at some point because they gave it to me to keep safe and told me if anything ever happened to them that you were to get it before your twenty-first birthday."

My birthday was Saturday, the next day, but why did

someone give my parents such a thing? Why did they hide it from me? Why were they fearful enough to hide it with Aunt Rose?

I was full of questions but just one came out. "Where is it now?"

Aunt Rose sat up even more. "I had to hide it, but your parents made it seem as if the obvious places wouldn't be safe, so I buried it."

I felt my brows pinch together. "Are you messing with me? This is a joke, I get it. You're making a point, it's crazy, I'm being crazy. It's fine, you could have just said that, Auntie." I rolled my eyes and adjusted in my seat.

"Vivian, this isn't a joke. And I need you to promise that you won't tell anyone. Your parents were certain someone was after it. That's why when the man came in, I was tense. I should have told you then, but I didn't want you to worry more than you were." She paused again, her face betraying her guilt as she avoided eye contact.

"Anyway, there is a satchel with it that I didn't open but they said you need to see." I sat for a moment still and silent. If she wasn't joking, this was a lot to process.

Finally, a particularly important question came to mind. "Do you think this had anything to do with their accident?"

She nodded slowly. "I can't be sure of course, but based on what they told me, I got the feeling it did. They were scared of something or someone."

I stood up as anger bubbled up inside of me. "Wait, if they were scared, why didn't they call the police? Report it. I don't understand. This is nuts." I paced the room as my mind raced. "So, you're telling me some random person gave them a gemstone worth thousands of dollars while they were overseas, but they had to promise it would be given to me? Specifically, *me*? And then someone here was basically chasing them for it, so they trusted you to hide it and give it to me on my twenty-first birthday? Oh," I added sarcastically and waving my arms, "and it quite possibly was the reason they are dead? Do you hear yourself?" I continued pacing, and my mind was reeling. Why was she saying this? Was she having a reaction to anesthesia? I felt blood rushing to my face, but I wasn't sure if it was anger or worry.

"Honey, I know this a lot and it sounds absurd, but it's true. You can find it under the azalea bush in the back corner of the yard." I stopped and stared for a moment.

"Are you ok, Auntie? Do you need me to get a nurse?" I walked over to her and grabbed her hand and put my other one up to her forehead to check for a fever. She grabbed it down and held both tight in her fragile, cold hands.

"Vivian, listen to me. I am fine, this is true. If you go to the azalea bush, you will find the box with the gemstone and the satchel. You need to find the box, get the satchel out, and see what it says. Promise me you will. But be careful; do it after dark."

She was serious. Or at least she really believed it. Her hands were still tightly wrapped over my hands, and she was shaking.

"Okay, Auntie. I'll do it tonight when I get home. After dark." She was shaken, but she seemed so genuine, so serious.

The worst that would happen is I would get dirty if she were wrong. And I would freeze. But this seemed important to her.

A nurse came in to check on Aunt Rose, so I stepped into the hall.

When she came out, I stopped her and asked that she keep an eye on her; she didn't seem like herself. The nurse assured me they were taking good care of her but sometimes the meds do tend to make people a little loopy, but she would be sure someone assisted her to the restroom and checked on her regularly.

I stepped back in, made sure Auntie's water was full, and found the book from her bag for her. "I have to get going since you want the shop open, but I'll check in with you later so keep your phone handy." I leaned down and squeezed her neck and gave her a peck on the forehead. I reached behind her, fluffed her pillows, and took a sip of my coffee but put it back on her tray. She was still so shaken. I hated to leave her like that. But I had to get going to make it there in time to open and get everything up and running before unlocking the door.

I drove to the shop replaying all she told me. I was incredibly distracted all day. We had a few customers here and there, so I tried to be attentive to them. In between customers, I stared aimlessly, I'm not even sure at what.

I kept replaying the conversation with Aunt Rose, the dream, the man, the blog, all of it. I had to know if there was really a box and what was inside the satchel. *And Jake.* I was supposed to be having dinner with Jake tonight. But I needed to know. It was such a crazy story, but a part of me did wonder if there was any truth to it. So many strange coincidences kept happening and the recent dream only made it more confusing.

Viv, no. This is insane.

I heard the door jingle and looked up to see Jake. He came with a bouquet of flowers, a drink, and a bag from the sandwich shop. He bit his lip with his head hung as he walked to me.

He put the bag and drink down and cleared his throat before he finally looked at me. "I know last night I upset you, so I hope you can forgive me," he said as he handed the flowers to me. I still felt embarrassed. I was also nervous about digging up an azalea bush in the dark later.

I took a deep breath and grabbed his hands, still cold from outside. "I know you're going to think this is because of what happened but it's not; I can't have dinner tonight." I looked up into his eyes, noticing some of the gold specks, along with bags under his eyes; he didn't sleep well. "But I promise we will still do our plans tomorrow, whatever they were."

He put his head down for a moment then looked back up at me to ask, "Is everything ok? If it's not me, is there something wrong? Can I help?" His voice broke as he spoke.

I shook my head and tried to sound normal. "No, everything is fine. I just need to take care of something that just came up. It's a favor for Aunt Rose and I promised her I would get it done."

He stepped in closer and pulled me to him. I could smell him; that manly but citrusy scent that he wore everyday mixed with a hint of strawberry lip balm he used. I could feel the cold on his clothes still but the heat from his face.

"Vivian, I worry about you being out late alone, are you sure I can't tag along?" The timber in his voice deeper this time.

When he said my name, every time, waves of excitement flowed through me often leaving me momentarily speechless. Everyone just called me Viv, but he always called me Vivian. So that only made it harder to break our date.

When I gathered my words, I finally got out, "Don't worry, it's not an errand. I'll be home. And I'll be perfectly safe. But definitely meet me here tomorrow afternoon and I'll be your beckon birthday girl."

He wrapped his arms around me, hugged me tight, and put his head into my shoulder. It was a passionate embrace, but it also felt comforting and safe. Like he was telling me with his body he would take care of me. But the feeling that he was holding back something was creeping up again.

He finally pulled away, kissed my forehead, and told me he would see me tomorrow then left the shop without looking back. He thought I was blowing him off. But Aunt Rose insisted I didn't tell anyone. Which was still so nuts; I couldn't believe I was even entertaining her nonsense. And ditching a date for it. I almost called him to keep our date, but then I decided I needed to be done with this so Aunt Rose could let this go. The sooner I proved nothing was buried, the sooner we both could move on.

It was steady for the rest of the day which helped time go by faster. I texted Aunt Rose to check in at some point. I promised to bring food after closing up tomorrow before I went out with Jake if her doctor didn't care.

I texted her again not long before closing time to tell her goodnight and I love her. We didn't mention our discussion from the morning in any of our text exchanges all day, not even a coded reminder. I figured with the way she had acted it was best not to have that in writing.

When it was time to leave, I locked the door but did a walk through. The trash could wait until tomorrow, but I grabbed the food bag that Jake had brought me to take home. I had only eaten half the sandwich so I could finish it later. I turned the lights off and left after locking up. I stepped outside and, for a moment, wished I had just gone with Jake.

Happy couples and groups of people walked around the square, some waiting to be called to their tables, others weaving in and out of the crowd with shopping bags in hand. It was a Friday night. The square was bustling, all lit up with holiday lights, and it was cold. Perfect night to be walking arm and arm with a good-looking man that sent electric waves throughout your body. Instead, I had to go home and dig a hole. I shook my head to snap myself out of my pity party and headed to the car to drive home alone to an empty house.

Chapter 10

It was dark inside besides the soft light of the over-the-stove lamps. It was also quiet and cool. Aunt Rose never made a lot of noise, but the house seemed much quieter without another person in it.

I made a glass of water and sat at the kitchen table to finish my sandwich from earlier. I sat there when I was done slowly folding and flattening the wrapper, contemplating whether I was going to go dig up her azalea bush. It hadn't been blooming of course, but it was huge and if I damaged the roots now it may not grow back. I had also considered that it was literally freezing outside. It was past nine now and the temps had dropped to twenty-five degrees.

I stood up and looked out the kitchen window to the back yard after I turned the flood light on. I could see the bush in the back corner of the yard. There was a huge wall of trees surrounding the back yard and of course the privacy fence. Aunt Rose had a green thumb so even in the dead of winter, evergreen bushes were thriving and covered the yard. The light gave a glow across the yard, so much of it was visible. Of course, the further from the house the darker it was. There weren't many colorful flowers but there were a few red dots popped on the holly berry bushes.

My phone dinged so I grabbed it, hoping maybe Jake was messaging me to look outside to see him standing there. But it was Aunt Rose. All she typed was, "I love you." It was late and we had said goodnight earlier. It was a reminder. It was her telling me to do it. *Now or never, Viv.*

After donning my coat and gloves, I went to the shed to find the shovel. Luckily, it was right by the door. Walking to the backyard, I headed to the azalea bush. I stood for a moment, considering the massive plant, then decided to dig behind it. The bush had been here much longer than since last summer so she would have buried around it, not under it and I didn't want to destroy the roots. And if you were hiding something you wouldn't do it in the front.

I had to shimmy my way behind the bushes and evergreens. I stood looking down, trying to figure out where to even start, then marked a line with the shovel and started digging. I wasn't in terrible shape, but I didn't do much manual labor and digging into such cold ground was a task. I was winded quickly and had to take lots of breaks. I had dug for what seemed like an eternity, but it was probably just five minutes. Still, I hadn't dug very deep. I stopped to catch my breath and considered wetting the ground as I tried to catch my breath, but then decided against it since the temps were below freezing. Even though it was so cold sweat was building on my brow. I wiped my face with my coat arm and took a deep breath, but finally started again.

My arms were getting tired, my back was hurting, and I was almost ready to give up when I hit something. It was a dull thud, not a sharp sound like a rock. I carefully lifted some more of the dirt up around whatever I hit and at first all I could see was a plastic wrapping. I knelt down and took one of my gloves off and shoved it in my pocket then swept some of the dirt away and realized there was a wooden box in the plastic. It was a cherry-wood-colored decorative box. *Could this actually hold some gemstone, hundreds of years old?*

My hand shook, and I couldn't be sure if it was from the cold or because I found something. I stood back up and dug up the ground around it so I could grab it up. Once I could get the shovel under the box, I put it down and grabbed the plastic and pulled the box up. It certainly wasn't empty. It wasn't terribly heavy, but it wasn't light either. I sat there for a moment and just looked at it.

Suddenly my mind was going a million miles a minute. Was there a gemstone in here? Was it the same one from my dream? Was it really for me? Most importantly...*Why am I still sitting in the dark yard in the freezing cold?*

I grabbed the shovel, pushed the pile of dirt into the hole while still holding the box, took the shovel back to the shed, then went back inside, locking the door.

I sat the box, still inside the plastic, on the table and looked at it for a moment. *Maybe I should do this upstairs.* Looking out the window, I became paranoid that someone may happen to walk by and look in the kitchen window.

I took my other glove off, shoved it in the coat pocket, and flung it onto one of the chairs before I grabbed the box and went upstairs. The dirty plastic was still around the box, so I went to the bathroom and disposed of it. After walking the box to my bedroom, I closed and locked my door. I placed it on my bed and stood there looking at it. *Did I really want to open this?*

I decided to change into my pajamas first, the whole time watching the box as if waiting for it to open on its own. Finally, I sat on the bed, the box there before me. I pulled it closer to me, rubbing my fingers over the carvings of the beautifully crafted box, then tapped it gently. *What did this box hold?*

Slowly, I lifted the lid and at first only could see a large object in a beige silk bag sitting in the black velvet lined box and next to it a weathered and small leather pouch. I ran my fingers over the silk bag and could feel edges and then large flat pieces inside. It was cold. My fingers moved to the small pouch. I pulled at the tattered strings and slowly untied it. Inside was a piece of paper rolled up. I pulled it out and slowly unrolled it.

Vivian Acworth Adams of Devon, UK 1560

Vivian, we've met before, and we will meet again. I hope if you are reading this that means you have found The Anam Cara. It was named such as it was found in a mine by a group of men, some Scottish and some Saxon, and they presented it to the Lord overseeing the mining. He presented it to the woman who later became the Lady of his estate. It has been passed to Vivian Acworth for decades and must always find you by your 21st birthday and remain in your possession until you depart that life. Hopefully, the stone will remain with our family until it can find you again. It is the key to your dreams and the truth to your tragedy. Without it, both will be lost forever.

I sat and reread this over and over as my heart began to race. It was handwritten in calligraphy and the paper was old and dingy but still intact. *What is this?* This made no sense at all. *1560?* Passed down to my namesake for *decades?* And Adams...*Jake's last name.*

Sharp pangs filled my chest, my breathing fast and shallow. My fingers and lips started to feel numb. *Not now damnit.*

My first panic attack was the day I learned of my parent's death. I had several after I moved in with Aunt Rose as well, so I knew what it was, but it was still scary, albeit warranted in this situation. I threw my legs over the side of my bed and put my head down between my knees and took slow, steady breaths for a few minutes.

The pangs started to subside and slowly I got feeling back in my lips and fingers. I slinked down the side of the bed and sat on my knees facing my bed. The paper and the box were still there. So, I didn't imagine all of that.

I sat up a little, enough to reach for the box and pulled it to the edge of the bed in front of me. I sat back down on my knees and stared at the silk covering for a few minutes, like if I looked hard enough, I could see through it. A strange noise caught my attention, forcing me to jump up. It took me a moment to get my wits and realize it was just the old pipes.

I drew in a deep shuddering breath and slowly reached my shaky hand out and picked up the object, slowly untying the silk covering. I slid the object out onto the bed. *Oh my God.*

There it was. *It was real.*

It was dark pink. A large chunk of beautiful stone, almost hexanol shaped but with a few pointed edges on the ends, not perfect points, about five or so inches long and maybe two inches in width. No extremely clean cuts across it but some flat surfaces all around with small little edges here and there. It was mesmerizing, and light bounced off the flat sides or facets.

I gazed at it for a moment, my heart racing again. I sat up more on my knees and reached out slowly with both hands then after a brief pause, picked it up and held it in them, still holding it over the bed. It spanned across my palms together. I rounded my fingers over it, grasping it tightly with both hands and suddenly my eyes fluttered closed.

I felt a pull somewhere, then I began to have flashes. Vivid flashes of the dreams I had been having for months. First it was just the locations moving quickly, then I could feel that I was there. Then there he was, my mystery dream man. My mind was still playing it all in short clips and flashes and he was unclear just as in my dreams.

I don't know why or how but I was scared, or maybe just nervous, and my body pushed back against whatever had pulled me and I opened my grasp, dropped the stone onto the bed, and it all stopped.

My eyes were open, my breathing was labored, and I was alone in my room in the quiet house. I leaned back and sat all the way down and moved back from the bed a bit more. I didn't understand what just happened, but it all felt so real. Like I was there, *really there* in those places. And with him. And he was even more familiar than before. I felt like I knew all the places, and him, like I knew my own home. I placed my trembling palms on the floor, making sure it was still solid beneath me.

I looked up at the gemstone sitting atop my bed. How could I put it back without touching it? How was I supposed to sleep now? What do I do with it? *It was real.*

Aunt Rose was telling the truth. It was all true. I had to go see her in the morning and I couldn't leave this here now that I dug it up.

Once I got my breathing back under control and trusted my footing, I stood up and went downstairs, grabbing the silicone oven mitts and ran back upstairs. Surely, they would protect me from whatever strange flashbacks just happened. I put the mitts on, grabbed the gemstone, and put it back in the silk covering and placed it back in the box. I wasn't taking any chances touching it again. I then rolled up the paper, very carefully, and put it back in the little pouch and tied both back up, put it next to the stone, and then closed the box. I hid the box under the pillow on the other side of the bed then took the mitts back downstairs.

I don't know why or what I was planning to do with it, but I grabbed the carving knife out of the knife block and took it back upstairs with me and locked my bedroom door. I carefully nestled in my bed, knife in hand, and tried to get comfortable. Instead, I lay there for over an hour just staring at the pillow covering the box.

I was afraid to close my eyes. Partly afraid of what I may see again, and partly afraid to fall asleep. What if someone was watching me or had seen where I dug? I tried to cover it back, but it was still obvious the ground was freshly disturbed. If someone was looking for it, they may be following me.

I rolled over to look at the clock. It was already midnight. I was supposed to be up in seven hours to get ready to see Aunt Rose. And worse, it was too late to call Jake. I had an intense urge to call him to come here and just be with me or to go to him. I always felt safe with him. But I blew him off, at least he thought so, and it was the middle of the night. Jake had been acting strange, but was that in my head? Or was it valid and I should question it? No, even if something was bothering him, I'm sure it was nothing. *No sense in worrying until there was something to worry about.*

Still, maybe Aunt Rose was right. I should keep this to myself. I sat a while more staring at the pillow and my eyes were very heavy, so heavy they were closing involuntarily, and I was fighting to keep them open.

Chapter 11

I stood in a small room dressed in a very ornate gown with huge skirts that were luxurious with green and gold silks and intricate stitching with gold ribbon used to tie my bodice. My hair was piled up beautifully leaving my shoulders bare.

Sun shone through the high stained-glass windows surrounded by stone walls. There was a small table covered with delicate tablecloths and runners designed with blue, gold, and green. Fresh cut flowers adorned the table but in the middle was a decorative pillow. I stepped closer to the table to see the pillow was holding the gemstone.

I continued closer and reached toward it, there was a knock on the door. I turned and saw two guards on either side of the door, but they didn't move. The knocking continued and got louder and louder. I couldn't understand why the guards didn't open it. I looked back toward the table and noticed a band on my ring finger. Then I heard my name being called and the knocking became louder still, so I turned back to the door and began walking to it. I reached out to open it and then...

I woke, not to my alarm but to loud knocking on my door. Not the front door...my bedroom door. I locked up when I came in. I sat up in my bed and realized I was still gripping the knife I grabbed from the kitchen. I reached over to my nightstand to feel for my phone and noticed the clock. Half past two. My heart was beating furiously, and I was trying not to breathe loud or knock anything over while I felt around for the phone when I heard my name, muffled through the door.

"Vivian, are you in there? Open the door, say something, or I am breaking it down!"

That was Jake.

I jumped out of the bed and stumbled over my slippers, but I managed to find the door as my eyes adjusted. I unlocked it, flinging it open still holding the knife.

"What are you doing here? How did you even get in? Do you know what time it is?"

He didn't reply but stepped past me and looked around the room like he was looking for something. There was a soft glow from the nightlight in the bathroom.

"Are you alone? I tried calling and texting, so I decided to come here just be sure you were safe. There was dirt tracked in from the back and all over the door."

I went over to the nightstand and turned on my lamp. I blinked as my eyes adjusted to the light and my brain was processing what the hell was happening.

"Why are you holding that? And what's all over your face?" he asked.

I hadn't showered when I came inside. I must have rubbed dirt on my face. And I was still holding the knife, like I knew what to do if someone had actually tried to harm me.

I talked fast as my brain still decided if I should be mad or happy that Jake had come. "I did some yard work for my aunt after work and was tired. I forgot to go wash up and I have this," I said, waving the knife, "because I don't like being here alone. You didn't answer *my* questions. What are you doing here, Jake?"

He stood motionless and silent for a few moments. He had an intensity in his eyes unlike any I had ever seen. His jaw muscles flexed behind his short beard, but his lips were so tight they started to lose color. He swallowed and his lips gained color back, though they were still tight, and he walked to me, gently pulling the knife out of my hand then put it on the nightstand.

He cleared his throat. "It was easy enough to get in, the house is old, and I *was* a police investigator."

Anger filled me, but so did relief. I had wanted him to be here, but he broke into the house in the middle of the night, so it seemed appropriate to be mad. He was quiet as he shifted his weight from one foot to the other, like he was buying time to gather his words. The longer he took the more aware I was that I was in my ratty old comfy pajamas and probably looked as I normally would when I rolled out of bed. The tension radiating off him was making me feel small and unsure of myself. I couldn't tell what he was thinking, or why. *Why the hell was he here?* He was acting so strange and hadn't even tried to touch me since I opened the door. I got a sinking feeling as he stood rigidly in silence.

I cleared my throat, hoping that would get a reaction from him or at least break the tension that filled the room.

He let out a loud sigh, his hands at his hips, his eyes softening. "Can you sit and just listen? It may sound bad but if you let me say it all you'll hopefully understand."

I slowly sat on the edge of the bed, nervously pulling at my shirt, hyper-aware that it was incredibly thin, and I didn't have a bra on. He started pacing back and forth in front of me, never making eye contact. He often stared at me openly, so it was making my skin crawl that he didn't even glance at me.

My stomach was in knots as he walked back and forth. I dramatically cleared my throat again to break the silence and he finally stopped pacing. His hands went to his face, covering his mouth. He slowly moved them down his face, running down his neck as his eyes roamed everywhere but at me.

He began pacing again but also started to speak in a very calm and even tone, "Vivian, you know I came here to work for my dad as one of his investigators. And I need you to know up front, everything I've told you has been true. I am who you think I am."

He stopped pacing and finally looked at me, his voice more certain. "But I gotta explain something, and this is the part I need you to just listen to the whole thing, can you do that?" He was cutting the words with firm palms in the air to show me the importance. I nodded my head in agreement, still tugging at my shirt. After the last few days especially, any explanation, for anything, would be helpful.

He began to pace again, hands back on hips. "A few months ago, one of my first jobs was to investigate your aunt and her shop but nothing specific. I was supposed to visit the shop, follow her a few places, then report back. Which I did." He slowed again, turning to face me, his brow furrowed, wringing his hands together. His voice was no longer certain, it started trembling, but he continued.

"I ran into you at the donut shop, and I didn't know who you were then but when I went to walk past your aunt's shop, I saw you there behind the counter. So, I made sure we ran into each other again." He started toward me, but rage filled me as I digested his words, so I waved him back, shaking my head as I tried to understand what I was hearing.

My voice shook as I spoke. "Wait, you were spying on us? On me?" I stood up and quickly was in his face waving my hand at him. "You were using me to get to my aunt? I can't believe this. You need to leave, now." I pointed my whole arm toward the door.

He firmly grabbed my shoulders and leaned down, his eyes darting over my face, his voice higher and soft. "Vivian, you said you would listen, and I said it was going to sound bad, please let me finish, let me explain."

I wiggled to shake free from his strong grasp on my shoulders but couldn't. I pushed his chest, but his sturdy frame was unyielding. I started grabbing and pulling at his arms to get them off of me.

I practically growled as I scrambled to escape his grasp, "Let me go, you lied to me, you used me, there isn't anything left to explain." My demands got louder as I fought to get out of his grip, but he quickly reached his long arms around me pulling me close to him. My head was buried in his chest, but I wiggled harder to get loose, now kicking and flailing as my arms were restrained. *So not only did he lie, he's holding me hostage?*

He started talking over our tussle, still holding me tight as I continued to fight to break free, "You said you would listen and if you won't sit still, I will just hold you until I'm done."

My arms were restrained by my side, and he was much larger and stronger than I was, but I kept fighting to get loose, not speaking to save my breath for energy but letting out grunts as I worked. I couldn't help but inhale his scent as my body and face were being held right up against him.

He grunted trying to get a better hold of me then continued, "Vivian, I was told to do a job and I didn't know your aunt and I didn't know you." He had to keep adjusting his grip as I continued to struggle, letting out a small growl each time. *Good, I was annoying him at least.*

"But that first time I touched your hand at the donut shop and saw you, I don't know how to explain it. I've never felt it before, and when I saw you again, I knew I had to talk to you. Not because of the job but because I had to see *you*, I had to be with *you*." He paused again.

He drew in a deep breath and his voice was getting shaky again. "When I touch you, the world stops. I kept seeing you because I had to, for me, not for them. I told them nothing more than I had already. I didn't tell you because I didn't want to upset you and I thought they were done with whatever they wanted because I had nothing new to tell them." He adjusted his grip again, but I wasn't wiggling as hard now.

"But they came back to me with something more specific and I never saw or heard you mention anything like that, so I told them that and let it go, until you had written it down. So, I snuck the file and found something. It was vague and I can't put much together on who it is, but someone thinks whatever you wrote down is theirs and that you have it." He took another deep breath and blew it out hard. I was tense and still had my fist balled but I stopped trying to get away from him. I was so confused. I felt betrayed and hurt, but something inside me knew he was being sincere.

"Tonight, I had a weird dream that scared me. I woke up needing to know you were alright. So, I called but you never answered or called me back, so I had to be sure you were safe. But when I got here and saw dirt everywhere I dunno, I got nervous. Your car was outside and there was a trail of dirt leading into the house. I tried knocking and calling again and you didn't answer so I picked the lock to check the house. And I know that's shitty and impulsive, but I had to know you were fine."

I loosened my fists and listened.

"Then I saw a dirty plastic bag in the bathroom and more dirt leading here and the door was locked, and the other bedroom was empty, so I had to assume this was your bedroom. So, I thought," his voice broke, then he stopped talking. I felt his diaphragm shaking, and I could feel the muscles in his arms shivering. It wasn't from the cold, he was crying.

His arms were still tight around me, so my face was snuggled into his chest, and I felt warm tears fall on my forehead then he leaned his head down to my shoulder, snuggling his face into my neck and loosened his grip. I stood in the same position I had been held in for a moment, but finally I couldn't help but move my arms around his back, still under his arms, and pulled him tightly to me. His shoulders were bouncing, and I felt him trying to hold his breath to hold back the tears and cries, so I squeezed him tighter and nestled my face back into his chest, this time intentionally breathing him in. He finally let a shaky breath out and I felt a flood of warm tears on my neck where he had nestled his face. He squeezed me tight, but not the same as he was moments ago–this was him embracing me.

My anger was subsiding. I began to feel a sense of relief but also heartache as I held him sobbing in my arms. I knew deep down he was holding something back, and now I know what it was.

"Why didn't you just tell me before?" I whispered to him.

"I didn't want to lose you."

I needed to know more. "So why are you telling me now? You had to know I would be upset, and can you blame me?"

He lifted his head, but he still didn't look up at me.

Sniffling and still shaking he answered, "Like I said, I don't know enough to really know the extent or details, but I don't think you're safe. And I have to protect you. I had to come tonight. And there was no way to explain why I broke in without coming clean. But if protecting you means losing you, then that's what I'll do."

My heart and stomach fluttered. His hands shook on my back as he held me. My anger was replaced with a new fire, and it was getting more intense as he continued to confess and cry in my arms.

He finally looked up at me, the blue in his eyes popping against the redness and I wanted so badly to comfort him. My heart was breaking as waves of electricity were crashing through my whole body. My brain was telling me to still be angry but every other part of me had already forgiven him.

He took a moment to take a few breaths to calm himself then continued, "I told you on our first date I believe in fate and that was true. And I can't explain it, but I know I have to be with you. I can barely control myself when I'm with you, Vivian." He looked down again, his bottom lip trembling briefly.

"Just holding you right now, I have to force myself to breathe, force myself to not run my hands all over you, to not just take you. And when I got here and thought something happened to you I..." his words trembled. I felt him shaking again as he fought off new tears.

I couldn't stand it any longer. I was encompassed by his large body, feeling his warmth, his emotions. As crazy as it all was, I believed him. And having him there against me, feeling his strength and weakness all at the same time drove me mad. My body was ready for him, desperate for him.

I moved my face close to his and I could barely breathe. I reached a hand up to his face and he rubbed it into my palm, closing his eyes as my thumb glided over his cheek. I moved in closer and found his lips.

He kissed me back, at first gently, but then I reached up and grabbed his neck to draw him into me. He became ravenous and kissed me deep and hard, grabbing a handful of my hair in one of his hands as he pulled me deeper into him. *This was it.*

I forcefully pushed his jacket off his arms then reached my hands up into his shirt and could feel his warm skin and ran my hands over his tense muscles before finally pulling the shirt up over his head. He then moved his hands to the bottom of my shirt but stopped, looking at me as if waiting for my approval so I nodded my head and put my arms up to let him know I was ready.

I felt the cool air hit my skin but then I was warmed by him. We were belly to belly, chest to chest and his arms were wrapped around me. I ran my hands over his chest and felt little hairs right in the middle of rounded muscles. He leaned down and kissed me hard again, pulling me even closer to him. I ran my hands down to his chiseled abs and finally made my way to his belt buckle. As I worked to unhook that, I was working off my own pajama pants with my feet. I finally felt the leather separate and unbuttoned then unzipped his jeans and began to push them down over his hips, pulling mine down at the same time.

He grabbed me back up quickly then put one large hand under my ass and picked me up, so I instinctively wrapped my legs around him, my skin tingling against his. I could feel him holding something against my back; I assumed his wallet.

He gently laid me on the bed and leaned down to kiss me, holding his weight up on his own arm while I could feel the other pushing his underwear off. I reached down and felt him, hard and throbbing and he let out a small, low moan which sent a new bolt of electricity through my whole body.

Our kissing was ravenous again and I wasn't sure how much longer I could take this. I wanted him inside me so badly. He slowly ran his hands over me supercharging each inch of skin he touched. He cupped my breasts, caressed my skin, and tickled my hips under the edges of my panties. I ran my hands over him, reveling in the feel of his bare skin. *I couldn't believe we were finally here.*

I wanted him now, but also wanted the moment to last forever. His skin felt warm and soft under my hands. I rubbed every inch of him. I felt his hard back muscles, cupped his round ass and I pulled him closer. His shaft was firm against my center. The only thing between us and what I knew would be pure ecstasy was a thin piece of silk. As if he could read my mind that I was ready, he reached and slid the silk barrier down and I kicked them off my feet gently. I heard the sound of a wrapper and felt the movement of him sheathing himself.

Suddenly we were frozen in time, gazing into each other's eyes while we both were taking deep, long breaths. I began shaking as my want had turned to primitive need. He tucked some loose hair behind my ear, his touch almost a tease.

Finally, he leaned down again to kiss me, then pulled away just barely. "Vivian, you're shaking. We don't have to do this."

I nodded as I whispered, "I need you, Jake. Please."

He pressed his lips to mine as he ran his hand down my body until he found my center. He slowly ran his fingers over the slick folds gathering wetness, then stroked up and down causing my back to arch as I sucked in a breath. I didn't want to wait to feel him inside me, so I reached around him with one arm and guided him inside with the other. As he entered, an intense wave crashed over me.

It was like nothing I had ever felt. Like the electricity I felt every time he touched me had been charged by a bolt of lightning. My breathing stopped for a moment as my body absorbed the new energy. He came into me fully and stopped.

He put his mouth against my neck, but then whispered in my ear, "Breathe, Vivian."

I let out my breath and took in another, trying to breathe as instructed, although I was finding it difficult with him inside me. We both reveled in that first moment. When I was breathing again, he began slowly kissing my neck before he found my mouth and kissed me again, slow and passionately.

Eventually we both slowly started swaying our hips rhythmically together and continued kissing, deeply. He ran a hand over me slowly and carefully like he was trying to remember every curve and nook. I caressed him slowly, kissing and gently biting his shoulder. His smell was even more intoxicating on his bare skin. We were moving together for a while, slowly increasing our rhythm. I was completely lost in him as we melded together perfectly. Prickling heat moved from my core outward, pulsating further into my extremities with each thrust.

As the waves began to intensify, I wrapped my arms around his lower back and pulled him deep into me. Suddenly I was quivering inside, and he let out a deep sigh and I knew he was also there. A small whimper escaped my lips.

He was still holding his weight off me but wrapped an arm under me with the other gently moving stray hair away from my face. We were staring into each other's eyes, and he gave another deep thrust and my whole body tingled, like the feeling when you wake up a sleeping limb, and all I could see was black and white static. Satisfied sighs released from both of us. Our breathing was labored but we recovered there still perfectly melded together. He held me tightly, but I was so spent all I could only wrap my arms around him as I fought to catch my breath.

When my eyesight returned, I looked up at him and a weird sense of deja vu hit me; this wasn't the first time I had felt this. Him over me. His arms around my naked body. *But this was the first time, now.* That didn't make sense, but we did. This did. It felt familiar and right, perfect. I couldn't explain it, so I decided to not give thought to it right now and just be in this moment.

He had gently laid his weight on me without crushing me. He made a small move to roll away from me, but I tangled him with my limbs to hold him there to me, at least for a while more. He lifted his head and gazed so deep into my eyes he could have seen right into my soul, then he leaned down and softly kissed me as he brushed my hair away with his hand. "Vivian, I promise you now and forever, I will never keep anything from you again. I hope you'll believe me."

I pulled his mouth down to mine for a kiss, then said, "I

do." With that, I finally released my grasp on his body, and he rolled next to me, and I looked over at the clock. It was three fifteen in the morning.

"You'll stay here, with me." I wasn't sure if I was asking him or telling him.

"I am staying. I'll be right back." He quickly bounced from the bed and into the bathroom.

He came back in a few minutes, more casually now and providing an amazing sight. I hadn't even seen him shirtless before and I got a full view as he left and a full view as he came back. He climbed into bed and turned the lamp off. We scooted closer together and I was getting comfy in the nook of his arm, shoulder, and chest when I felt his arm moving. Then he leaned toward me and reached his other hand under my pillow.

"What's that?"

Panic filled me. I completely forgot I had shoved the box under the pillow before I lay down earlier.

"Um, it's the thing I did for Aunt Rose earlier."

"Vivian, you had a knife when I came in and there's something tucked under the pillow. What's going on? You can tell me. I hope you know that now, you can tell me anything." I grabbed the covers close and leaned over him to turn the lamp back on then reached under the pillow for the box. I handed it to him while keeping the covers tucked close to my chin. He sat up straighter in the bed and put the box on his lap and opened it.

"Is this what I think it is?" I nodded hoping we were talking about the same thing.

"Aunt Rose told me to keep it completely secret, but I just found it tonight. I didn't know anything about it until a few hours ago. She told me, well now I guess it was yesterday morning, but I didn't really believe her until I found it." He didn't open the satchel or the bag and just closed the box.

"We need to keep this, and *you*, safe. Let's get some rest and we'll sort this out tomorrow." He leaned over and tucked the box under the far edge of the pillow but enough it was still covered. He turned the lamp off, rolled back over, and pulled me close to him. He kissed my forehead and brushed my hair back out of my face and I nestled in under his arm, my face on his chest.

I was exhausted. And I still had to be up in a few hours to open the shop. But I didn't care. I felt whole, calm, and safe as I lay there with him. I finally closed my eyes and let out a small happy sigh.

He ran his fingers lightly over my back and before I drifted off to sleep he said, "Happy birthday, Vivian."

Chapter 12

I stood at the door, guards standing on either side. I turned and the table was there, flowers and all, along with the stone atop the pillow. I was still in the green and gold gown. I turned back to the door and gently pulled it open.

Sunlight from the hall was beaming in so I stepped out of the room hoping to lose the glaring light. The light was from a huge window to the left, so I turned, putting the light at my back and a large familiar hand awaited me. I instinctively placed my hand into it.

The hand was met with a long ruffle coming from under a dark blue sleeve. The figure wore a vest with white embroidery that fell close to his knees, all very well-tailored. Long and muscular legs were covered with white stockings and the feet had black dress shoes. I finally looked up after inspecting the attire to find his face. No beard this time. But it was most definitely him. The same man who handed the stone to me before. The one in all the dreams. I could tell he was smiling, even as he bowed before me.

I curtsied and as I did, he looked up without standing and we were eye to eye. I couldn't believe my eyes...

The alarm blared, but Jake was between me and the nightstand. I tried to carefully lean over him to tap the snooze but as I did, I felt his arms close tightly around me. I hit the snooze lay over him. I looked down, still trying to make sense of it. He slowly opened his eyes and smiled at me. I sucked in a breath as my heart jumped into my throat.

It was him.

My faceless dream man finally revealed himself, but why? Was it my mind just inserting him because of what happened? But even if that were true, *it was him.* His hair, the shape of his face, his body, his hands, his stride, all of it. It all fits. *It was him all along...*and now I knew.

I stared down at him not knowing what to say or do. He'd think I was crazy. I couldn't tell him. He lifted a hand to my face and moved some hair behind my ear.

With a sleepy but satisfied grin, he told me in a low voice, "You have dirt on your face." *Oh my God.*

I had to be a mess. I tried to jump up, but he pulled me back down and gave me a sweet and soft kiss.

"First, good morning birthday girl." I smiled and flushed a little. Oh, how I wish I didn't have to open the shop today.

"I have to shower and go to the shop or Aunt Rose will kill us both." I gave him one more kiss then slipped off the bed, keeping the top blanket for me to wrap up in. He stretched out with a loud morning yawn, then threw his legs over the bed and grabbed his boxer-briefs from the floor.

"Should I go make some coffee then?" he asked.

"It should be ready. Help yourself and I'll be right down." I tiptoed off to the bathroom and turned the shower on.

While the water warmed up, I stood there thinking about the dream. *It was him.* I knew it. But how was I dreaming of him before I had met him? I know his face just finally revealed itself, but it was the same man from head to toe every time. All that was different last night was I could finally make the facial details out this time. As I thought of his face in the dream, the memory of his face last night crept into my mind.

He had been so open and vulnerable. Two things I hadn't seen on him before. And then, the way his eyes seared into mind as we were tangled together. More than the shower was heating up now.

Steam began to build in the bathroom and snapped me out of my daze. I dropped the blanket, stepped into the tub, and pulled the curtain. I tried to hurry, but I had to wash excess dirt off thanks to my backyard excursion. I was just about finished when I heard the door open, and I froze.

"Special delivery," he said cheerfully, and I heard a clinking sound. Even though we had been together several hours ago across the hall, I felt goosebumps pop up on my skin and knots started tying in my stomach. This was in the cruel light of day, in the even less forgiving fluorescent bathroom lighting.

I began rinsing the conditioner out of my hair when I felt a draft in the shower. I couldn't force myself to turn around, so I just stood with my face in the water and felt his arms reach around me, one grabbing my breast, and one moving between my thighs. A new shock wave was rushing through me, and I was paralyzed from the excitement. I stood with the shower beating down on me, enjoying his hands gliding over my wet soapy skin.

Suddenly his hands were moving down, I felt him coming around in front of me and he was slowly dipping down. He was kneeling before me and quickly his hand was replaced with his mouth. I could barely stand and there was no railing or anything to grab onto without pulling the shower curtain clean off the hooks, which I almost did.

He lifted one leg over his shoulder and held me from behind on the other. I tried to call his name out but was overcome with the intense rush of blood pulled away from every part of my body and being sent to my center. He ran his tongue from my opening to the sensitive, swollen nub. As he gently suctioned it, I began to pant. He then ran his tongue up and down again, slowly at first then with each stroke he picked up speed. He circled the engorged nub with his tongue before gently sucking it again. My legs began to shake, and he worked more furiously until I let out a whimper, unable to hold it back or stay quiet. He slowed his work and gently pulled my leg off his shoulder and back onto the tub floor. He kissed his way up my body slowly until he was standing in front of me. I was still catching my breath and trying not to lose my footing. He smiled smugly then grabbed the shampoo bottle and started bathing.

I was still standing there gathering my wits when he finished up and turned the water off. He reached out and grabbed my towel and wrapped it around me.

"You're going to be late if you don't get a move on." He grinned down at me, still looking pleased with himself.

I slowly stepped out of the tub and went to the sink to brush my teeth, trying to snap back into reality. He had grabbed a towel and dried off before he came up behind me.

"Any extra toothbrushes by chance?" I looked around and found a spare one someone brought home from the dentist and handed it to him, still unable to speak. He grinned as he brushed his teeth and toweled his hair dry then wrapped it back around him.

"Here's your coffee, hope it's not cold." He gave me a quick kiss on the forehead before he walked back across the hall.

I took a sip of coffee, and it was warm but didn't mix well with toothpaste. I went to my room, and he was dressed.

"You may not believe this, but I didn't plan to sleep over," he said as he tied his shoes. "I don't know what I planned at all really. So, I need to run home and change. But if you don't mind, I can come straight to the shop when I'm done."

I nodded my head as I stood there wrapped in a towel. He

stood then pulled me up against him. His face appeared softer and satisfied, like he was overall lighter.

"You may think this is crazy, but I dreamt about you last night. I had on stockings and a man-dress," he chuckled and gently pushed my wet hair off my shoulder, reigniting the electric surge inside down my neck into my abdomen. "But you looked beautiful in this old-timey dress and your hair up so I could see your face and your shoulders." He paused and his head tipped down. He was blushing. "I don't know why I just told you that."

My head was spinning. *Did he and I have the same dream, at the same time?*

"I know, crazy, forget I said anything." He was quick to change the subject. "I hate to leave you now, but I need a fresh set of clothes. I'll see you over there soon, okay?" He grabbed the back of my head and pulled me in for a toe-curling kiss. Once he had managed to get me off balance, he pulled away with a look of achievement on his face and started to leave. He had made it down several steps then he turned back.

"Oh, do you have a bookbag or something? You should bring that box with you. I wouldn't leave it here under the pillow."

I thought for a second and finally managed to utter words. "I do, in the closet downstairs. I'll grab it before I leave."

He turned again then once more turned back. "Take the car, too." Then he finally turned and made it down the stairs and out the door.

I threw on some jeans and a long sleeve shirt then went downstairs for more coffee and found the bookbag. I took it back up, along with my hot coffee, and put the box in and zipped it up. I finished getting ready then took the bookbag and my coffee downstairs. I sat my phone down to put my coat on and saw the calls I had missed from Jake last night and a good morning text from Aunt Rose. I must have turned the ringer off and didn't realize. *Shit.* I didn't have time to go see her.

I texted Aunt Rose I woke up late but would be by in the afternoon. Then I headed out and locked up, not that it did much good since Jake so easily broke in. We needed to check that out once Aunt Rose was feeling better. I got into the car, bag, and coffee in hand, then took off toward the shop.

Chapter 13

It was even colder today than it was late last night. I went in, bookbag in arm, and turned the lights and computer on then turned the heat up a few notches to quell the chill. There were still decorations I needed to put up. I had spent so much time organizing the boxes I found the other day that I never got started decorating. But today was Saturday and it was always busy so I wasn't sure I could get it done unless I stayed past closing time.

I put the bookbag behind our mini fridge under the counter and pulled the boxes up front just in case I had time between customers. It was almost Christmas, so it was shameful I hadn't done this sooner.

I went to the front, unlocked the door, plugged in the open sign, and walked back to the counter. As I was logging into the register the door jingled. Jake strolled in with fresh clothes along with two coffees and a little bag. *God he was perfect.*

"I knew you didn't have time to eat yet, so I grabbed a birthday donut for you and some hot coffee." He was grinning ear to ear as he handed the bag to me but as I took it, he put the drinks down and stepped in close to me, wrapping his arms around me. He smelled amazing and I could have been imagining it, but I think he was more gorgeous now than when I saw him this morning. He let out a moan, filling my abdomen with heat.

"So, birthday girl, you sure you don't mind me hanging around all day?"

I pulled him even closer and enjoyed the long embrace, breathing him in. I knew he wasn't property, but he felt like he belonged to me. And I belonged to him.

After a moment, I looked up at him and with a bossy tone replied, "No, because you can help me with decorations." I laughed and he smiled then leaned down and picked up a box.

He took it to the front and started pulling out lights. I took some tape and tacks up to him to use to hang them. Customers started coming in, so I left him to the decorations and got to work

As customers shopped, I finally started picking at my donut and enjoyed the piping hot coffee. The day was going fast, and he made quick work of the decorations. He motioned for me to come up and see what he had done. They looked good from inside, but he wanted to look from outside.

"Ok, but we won't be able to see them well until it's dark," I told him as we walked out. Neither of us took the time to grab our coats and we quickly walked out and turned to see the storefront. It was really beautiful, even in the daylight.

The lights actually were visible against the inside of the shop. He hung some paper snowflakes and multi-colored bulbs dangled across the windows. My teeth chattered and he said it was too cold for me to be standing there and he pulled the door open for me. I went to step in but turned to smile at him. As I looked past his shoulder into the square, I stopped dead in my tracks. The man that had come in asking about the gemstone stood on the sidewalk across the square.

"Vivian, what is it?" Jake moved toward me, blocking my view so I pushed his shoulder to look again.

He turned to look at what I was searching for but as we both looked, he had gone.

I looked around anxiously. "He was just there. It was him, the man that had come here asking about the stone a couple of times."

Jake turned, looking around. "Are you sure?" He asked as he turned to look again. I didn't see him anywhere. I took another look around, but he had vanished somewhere. I shook my head and then shivered from the cold, so I stepped back into the shop.

Jake walked into the back and made sure the back door was locked.

"We never use that door. It's always bolted," I said as he walked back to the front and looked out. He walked to the counter and asked if I could describe the man, his demeanor no longer light but rigid and serious.

"Well, umm, I would say he's only a couple of inches taller than I am, older, but not incredibly old, maybe 50's. Sort of unassuming, no facial hair, dark eyes, round face, he wore a tan hat and tan dress coat both times I saw him, but he had removed his hat the first time he was here, and his hair was brown and thinning, but he wasn't bald. Other than that, I don't know how to explain." I paused, trying to think of anything else. "Oh, he wasn't a large build or overweight but not thin. But that's it." Jake had found a pen and pad and wrote as I spoke. I hope I never had to describe anyone for a lineup. But Jake seemed to make sense of what I said.

"I don't recall anyone like this, but I'll keep an eye out at work next week. My guess is he won't be going in. The file I found was small with very few details and I guess that was on purpose. But you never know, maybe he will go by. But I'm not even sure it's connected." His eyes seemed dark so I stepped a little closer and could see his pupils were dilated. His jaw was clenching, and he ran his hands through his hair.

"It has to be. What are the odds that more than one person is looking for it?" I paused, then wondered out loud. "So, you don't know who hired you? Did you never speak to them?" I asked urgently.

He shook his head. "No, I'm not an attorney, I'm just an investigator. Unless it's for a hearing I don't typically speak to the client. I just get the file once the attorney and his assistant get the info, and the payment."

I thought for a second and got nervous. "What if he *has* been there and knows who you are and just saw you here with me? Won't that be a problem?"

He shook his head. "No, because as much as I didn't want to bring that back up, I was supposed to be around." That stung a little, but I believed him wholeheartedly and then decided maybe that could work to our advantage.

"What if you told them you may finally be onto something? Not tell them we found it but just mention a conversation or something. Maybe that would draw him in or at least more of the details could be put into the file? My Aunt thinks whoever is looking for the gemstone may have had something to do with my parent's death." He looked at me questionably so I told him it was kind of a long story, and we could catch him up later, but we probably shouldn't keep discussing it at the shop. I forgot he didn't really have the backstory, just that I had whatever it was someone was looking for. He came closer, gently rubbing my arms and shoulders, looking me over as if I was an injured bird.

"I'll figure this out. And I'll snoop around with the assistants, see if anyone can tell me about the client. I won't let anything happen to you, Vivian." He had an absolute tone. His intensity was increasing. The electricity rushed through me, and I could feel my muscles begin to quiver. Some light reflected off one of the decorations pulling me back to reality.

"I almost forgot, I told Aunt Rose I would bring her lunch after I closed up. She is miserable there and hates the food. Do you mind if we go?"

He looked at his watch. "I'll take care of it, be back soon." He swiftly grabbed his coat and took off before I could stop him. I didn't mean for him to buy the food.

It was close to closing time, so I went around to be sure things were in order so all I had to do was turn the lights off and leave in a few minutes. I started toward the front of the store and saw Jake jogging toward me with a big bag and a drink carrier.

I pushed the door open, and he lifted his arms up to show me his accomplishment. "See, taken care of! Go ahead and finish closing up and I'll be at the car so we can take this to her."

I grabbed the bookbag from under the counter, put on my coat, and headed out to lock up. I unplugged the open sign but left the Christmas lights on so people could see them once it was dark.

He put the food and drinks in the back and was waiting outside the car for me.

He opened the passenger door. "Would you like me to drive you, ma'am?"

I had never ridden with him even though he had a car. Just like me, he often walked everywhere.

"I left my car at home. I figured you wouldn't want to leave yours here all day." With everything going on, I didn't like the idea of leaving the car in the square. It wasn't much but it's the only one we had. I handed him the keys and gladly sat in the passenger seat. He closed my door and walked around the driver's side.

When we found a parking space, he turned off the engine but told me to hold on a second, so I sat there. He jumped out and ran around the back of the car and came to open my door and reached his hand out to help me out. The chivalry was making me uncomfortable. *How sad was that?*

I wasn't far removed from high school where chivalry was never alive, and the college guys never acted like this where I went to school. But I still took his hand and stepped out.

He reached in and grabbed the bookbag and threw it over his shoulder. "Don't want to leave this out here." Then he reached into the back and grabbed the food and drinks. He refused my offer to help, so I made sure to at least get to the elevators to hit the button before he could.

We walked quickly through the bright and sterile hospital and went to Aunt Rose's room. When we got there, he told me to take her the food and grab her drink.

"What? Don't be silly. Come on." I urged him to follow, but he didn't want to. I walked in and immediately told Aunt Rose he was with me.

"Don't be shy dear, come on and stop lurking in the hall!" Aunt Rose shouted out. He slowly walked in and sheepishly smiled. I gave her a hug and she immediately opened the bag of food I had set down on her tray.

"Oh, my goodness, you got me Vincent's! And it even has the breadsticks in here."

I shook my head. "I didn't get this, Jake did."

She smiled at him and reached her arms out. "Oh, you dear boy, you come here to me! This is amazing!"

He seemed nervous so I nodded him over. He walked over to the other side and leaned down. Aunt Rose gave him a good hug and kiss on the cheek. He started to blush but smiled and stepped back, so he was still standing by her. She sat up in the bed, so I adjusted it up a bit more and fluffed her pillows.

"So," she started to say as she was shoveling pasta in, "what have you kids been up to? How was the shop today?"

I started to feel flushed, and I think Jake could see that, so he chimed in. "We put up some decorations today and had a good bit of customers." She smiled at him and thanked him for the decorations.

"Viv, I didn't know you were bringing me eye-candy today. I had hoped we could chat." I put my hands in my pockets and took a deep breath. She wanted to know if I found the box.

"We can catch up soon, but everything is as you said. I didn't know I would have company today until later." I looked up and smiled at him. "But he wanted to spend my birthday with me."

Aunt Rose practically threw her fork down and waved both arms up. "I am *the* worst! I can't believe I didn't acknowledge your birthday, honey. I am so sorry." She reached out for me to hug her and squeezed me tight then planted lots of little pecks on my cheeks. I was giggling and told her it was fine; I think she mentioned it last night anyway.

"No excuse! I just can't keep up with what day it is in here. We will do something great once I bust outta this joint, to make it up to you, I promise!" I grabbed her hands and told her again it was more than fine, and I just wanted her to get better.

"Jake, since I completely failed, I expect you to make it up to her." She went back to eating and he was grinning at me from across the hospital bed. The thought of him making it up to me was more than I could stand to think about standing next to my aunt. I pulled the chair up and sat down so Jake pulled the stool over and sat on it.

"So, are you still doing well? Everything healing up nicely?" I asked her.

"So far, so good. Still looks like Monday, but they told me they don't know the time yet. I'll order a cab. And of course, I am to take it easy a few days more so I will need your help next week."

I was about to protest the cab when Jake leaned over to her. "I can come and drive you home Monday, this is my number," he said as he handed her his card.

She looked at me smugly and with that same smugness dripping off her words asked, "Well, how could I ever turn down that offer?"

He smiled and said, "Just call me when you're ready, ma'am." I had to figure something out, but I didn't expect him to go get her but didn't want her taking a cab after surgery. We sat for a while more and she and I chatted about the shop and how quiet the house had been without her there.

"Well, kids, I appreciate the meal, I really do. But I'm tired and it's your birthday, so you take this man and go have fun." Aunt Rose said with a shooing motion. "Enjoy your day off tomorrow! I will check in with *you* later."

I stood up and leaned over to her and we had a long, tight hug. When I pulled away, she looked me in the eye and gave a small nod and I knew she was asking if I found it, so I gave her a small nod back. I couldn't tell her, yet, that Jake knew. She needed to get better and didn't need to be upset at me, at least not now. Jake also leaned in and gave her a small hug and then walked around to me. We grabbed our coats and headed down the hall.

I was putting my coat back on and asked him, "So what now?"

He smiled and put his coat on before we walked outside back to the car. "You'll see."

Chapter 14

Jake drove us away from the hospital and headed to the market. He told me to wait in the car and was back quickly.

"Gotta love advanced ordering." He put the bags in the back, and we took off.

We headed down the street and were just a block off the square but pulled into a parking deck that required a key card to get in. It was an upscale apartment complex, at least compared to the typical buildings near the square. Most didn't have gated parking and the signs alone screamed fancy with the calligraphy style writing set against marble backing. He got out quickly and opened the door for me. He was grabbing the bags out and I offered to help but he once again told me he had it. As he gathered the bags I looked around.

Besides the concrete, it could have easily been part of the hospital. It was bright and clean. Way too clean to be a parking deck. Most parking decks reeked of oil and exhaust and had trash, at least in the corners. Besides Jake's cologne and something sweet from one of the bags, the whole space was void of smells. And not one stray piece of paper could be found.

"Is my car okay here? You paying if it gets towed?" I jokingly asked not knowing what else to say.

"It's fine, it won't be towed." He lifted the bags. "I think this is it, let's go."

He was carrying the bookbag and the groceries, so I grabbed the doors as we entered using the keycard that he handed me. He told me to hit the fifth floor on the elevator, which appeared to be the top floor of the building, although the building seemed much taller than just five floors.

Once the elevator opened, I followed him down a long hall with only four doors total, two on either side, with very crisp and modern décor along the walls. When he got to the last door and stopped, I tapped the keycard to his door and opened it.

The space was huge with high ceilings and large windows. Mostly basic furniture but tidy. The kitchen and living room were in one large area and there was a dining table near the floor to ceiling window closer to the kitchen side. One sofa, a chair, and of course a television in the living area. Not surprised to see a sports magazine on the end table. There were two doors so I could only assume one was the bathroom and one was the bedroom. *Definitely a single man living here.*

He put the bags down on the kitchen island and turned on the lights. He cleared away a coffee mug that was on the island then hurried to the table and pulled a jacket from one of the chairs. I chuckled as I looked out the window. Aunt Rose's house was "lived in" so a mug and a jacket didn't seem like an issue to me, but he was rushing to move them from my sight.

After he put his jacket on a hook by the door he returned to the kitchen. He began clinking around and started pulling out pots and pans, then he also pulled out two wine glasses and pulled a bottle of red out of a cabinet. He opened it, poured into both glasses, and handed one to me while still holding the other.

"I had some other plans for your birthday, but a few things had to be rearranged since your aunt needed to have her procedure. So, I'll do my best." He grinned in a way that told me I would enjoy his best. He then raised his glass. "So, cheers to your first drink, that I know of, but for sure the first with me, and many more to come." We clinked glasses and I took a sip.

I had only had beer and college concoctions before, but

this wasn't bad. I hadn't had any alcohol in months since I'd left college, so I knew I better take it slow. He motioned for me to come over to the kitchen area and pulled a stool from the island for me to sit on.

"I hope you like steak, I figured staying in may be a good idea in light of recent developments. And I can cook a mean steak. Plus, it's good with wine according to the folks at the market." He shot a quick wink at me. *Act natural, Viv.*

I smiled and nodded. "I love steak. So, you're cooking me dinner? That's a first for me."

He grinned as he tilted his head. "Well, I'm surprised. But I like being the first for all this stuff for you," he said while he was seasoning food. He then stopped and looked right into my eyes. "Hopefully, it'll help you remember this birthday."

I could hardly contain my nervous energy, so I slid off the stool and started to look around his apartment, checking out the pictures. He was still puttering around the kitchen preparing the meal. He did take time to stop and put some music on, not loud but just enough where it wasn't quiet. eighties, nice touch. Specifically, The Smiths to start. The car is pretty much fixed on the station that plays mostly eighties and nineties so he must have been paying attention.

There was condensation on the windows, but I could still see out a bit.

"This is some view of the town you have." I twirled around, still holding my wine glass. "I see why you left the cop's salary."

He grunted a little but not in an upset way. "Well, Dad of course offered for me to stay with him but it's a little cramped there with his new wife and their kids. They're only ten and twelve and Karen and I don't necessarily see eye to eye. So, I made sure to secure a place of my own before I moved," he said, still cooking away.

I strolled back to the island as he spoke. I leaned over it, listening intently and watching him. He had talked a little about his old job, but not his family before.

"I worked in high school, and he paid for college so all the jobs I had, I just saved the money. And even though I wasn't a detective for long, I made a decent salary. It's not really as much as it looks." He leaned over and topped off my glass even though it wasn't empty.

"It'll be a while before I finish dinner, but I have a few things to nibble on for you at the table, want to come sit?" He motioned to the table by the window. He carried a premade snack tray, but it was nice. Lots of cheese, little meats, grapes, and crackers. I hadn't had much all day. In fact, just the donut, so I needed to eat something, especially with the wine. I slowly nibbled on the snacks trying to get a handle on the knots in my stomach and the lightheadedness that was growing as I drank.

"So, tell me about college. Think you'll go back?"

Wow, I wasn't expecting that. But I suppose the details haven't really been filled in yet except my little outburst about my parents at dinner a couple weeks back. And he shared a little more with me.

I pulled in a deep breath and shrugged. "Well, I'm really not sure. I don't exactly even know what I want to do. I came here after the accident mostly because Aunt Rose asked me, and I didn't really know what else to do."

I took a small sip then continued, "We sold the house, so I was essentially homeless, but I wasn't destitute. I was already struggling when the accident happened. When it was time to register for fall, well, I just didn't. I didn't really want to be there toward the end anyway. I was just there because it's what I was supposed to do, ya know what I mean?"

He swirled his wine around in his glass while he was listening but set it down before answering me. "I do. The only difference is I stuck out the four years and didn't disappoint Dad *until* I told him I wasn't applying to grad school."

He dropped his head a little before he took a sip of his wine and continued. "He was dead set that I would take over the firm when he retires. He had his plans, but never really asked me mine. I always wanted to be a detective and while I told him, I was with Mom a lot more, so I think he assumed it was a phase or I was just saying that to irritate him. But it just felt right." He shrugged. "So that's what I did."

I finished chewing my last bite of unidentified but delicious cheese. "But if you loved that so much and had a job you really wanted, why did you come here?" Now I was staring into his eyes, and he squirmed in his seat.

He cocked his head to the side a bit and his brow scrunched down. He looked back up at me, his blue eyes deep and his voice low and serious. "You may think this sounds crazy and it's hard to explain. I had a hard time leaving my dream job. Most folks gotta wait for a spot to open so they work patrol until then, but it just worked out for me fast." He had a hint of sorrow on his face briefly, but then that turned to a confused look.

"But Dad had asked me to come work with him as soon as he knew I wasn't going to grad school–several times–and I blew him off at first. But he asked me again a few months back and before I even had details, I just said yes. He was even a little shocked, I think. I don't know why but I just blurted it out."

He stopped for another sip, then his voice was more even again. "I, of course, called him again the next day and explained I was going to give a notice at my job and find my own place, but I just felt like I had to be here suddenly. And I don't know why. Have you ever felt like you had to do something but couldn't explain it?"

I was staring across the table at him, my heart fluttering. "Yeah, I think I do." I started to feel my cheeks get warm, so I tried to continue the conversation. "So, does he think by working for him you'll see the error of your ways and go back to school?"

He shrugged and grinned then stood to go grab the wine bottle. He poured a little more in both of our glasses.

"Sort of off subject, but Aunt Rose is supposed to come home Monday and you broke into my house." He looked like he was going to apologize so I quickly stopped him, "I'm not complaining that you did. I just worry it may be easy for someone else. Is there a way we can change the locks or something? I don't like the idea of her there alone and vulnerable."

He nodded. "Absolutely, we can go tomorrow and grab the things we need" His serious face turned more mischievous. "But if she's alone, does that mean you'll be here with me?"

That look sent a nervous laugh out that I couldn't control. "Well, I suppose sometimes if you don't mind me, but I just meant during the day after she gets home. I'll have to keep the shop open while she recovers for a few days. And with the commotion lately, I just want to be sure she's safe."

He leaned toward me over the table and grabbed my hand. "Vivian, I told you I won't let anything happen to you and that goes for her, too. She's your family." He started to blush a little and his head dropped for a moment but then he looked back up at me. "Maybe her bringing you here is what pulled me to this place?" He sounded only half-joking. At this point I couldn't rule out anything. So much in the last few months has not made sense and the last few days have been particularly odd.

As he held my hand the normal shockwaves that accompany his touch were flowing through me. I wondered how obvious it was to him that I was so affected each time he touched me. And it also became clear to me suddenly that I have had at least two glasses of wine with extraordinarily little food all day.

I pushed my glass to the middle of the table. "Maybe I should slow down on that until we have real food." He apologized for topping it off and jumped up and walked to the kitchen. He made me a glass of ice water and brought it back to me.

"Here, sip this. I'll go ahead and start cooking but you keep snacking." He leaned down and gave me a long, but closed-mouth kiss then turned back to the kitchen.

I sat watching him work as I kept nibbling. He was moving things around and turning on burners then asked, "So what was it you were saying at the shop earlier? About your aunt thinking this all has something to do with your parents." I sat up a bit straighter and took a long sip of the cold water.

"Well, it all happened so fast I honestly don't know much. But the other day when I visited her at the hospital, I was mentioning that someone was searching our website for the gemstone. Just the day before her surgery that man was in the store again asking for it."

I stopped, trying to recall details. "Looking back, she was tense when he was there but told him she had no such thing and he left. So, she got really weird when I mentioned it again at the hospital and broke down and told me about the gemstone. She told me my parents had gotten it overseas and sent it home to her for an appraisal since she deals with antiques. Then after that they told her to keep it safe and hidden. She said she didn't know the ins and outs, but it seemed like my parents were scared or something and even told her if anything happened to them to be sure I got the stone by my twenty-first birthday." I took a long sip of water before continuing.

"So, she told me all that, where it was, and that I needed to find it. But she also swore me to secrecy which is why I didn't tell you *and* why I didn't meet you last night after closing time. She seemed really scared. I hated to blow you off, but I promised her. I guess I still ended up breaking that promise, though." He was listening but still cooking and tending to the meal.

"I get it, Vivian. It's all a little strange. And I hope you know your secret is safe with me. I will admit, though, I was a little put off yesterday. I thought you were mad about the night before, and it was tearing me up."

I felt myself blushing. "No, not mad, or anything. In fact, I almost blew off finding it because it all sounded so crazy, and I really wanted to be with you."

He fought off a smile as he kept stirring and flipping things on the stove. I reached back for my wine glass and took a sip, then another.

"So, did you look at it, the gemstone?" He asked, catching me off guard.

"Well, I had to see what the fuss was about, I suppose. Once I found the box, I took it inside and opened it to find the two bags of different sizes as you saw. So, I opened them but then just put it all back how I found it and tucked it under the pillow. I wasn't sure what else to do with it." He kept tending to the food and occasionally took a sip of wine.

"So, you said again, the man was there before?"

"He had come a couple weeks back asking for a red or pink stone and looked around some but that was all. I didn't think much about it until he came back." He stopped his stirring for a minute.

"I'm not a betting man but I'd say he isn't the one actually looking for it, he's probably working for the person who is. If it's as valuable as you say I doubt the person wanting it does their own leg work. But then that's odd they would have me snooping around as well. Or maybe they were getting restless. There just isn't much to go on." He turned the burners off, took several purposeful steps to me, knelt by me, and grabbed my hand.

His chest was heaving, and his eyes were locked onto mine. "Vivian, I have a bad feeling about this and there is a lot I don't know, but I do know this...I will not let anything happen to you, your aunt, or that box. I promise you that." He squeezed my hand a bit harder. "And I *will* find out who that man is."

I don't know if it was the wine, the words, or just him, but I couldn't control myself. I slid down to my knees to be face to face with him then grabbed his face and drew it to mine. He put his hard arms around me but once I felt them, I wanted to feel his skin. I ran my hands up his shirt then pulled it up over his head. He wrapped his arms around me, and I ran my hands over his hard back, pulling him closer. Our lips met urgently sending heat throughout my body.

He shifted, beginning to stand. A small growl escaped him as he reached under and picked me up. Goosebumps ran up my arms. I wrapped my legs around him as he carried me toward one of the doors. He walked backwards into it and even though it was dim, and we were still lip locked, I opened my eyes long enough to see it was his bedroom.

Once in the room he turned to walk forward to the bed, and he gently placed me down. He was laying over me holding himself up with one arm and using the other to feel the skin under my shirt and somehow managed to unhinge my bra even though the clasps were in the back. He sat up on his knees for a moment to help me pull my shirt off and I pulled the straps of my bra down off my arms. He leaned over me again but started kissing my neck, my breasts, my tummy, and I could feel him unbuttoning my pants, sending heat and moisture between my thighs. He slowly worked my pants and panties off. I leaned up just enough to desperately unbuckle his belt, then opened the button and started pulling his pants and boxer-briefs down as well. He reached into the nightstand and pulled out a foil square.

He leaned over me, his warm taut skin against mine, kissing me intensely, as he rolled the condom over his shaft. Then he moved his large warm hand between my legs, and it reached down into the wet folds, sending a small moan from my mouth. He gently rubbed and caressed as my body became swollen around his fingers, his thumb rubbing over the engorged nub. When I tried to reach for him, he twisted so I couldn't, but he continued to stroke me. We were still kissing hard, tongues intertwining, and I could taste his lip balm but also the red wine we were drinking. He was still stroking and rubbing, and my legs began to shake, and I was starting to feel like I was about to unravel so I made a quick move and rolled us both so that I was on top of him.

Once I got my balance I reached down and guided him inside and slowly lowered all the way down onto him. He let out a low moan as I did, and it excited me even more than I already was. His hands were resting on my hips as I began rocking. I moved slowly at first, allowing myself to feel him inside me. Gradually, I increased the pace, and we were moving together, the tension building. I grabbed his hands and moved them both to my breasts, so he was kneading and massaging them. We kept our rhythm together, me swaying my hips, him thrusting from below. His face was intense, his sultry eyes locked onto mine.

I started to feel my core beginning to lose control and my eyes involuntarily closed as I was ready to let it happen. But he grabbed my hips and stopped me, biting his bottom lip with a vexatious look in his eyes. He squeezed my hips, made a quick move, and rolled me onto my back. We were still melded together as he did, but he didn't immediately start rocking or thrusting and still gripped my hips.

I felt as if I would burst if he didn't let it happen soon. I needed the release. I felt my face contort in desperation and I moaned out his name and dug my fingers into his back.

"Jake...please."

He finally slowly started pushing himself in and out and his mouth was gently on mine. Everything down to my toes was aching for release. I wrapped my arms and legs around him to pull him in close.

He stopped again for a moment and looked into my eyes, grinning at me as he teased me. I squeezed my legs around him tighter, barely able to breathe, then he came down and kissed me hard and began thrusting just as hard. I moaned through his kisses and my entire body was stiff from the waves of pleasure running through me.

'Oh, Vivian," he let out in a low rumbly voice as I felt him quake inside me just as my release finally was granted and my eyes filled with black and white static.

He stayed over me catching his breath then leaned down and kissed me softly and slowly. Static lingered behind my eyelids. My arms and legs were wrapped tightly around him. He slowly lowered himself onto me but made sure he wasn't crushing me below him. *God his weight on me was amazing.*

As my breathing calmed, I finally loosened my grip but still held him, running my hands up and down his back. His arms were tucked under me, holding me to him. His head resting on my shoulder with his warm breath and beard tickling my neck. Even though I had my release, electricity was still firing through every nerve in my body as we lay there, intertwined with one another, like pieces of a puzzle. I felt something over his normally smooth back and kept rubbing the spots to figure out what they were.

"I think you got me with your nails," he grumbled with his face still tucked into my neck.

"Oh my God, I'm so sorry! I swear I didn't mean to do that!"

He chuckled. "Oh, I don't mind. You do whatever you want to me." I felt blood rush to my cheeks, so I was grateful for the darkness of the room. We lay there in silence for a few more minutes.

"Oh no! The food!" I blurted out.

"I bet you're starving. Let me turn the stove back on really quick." He stole another juicy kiss and I reluctantly let go of him so he could get up.

He jumped up off the bed and pulled some grey sweatpants from a drawer. I couldn't help but take a good look at his physique as he did. He had a beautifully sculpted V-shaped back with perfectly rounded ass leading to large but lean legs. I got a good look before the sweats were pulled on and he walked to the bathroom, then out to the kitchen.

I got up, with the blanket, and walked to the chest of drawers he pulled the sweats from and found a large t-shirt to toss on before pulling my panties back on.

He came back and laughed as he looked me up and down. "I see you found my shirts, and you look sexy as hell, but I actually planned ahead a little." He pulled a bag from behind his back. I wasn't expecting that, but I reached for the bag, almost afraid to pull out whatever crazy lingerie he must have gotten for me to wear around his apartment. I reached my hand into the bag and felt soft cotton, so I grabbed the material and pulled it out. It was Christmas pajamas, a long-sleeved shirt with pants. Little gingerbread men and candy canes were all over them.

"I had hoped I would convince you to sleep over, so I figured you'd need something to sleep in. And it's hard to find non-holiday pjs right now but they're kinda cute, right?" He was looking down at me with a childlike curiosity, waiting on my approval.

I laughed a little and hugged him tight. "I love them. And I suppose I'll stay; you *are* feeding me." I stood on my tiptoes with a grin and gave him a kiss then pulled away and walked toward the bathroom to change and freshen up.

I came out of the bathroom in my new pjs, and he had set the table and even had a candle lit. It was already getting close to sundown now since it was winter, and the days were short. I went and sat before he could pull the chair out, but his hands were full anyway. He put a shirt on while I was in the bathroom. *What a tragedy.*

"Sneaky, I didn't even hear you come out. Oh well, hope you're hungry!" He had some veggies on the table and was carrying the steaks over. He served them up before taking the large pan back to the stove. I started putting some veggies on his plate then on mine and he walked back over and sat.

"It's your birthday, so stop. Let me serve you ma'am." I had already finished filling the plate, so he poured us both some more wine and he held up his glass.

"To the birthday girl, and the first of many we will spend together." We clinked glasses and both sipped then I grabbed my utensils to dig in.

Between barely sleeping or eating all day, the wine, and the extracurricular activities we just had, I was starving. Everything was so delicious, and he was right, the wine was good with the steak. I could just hear Aunt Rose in my mind, "You don't want to look like a pig." Oh well, he cooked, and I was starving. He must have been as well, as we both were quiet through most of dinner. I finally put my fork down and leaned back in my chair when I was full.

"Are you ok?" he asked.

"Oh, I am more than fine. I'm stuffed!" I patted my tummy. "That was delicious. How did you learn to cook like that?"

He smiled. "Well, being the only man around my house

growing up my mom made sure I knew how to cook and clean."
He smiled a little while talking about her, his eyes warm. "She
always said a wife isn't a maid, so I needed to be able to do these
things."

"She sounds pretty smart."

He let out a small laugh. "She is. I didn't appreciate it back
then, but when I went off to college and only had a microwave
and a hot plate it came in handy to know. And now I can cook for
you. I don't suppose you have room for dessert now?" I couldn't
imagine having one more morsel right now.

"I need to wait a bit if that's ok. I just hope I can stay
awake for a while. I didn't get much sleep last night, for various
reasons," I said as I waggled my eyebrows.

A devilish grin spread on his face as he stood up and
poured a little more wine for us both. He grabbed his glass then
reached his hand out to me. I grabbed my wine glass and then
took his hand. He led me to the couch and let go of my hand then
made a sweeping motion with his hand.

"May I interest you in some Netflix and chill?"

I laughed and nodded my head but motioned for him to
sit first. "You sit so I can get comfy." He nodded his head as if
obeying orders and sat down on the edge, so I nestled in right
next to him. He grabbed the remote, turned off the music, and
turned on the television. I was so cozy and relaxed sitting there
next to him, tucked under his arm in a little ball with my feet
pulled up on the couch, knees tucked up close to me.

He scrolled through some titles and chose some chick-
flick I had seen a million times, but of course one more wouldn't
hurt. I sipped some more of my wine, but my eyes were getting
heavy, so I passed the glass to him to put on the side table. I
scooted in even closer and laid my head on his chest and he was
softly rubbing my back with the arm he had around me.

The day was catching up to me quickly. So much adrenaline, so little sleep, so much intimacy, so much food, and so much wine. So much had happened in less than twenty-four hours and my body and mind were about to succumb to it all. It really was hard to wrap my head around all that happened just in the past day. I was trying so hard to stay awake, but my eyes began crossing and my eyelids were heavy. I moved a little hoping to jolt myself awake but it didn't last long.

As if he sensed I was fighting sleep, he rubbed my back and said, "shh, shh," even though I hadn't said anything. Before I knew it, my eyelids had closed, and I couldn't peel them open even if I tried. I was quickly drifting off to sleep there on the rhythmic movement of his chest from his steady breaths and soft sounds of a movie in the background.

Chapter 15

It was dark and eerie as I knelt on the forest bottom in front of a large fire. The fire was warm on my face and the flames practically licked the tall branches above. I felt cold air on my back even though I had a heavy cloak on. The fire not only had normal hues of orange and red, but bold flashes of blue and purple shot up inside the flames. The energy in the air made the hairs on my arm stand up.

I sat facing the fire, my hands tucked into the cloak leaving nothing but my face visible. Suddenly the flames were shortening, as if something had been previously forcing its height and ferocity. It calmed into a normal fire, no more blue or purple and it no longer teased at the branches above. As the flames became shorter and shorter, I could see across the fire and there was someone there. A woman.

She was also in a hooded cloak but while mine was plain hers was ornately decorated at the end of the sleeves and the clasps at the neck were large and golden. The hood was large and obscured her face. She had something in her hands, but I couldn't tell what it was.

The tiny figure turned and started to walk around the fire to me, so I stood and turned toward her. When she came to me, her tiny hands with delicate lines and obvious veins reached out, still holding something. I reached mine out toward her with my palms up. As she finally approached me, I could see she was holding the gemstone. She carefully placed it into my hands, and I held it tightly. A sense of relief washed over me. I looked past the woman and saw a familiar face that brought a sense of love and warmth immediately. Jake was looking around, wielding a sword and two horses waited just past him. He put his sword in the sheath and then reached his hand out toward me and began calling me to come, saying that we had to leave. "Vivian, Vivian, Vivian..."

I was coming out of my sleep slowly and realized I was still laying on Jake, but we both were more outstretched on the couch.

"Vivian, sorry to wake you. It's late." He was rubbing my back, speaking softly and smoothly. "Wanna have birthday cake then go to bed, in the bed? Maybe it'll be more comfortable in there." I rubbed my eyes a bit and looked outside and the sky was dark, but the city lights lit everything up brightly.

"How long was I out?" I leaned up a bit and pushed my legs back over the sofa so my feet could hit the floor.

"Long enough to miss the whole movie, but I figured you wouldn't mind." He stood up and reached his hand out, so I grabbed it and he pulled me up and to him for a strong embrace. He kissed the top of my head then grabbed my hand again and led me back to the table, pulling the chair out this time.

He went to the fridge and pulled out a pink box and set it on the island. Once the box opened a sweet smell emerged. His back was turned, and he was hiding something, then he turned and presented a small, round cake with white frosting and a candle on top. He placed the cake on the table and went back for plates, utensils, and a lighter.

He sat down, lit the candle, and recited, not sang, *Happy Birthday*. I grinned ear to ear and felt blood rush to my cheeks. Once he was done, I drew in a breath and dramatically blew out the candle. He grinned as he cut a piece of cake for me. He cut one more for himself and sat down across from me at the table.

"I can't believe you did this, or that you sang Happy

Birthday," I said jokingly.

"I don't sing, but I got the message out all the same. And you deserve a cake on your birthday."

I took a bite of the white cake with white frosting, and it practically melted in my mouth. "Oh my gosh, this may be the best cake I've ever had. This came from the market?"

He replied, "Well technically it came from Betty's Bakery but my friend who works at the market grabbed it so I could get everything together when I went by." I was impressed, he had been here a short time but made fast friends willing to do favors.

"You seem to have a lot of connections around here, dinner upstairs at Vincent's, special cake pickup. Are you bribing people or something?"

He chuckled. "No, a lot of it is just because of my dad but Johnny at the market, well, we've been friends for years. Growing up I didn't see him except when I visited Dad, but guys can pick up easily where we left off. He was happy to help." I nodded and finished off my cake. My water from earlier was still there along with the dinner plates so I took a big sip and stood up, starting to grab up our mess.

Jake quickly stood and grabbed my plate and cup. "I told you, you're the birthday girl so I am here to serve you. Just go sit on the couch while I clear this off." I rolled my eyes a bit but did as he instructed and went and curled up in the corner of the couch.

The cake was delicious but rich and heavy which made me more tired than I already was. I was struggling to stay awake again, so I tried sitting up straighter, but my eyes began to close.

The cloaked figure from my dream flashed in my mind. *Aunt Rose?* Had I had too much wine today? Was I that exhausted that my mind was playing tricks on me? Did I just miss her? So much from my dreams didn't make sense but then later did. Like

Jake's face finally appearing after all this time. But was it really him? How did he have the same dream I did? It must have been her. But why? And what did it mean? The fire, the stone, her, the forest, Jake coming to fetch us. And clearly it was the same time as the last dream according to the way he was dressed. *It was Aunt Rose.*

But why?

My eyes opened again and suddenly I was wide awake. I heard the clanking of things in the sink, so I looked over my shoulder and Jake was still cleaning up in the kitchen. I turned back to the television, but it was just running through different shows on Netflix we could watch.

I sat there trying to make sense of it all. I played it over and over again in my mind, trying to be sure I could remember so I could write it all down in my journal once I went home. This must be a piece of a puzzle. I was beginning to think that's what the dreams were, clues to something. But what?

Finally, Jake was standing in front of me, reaching out his arm. "You look sleepy, let's go to bed." My body and mind were exhausted even though I was still replaying my last dream. I took his hand and followed him.

The blanket that I had pulled off earlier had been put back on the bed. He walked over to the side closer to the door and flipped on the lamp, so I walked to the other side and pulled the covers back. The top blanket and pillow covers were a dark blue, but the sheets were white and soft like a t-shirt. I felt giddy as I climbed in and got situated while I waited for him to join me. We went from dates and kissing to sleepovers and lovemaking.

The bed was soft and comfy but of course the sheets and pillow were cold from the cool air in the room. I watched Jake as he picked up his pants from earlier, tossed them into a hamper by the chest of drawers, and then he took his shirt off and tossed it in as well. He was beautiful to look at, I couldn't help but stare as he walked toward the bed. He climbed in, with his sweatpants still on, and turned off the lamp. He reached over and pulled me flush against him before fixing the covers over me.

I was so tired, but my mind was still racing. I was snuggled up close to him with my face on his chest. The length of my body was right up against his, our legs tangled together. I almost couldn't believe I was laying there in his bed, in Christmas pajamas. The excitement of his touch was still there radiating through me, but also a sense of safety and home, like I was meant to be there. Not there in his apartment, but there in his arms. He was still, his breaths deep and steady raising his chest up and down. I could feel the little patch of hair in the middle of his chest and was breathing in his scent which was now a mix of his citrusy cologne, sweat, and even a bit of my body wash.

I thought he was drifting off to sleep but then he asked, "Vivian, are you alright?" At first, I nodded my head that I was, but he gave a soft rub to my back encouraging me to speak up and I could feel his beard brush my hair and knew he was looking down at me. I dug my head into his chest for a minute then put my chin up on it and looked up at him. My eyes took a moment to adjust in the dark but slowly I could make out his face and he was looking down at me, but with a curious look.

"I don't know, is this not all just crazy to you? Like, do you not think I'm crazy with all this?" He scooted a bit so he could tilt his head and get a better look down at me.

"No, I don't think you're crazy. I told you before I believed in fate, and that was true. You may think I'm crazy, but I think this was all meant to be. We were meant to be."

My heart sped up and I hoped it wasn't palpable to him since I was laying on his bare chest.

He was softly rubbing my back as he was speaking to me with his low but clear voice. "This may sound crazy, Vivian, but I've had dreams of you, before the one last night. And when I met you, something clicked. When I touched you that first time, I don't know how to explain it, it was like I already knew your touch. It wasn't an ordinary feeling." He paused briefly. "Ack, I need to shut up, are you ready to run out of here?"

I propped up a bit more, bending my back so I could see him better. "No, I don't want to run. I want to hear more." He continued rubbing my back and he turned his head a bit like he was considering whether he should tell me anymore.

"Well, I don't know, I mean that's most of it. I don't want to sound cheesy, but just touching you, it's so intense, like I can feel you all through my body and it makes me insane. Even now just laying with you, my muscles feel like they could jump right out of my skin. And it just seems right, that you're with me, here, and not just in bed but just *here*, next to me. Is that pathetic or nuts?"

I shook my head. "No, it's not pathetic or nuts, because I was thinking the same thing. I can't explain any of it either, but I think you're right. I think something drew us together. I've been aimlessly wandering through my life for the last several months, maybe even before that, and suddenly this makes sense. Even though there are things I can't explain, I think we're supposed to figure it out together." He pulled me up closer, pulled my head down to him, and kissed me deeply. I felt his arm trembling as he held the back of my neck.

He pulled away slowly, took a deep breath, and let it out. "We will, I promise. Now, let's get some sleep."

Chapter 16

I slowly opened my eyes; little beams of light were breaking through the dark curtains. I smelled something savory as well as fresh coffee. I rolled over and reached my arm across the empty side of the bed. I lay there for a moment and heard sounds coming from the kitchen. I looked over and the clock said it was just past ten. I hadn't slept that late in ages. But I also hadn't slept so soundly since before my parent's accident.

I sat up and stretched, quietly got out of bed, and tip-toed to the bathroom. My hair was wild, so I took a minute to try to tame it by wetting my hands and scrunching it a bit. A little better but not great. I realized my morning breath was out of control and frantically started searching for a toothbrush. I found one still in the box under the sink and the toothpaste was in the drawer, so I brushed and rinsed. *Ok, now I was sort of presentable.* When I found Jake in the kitchen in nothing but his sweatpants, he was pouring coffee into a mug. *Stop ogling him, Viv.*

"Good morning, I hope I didn't wake you. I was trying to be quiet." He handed me the cup and gave me a peck. The coffee was sweet and delicious. He must get the good kind. I went and sat at the kitchen table and looked out the window, so I didn't keep staring at him.

"Mmm, good coffee. You can see so far. The city looks so different from up here."

He came over and put a plate down in front of me. "I grabbed you some creamer. I hope it's the right kind. Breakfast casserole and before you say anything, I didn't make this, I just put it in the oven with the instructions on the box." It still smelled wonderful, so I dug in and was still enjoying my coffee. He came over and sat to eat with me.

"I had the foresight to get you pajamas but not an outfit. Why don't we run you to your house before we get the stuff to fix the locks?"

I nodded, I had completely forgotten about that, and everything else. I was in a fantasy land here, far away from everything and everyone. Even the coffee was better here.

"Sounds good, hopefully I don't see anyone from yesterday, with my walk of shame." Not that anyone would actually notice since I never really spoke to the neighbors.

He chuckled and with a few large bites finished his breakfast before taking the plate to the kitchen. I ate mine slowly, soaking in the calm and normalcy of the morning. I finally finished the casserole, and he came over with the coffee pot and topped off my coffee.

"No rush, enjoy your coffee. We can go whenever you want." He took the plate away, cleaned up the kitchen, and put the rest of the breakfast casserole in the fridge. I drank my coffee, enjoying each sip and taking in the view. The idea of leaving the warmth and comfort of the apartment didn't seem pleasing, but I did need clothes and we did need to go to the hardware store early enough for him to fix the locks. I stood up and took my cup to the kitchen and put it in the dishwasher. I realized then he wasn't in there with me when I heard the shower.

I walked to the bedroom and found my clothes and shoes from the day before and tossed them on then walked to the living room to wait. He was done quickly, and the bathroom door opened. I turned to get a quick glance of him in a towel walking to his room. I had some thoughts of what I would like to do to him, but my nerves got the best of me. Plus, there would be time for that later. I smelled his scent wafting from the bathroom. So manly and crisp. It brought up some recent memories of things we had done together. I was blushing when I heard his shoes walking up behind me quickly. He came up behind the couch and wrapped his arms around me and tucked his face into my neck. It took everything I had to not reach up and pull him down over the couch.

"If you're ready, let's go."

I stood up quickly and grabbed my coat then stopped. "Wait, what about the book bag? Should we take it or leave it?"

He shook his head. "No, I have it in my safe. I don't think we should lug it around the hardware store, so I put it away. It'll be well hidden there." He took my hand and walked me into the kitchen and gently pulled the fridge away from the wall just enough for me to see and pointed to a place on the wall. "See that faint square, if you pull that up the safe is under there and it of course needs a code." Even if you looked behind the fridge, if you didn't pull it out, you would never even notice the lines in the wall.

"Wow, that's pretty intense. Did you put that there?"

He smiled. "Yeah, it's where I keep my guns. I have a couple–former detective. They're worth a bit so I keep them locked up. But my building is pretty hard to get into anyway. Just paranoid I guess." I nodded and shook my shoulders. I hadn't been around guns much ever, so it sat well with me that they were locked up. He pushed the fridge back and led me out.

We walked off the elevator to the parking deck but instead of my car we got into his black SUV, which was much nicer and newer than mine. He drove out of the parking deck and turned to go around the square instead of through it. It took a few more minutes but it was still a short ride. He reached over and grabbed my hand, holding it during the ride. I gently ran my thumb over his hand back and forth as we rode, staring out the window.

We pulled into my driveway then walked to the kitchen door on the side of the house. I pulled my keys out and grabbed the knob with one hand before I pushed the key in. It wasn't locked. But I swear I had locked it.

"I locked this on the way out. I've done this so many times. Aunt Rose always leaves before me." He told me to wait there and first looked around the back over the fence then he walked past me, signaling to wait, and went inside. I stood there in the cold, and daylight, hoping nobody saw me with my clothes from yesterday.

He finally came back and opened the door. "Looks all clear. You sure you locked it? Yesterday morning was a little strange." He pulled me inside and shut the door.

"I know I locked it. You said it's all clear?" I put my coat on the coat rack and walked around the parlor and then upstairs. I turned the lights on in both rooms and the bathroom. It was all as I left it. And frankly was a bit of a mess. I walked back downstairs and found him still in the kitchen. "Everything looks okay, but I know I locked it. I need to clean up all this dirt before I shower. Is that okay? I know you wanted to get going."

He walked over and grabbed me. "We have plenty of time, and I can help. Just give me a rag and some cleaner."

I laughed then grabbed the cleaning spray from under the sink, the mop from the corner behind the door, and started to go upstairs.

"Hey, where's my rag?"

I came back down. "I didn't think you were serious; you can't clean my house."

He walked over and pulled the cleaner from my hand and then pulled a hefty amount of paper towels off the roll. He sprayed them well before he handed the cleaner back to me, opened the door, and started cleaning the outside of the door. I stood there for a moment in shock watching him, but finally walked upstairs and cleaned my mess along the way. Once I was done, I walked downstairs and Jake was still there but inside now, cleaning up my tracks on his hands and knees.

I held out the mop and he jumped up and grabbed it happily. "Much better than what I was doing. I got this, go shower and get dressed."

I hurried upstairs and hopped in the shower, cleaning quickly, then brushed my teeth again since I had some coffee before running across the hall in my towel to get dressed. Some jeans and a favorite t-shirt would work but I went ahead and packed a few things in case I stayed with him again. I also grabbed some mini toiletries Aunt Rose kept in the bathroom and tossed them in the bag with my clothes. From the top of the stairs, I yelled down to Jake that I'd be down in a minute.

After fixing the bed, I sat down and pulled my journal out of the drawer. I jotted down the last dream as best I could recall then stuffed the journal in my bag. Keeping track of these dreams had to be important. Maybe something would eventually make sense.

I jumped up and turned the light off then popped my head into Aunt Rose's room to be sure it was all in order for when she got home tomorrow. I started to turn off the light and leave but something caught my eye. Her bed was made, but there was an impression on the bed like someone had pushed on it. Not big enough for someone to have sat down, but like a hand propped up someone. I walked over and leaned down. Someone had put their hand there while they looked under the bed.

"Jake, can you come up here," I yelled down at him. I heard him taking quick strides up the stairs and he first went to my room and stopped but must have seen the light on in my aunt's room and came over.

"What's wrong?" he asked.

I motioned for him to come over and pointed down to the spot on the bed. "She made up her bed before she left. She wouldn't have leaned down for anything. I think someone was here and was careful not to disturb much, but this isn't right." He came closer and did the same I did and leaned down, bending his knees, and looked over. There was nothing under the bed, but it seemed someone had been looking.

"Maybe, but they did a good job if that's true. You didn't notice anything else out of place?"

I shook my head, but it made sense now that the lock was open. Someone else did come in here. He even said it was easy to break in. Maybe we should have changed the locks yesterday.

"This makes me nervous; she'll be home by herself until late. What if they come back?" I asked shakily.

He pulled me to him and rubbed my head to soothe me. "Most people won't break in during the day. And we can change the locks. We'll fix it all up so you both can be here. And if she doesn't mind, maybe I can stay over to be sure everything is fine?"

I nodded my head and started walking out of the room, grabbed my bag, and turned the light off and he was behind me. I made sure to lock the door and he checked it behind me.

"What's in the bag?" He asked as he pulled it from my shoulder to put it in the car.

"I grabbed a few things; in case we had an unplanned sleepover. But it's okay if we don't." *Why was I rambling?*

"Vivian, you could pack up all your things and stay with me forever if you wanted." He opened the door and I quickly ducked in hoping the flush in my cheeks was gone before he made it to the driver's side.

Chapter 17

We drove over to the hardware store, and he got a cart. He was tossing in all sorts of things as I walked along. I couldn't help but keep wondering who had been at our house. Was it the man that kept popping up in the shop? Someone else? Maybe a random intruder? Was it all really a coincidence? It had been a strange few days and I had very little sleep. Maybe I had left the door unlocked accidentally? Maybe Aunt Rose set something down shortly before she left. There wasn't anything else out of place that I could tell, but my room was left in shambles by me so it would be hard to notice if anything was out of place.

Then suddenly a thought crossed my mind. "Jake, the shop. We should go check on the shop. What if whoever was in my house went to the shop last night?"

He stopped pushing the cart and tipped his head a bit. "We can go check it out. I think we're about done here anyway. Let's go pay for this and we'll drive there first, okay?" He put an arm around me and pushed the cart with the other hand.

I must have been visibly shaken because he was practically cradling me alongside him. I hoped my gut was wrong, but I had a sinking feeling. Nothing there was incredibly valuable, pricewise anyway, but the idea of someone breaking in and snooping around just felt intrusive. It was bad enough I was almost certain someone was in our house. I tried to take a few deep breaths and stop overreacting while we were still at the hardware store.

Jake pulled items out of the cart and onto the counter for

the cashier. She was pleasant and made some small talk with us. Jake was cordial back and mentioned the cold weather. I was so preoccupied I said nothing; she probably thought I was a jerk. Before I knew it, she was giving the total and I reached for my bag, but he had already pulled cash out and paid her before I could find my wallet. He turned and smiled at me before I could protest, then grabbed the bags in one hand and grabbed my hand with the other, leading me back to the car.

The drive was short to the square, and it was brunch time on a Sunday, so we had to park down a side street and walk over. I pulled my keys out when we got to the end of the sidewalk of the block the shop was on. Jake was close behind me, making way for others to walk past us, but he had a hand on my hip the whole time and I could feel him towering over me from behind. As we got closer my nerves began to run wild and my stomach churned. I was a few yards from the door; any passerby wouldn't have noticed, but I had walked up to the open door many times and knew what it looked like when it was locked. It was not locked when we got there. I slowed a bit when I noticed this, and Jake bumped into me from behind.

"What is it?" He asked. I reached out slowly without even turning to him and pushed the door and sure enough, it opened. He grabbed my other arm and pulled me back to stop me from walking in. "Let me go first." I nodded and stood there for a moment as he walked in and initially, I couldn't see anything out of place.

I looked around the square to see if I saw any familiar faces, like a little unassuming man in a hat. Nothing but lots of people bundled up, going in and out of restaurants and looking in windows of shops. Most of the shops on the square were closed on Sundays. They were all small businesses and usually ran by the owners. Collectively everyone seemed to at some point agree that they would all close on Sunday's and people never seemed to mind. But many still window-shopped or wandered the square for fresh air.

Almost all the restaurants were open every day and every shop and restaurant were all decorated based on the season so you could come and just enjoy the scenery whether it was the middle of the night, the dead of winter, the blooming spring, the heat of summer, or the changing colors of fall. The streetlamps currently held colorful wreaths and lights running down them and all the shops had different holiday décor in and outside. The little "square" spot in the middle of town square had benches dressed in lights and there were large installations of Christmas Trees all decorated, Menorah and Kinara with faux candles in traditional colors, nativity scenes, and brightly colored "gift" bundles all around. The city already began erecting the large stand for the New Year Crystal Ball Drop. Even with no shopping there was plenty to do and see on a Sunday. It would have been such a beautiful scene to stop and soak in, but I was impatiently waiting to be called into the shop once it was deemed safe.

I still had my back to the shop while I was perusing the crowds for any signs of the suspicious man. With all the holiday fixtures, there were so many places someone could duck behind. I scanned the people walking, looking to see if anyone appeared to be watching the shop, or me. Jake had mentioned the strange man probably wasn't working solo, so anyone could be working with him. My chest became tight at the thought someone could be there in front of me right now, in plain sight, plotting their next move and I had no idea who they were. The doorbells jingled, startling me, and Jake gave me the ok to come in.

I turned and stepped in and locked the door behind me.

"Don't touch anything else, I should have told you before," Jake snapped quickly. "I'm sorry, I just mean we can't touch anything so the police can dust for prints." He came over and gave me a big hug. He was as tense as I was.

"You think we should call the police? They'll want to talk

to Aunt Rose, and she doesn't need that stress right now."

He shook his head. "For now, they'll be fine speaking to you, but we need to report it. I watched you lock up yesterday, so someone definitely came in here. I didn't check the front door well, but they seemed to have picked the lock, otherwise there would be obvious damage to the frame. I made sure nobody was here, but you should walk around and see if anything is missing or out of place. I'll call the police." He pulled his phone out and dialed so I took my coat off and set it with my bag down behind the counter.

I walked back up front and went up and down each row and shelf; everything seemed to be ok. I walked back to the counter and checked the safe and the drawer and both were undisturbed. I stood there for a moment, hands on my hips, then looked to the backroom. I went to check and there were boxes down that hadn't been pulled down before. All were open.

"Jake, come here when you're done." I heard him saying thank you and wrapped up the call as he came to the back and looked around. "We didn't leave these this way, right?" I asked, pointing to the boxes.

He shook his head. "No, I left the empty boxes down in the corner here. The rest were closed and stacked." I stood there wanting to go through the boxes, but he told me to not touch anything.

It wasn't long and there was a loud knock on the front door. We went together and I opened the door for the officer that stood outside.

"Morning, ma'am, I got dispatched here to check out a possible break-in."

I motioned for him to come in and then stuck my hand out. "Yes, I'm Vivian, my aunt owns the shop and she's in the hospital."

Jake stuck his hand out as well, "I'm Jake Adams, I called it in for her."

The office was writing down notes. "Ma'am, can I get your last name?"

"Acworth, Vivian Acworth. Sorry."

He looked up at me with his chin still tilted down. "Like, as in the city?"

"One in the same but they forgot to give me my key to the city."

He gave a short huff, but more like a chuckle than sarcastic in nature.

"I'm going to take a look around, but is anything missing or broken?"

I told him the store itself seemed to be in order but there were some boxes moved in the back, but I hadn't messed with them. He made some notes and then went to look at the front door then walked quickly to the back and did the same to the back door. He put his notepad away and pulled a cell phone out.

"I'm going to take some pictures before you look around and see if anything is missing from the boxes."

I nodded and stood there as he started snapping pictures of the doors and then came back to photograph the boxes.

He pulled a flashlight out. "Okay ma'am, push the flaps out completely and go ahead and look in and see if anything is missing."

I opened the boxes one by one and told him I didn't know for sure if things were missing or not.

"I just went through some of these, but my aunt didn't really keep a good catalog of everything. We get a lot of stuff in and out all the time." He huffed again and kept taking pictures then made some more notes.

"Here is my card, here is a case number. It'll take at least three business days for this to be loaded into our system and you can pull an official copy with this number. If you do find that anything is missing, or get any info, feel free to reach out to me at this number." He tipped his hat down and started to walk out.

"Wait, is that it?" I asked as he reached the front door. He turned and gave a forced smile.

"Ma'am, we have a report for you, but you even said nothing seems to be missing and sadly we don't have any cameras in here or aimed at the store, so there's not much we can do."

He nodded his head and turned to go, so I yelled out, "But you don't take prints or anything?"

The officer stopped again, slowly turning to me. "Well, we have little to go on and there is no damage to the doors or anything missing. Plus, it's a store so there are going to be endless amounts of prints in here. I'm sorry ma'am, but the report will be on file in case anything else happens. You may want to tell your aunt to get some kind of security system for peace of mind." He tipped his head one more time and swiftly left.

I turned around and found my face in Jake's chest.

"I'll be right back, don't move." He walked outside and I stood in the shop and watched out the window. He wasn't going after the officer but back towards the car. Once he was around the corner, I couldn't see him anymore, so I walked back to the counter and sat.

I was tidying the counter and must have hit the mouse because the screen on the computer came on. I could've sworn I turned that off. The lock screen was on where you enter the password.

I was about to start typing when the doorbells jingled and Jake yelled over, "don't touch that!" I moved back in my seat and had my hands up like I had a gun pointed at me. He came over eagerly, waving a small kit. "He didn't take prints, so I will."

"So, you keep a spy kit in the car?" I asked smugly. He smirked back and started dusting something over the keyboard then took a strip, which looked like wrapping tape, and placed it over the spacebar, the F key, the J key, then he did the same on the mouse.

"You use thumbs for the spacebar and your index fingers for F and J, easiest way to get prints." He then labeled them on a square piece that looked like cardboard. He went outside and did this to the door handle, above the lock, then inside on the handle and on the door frame that leads to the back.

"I'll see if I can get an old friend to help me run these just in case we can get a hit. We may end up with a bunch of women's prints, but it can't hurt to try." He was very matter of fact, like he was working a case.

"In the meantime, he was right, we need to secure the shop, too. We can get a cheap camera, but we'll need a locksmith for these doors. I can't get that kind of stuff at the hardware store. But I have an idea. Just wait here." He gave me a quick kiss and was out the door before I could stop him.

I walked to the front and locked the door to be sure nobody came in since the lights were on. Lots of owners took Sundays to clean or restock so it wasn't abnormal for people to be in the shops, but if you didn't lock up someone may wander in.

I walked to the back and stood looking around at the mess of boxes everywhere. I leaned down and started to close the boxes and stack them back on the utility shelves. I was nearly done tidying up when one of the last boxes caught my eye. I had sorted through it when looking for decorations. There was a large book that looked like an old photo album but had some pages inserted with writing and cut outs of papers and things. I had seen this a couple times before I remember it being brought in a few weeks back with another lot and I put it aside to go through later since it had pictures and clippings in it. I pulled it out and put it to the side before closing that box and the last one and stacked them up. I put the empty boxes at the bottom of the shelves and rubbed my hands together like I had just accomplished a lot.

I grabbed the book and took it up to the counter. I had to stop putting it off and it had been here for weeks. It was dusty inside and out and lots of pictures and papers stuffed the pages. It appeared leather bound from the look and feel of the material, and it was a ruddy brown color under the dust. Getting it cleaned properly would be a task. I ran my fingers gently over the old material then started to open the pages.

I was interrupted by the bells on the door. It was Jake so I left the book closed and went to let him in, making sure to lock it behind him. He put a large brown bag on the counter and was pulling small boxes out.

"What's that?" he asked, nodding to the book.

"Some book that came in a few weeks ago. It was in one of the boxes, I just kept forgetting about it, so I brought it up." I gently brushed some dust off the top letting out a sigh. "I need to clean it up and get all the contents sorted and tossed. Hopefully, I can get to it this week before Aunt Rose gets back and realizes I forgot about it." I made a face like I'd be in real trouble, but honestly, she wouldn't care. I grabbed a box he had put on the counter and opened it to look at the little device.

"There's three, one for the front area facing the door directly, one for the back facing that door and one for that corner that can capture the full interior of the store." He was pointing around as he explained.

"It'll take a few minutes to get them all installed. They'll record, but you can see real time if I do this the right way." He was pulling out wires and stands and asked if we had any tools. I gave him the small kit we kept in the back in case we needed to add or remove shelves or for small repairs to items we sometimes get in. I was just walking around the store aimlessly and my stomach growled.

"You hungry?" I asked as I grabbed my coat and bag.

"Yeah, just get me whatever, maybe I'll be done when you get back." He had started to reach into his pocket for his wallet, but I walked out and locked the door behind me. I looked around and decided on Bruno's, the burger joint we had just a few days ago.

I walked up to the counter and was looking over the menu. A young lady came over and welcomed me and took down my order, two cheeseburgers, two large fries, and two large chocolate shakes. After I paid, I was sitting at the counter waiting and my phone dinged. It was Aunt Rose.

She was feeling great and still planned to be discharged tomorrow, and of course asked how my birthday went. I replied that Jake would be getting her tomorrow and it was great, but I'd have to fill her in later. Before shoving my phone back in the bag, I sent another text saying I missed her and loved her. When I looked up, the young lady was bringing my food out with a dual drink carrier.

I quickly walked back to the shop and carefully unlocked the door while managing to not drop the food or shakes. Once inside, Jake immediately asked for my cell phone and took the items from my hands. I pulled my cell out and handed it over. He did a few things while I got my straw out and started sipping on my shake. It was never too cold out for a chocolate shake.

I started to open the bag to grab food out, but he handed me the phone back and said, "Okay, all set here. Let's take this to your house and I can change the locks there before it gets dark."

I was hungry but didn't want him to work in the dark and with it being winter, it did get dark early. Plus, I could snack on fries on the short ride over. We turned off the lights, he grabbed the food, and I made sure to lock the door behind me and pulled it just to show him it was locked before walking briskly to the car.

Chapter 18

The ride was quick, but it was so cold outside the food got cold. We pulled all the way into the driveway, and I quickly jumped out with the food and my shake and ran to unlock the door. He grabbed the bag from the hardware store, his shake, and hustled inside. I tossed the food in the microwave and shimmied out of my coat. Jake sat down with his still on.

"Want me to take your coat?" I asked him as I went to hang mine.

"Nope, I'll woof that down then get to work on the doors. I want to get done with our chores so we can have fun." He had a bit of a smirk on his face as I handed him the burger and fries and sat down. He shoveled it down fast and he took a long drink from the shake and stood up quickly but didn't move. "Brain freeze."

I laughed a little and kept nibbling on my food. He grabbed his tools and went to the parlor to do the front door first since I was still eating in the kitchen.

I could hear power tools and some clanking. I stood up and was clearing off my wrappings and fry container when he came walking back to the kitchen.

"All set at the front, why don't you go stay warm in there and I'll swap the locks on this door." He nodded toward the living room.

"I think I'll be fine in here with you but thanks for the concern," I replied with one eyebrow raised. He let out a small grunt and got to work.

As much as the shake was yummy, it did make me cold to the bone, so I made a pot of coffee because if I was cold, he must be freezing. He worked fast but I could see his hands were turning beet red.

He finally stood and checked the lock, then checked the keys to be sure they worked. Then he locked the door and stepped outside, and I watched as he pulled a card from his wallet and jiggled it in the door jam. He tried for a minute, and nothing happened, so he took a key and opened it then came back inside.

"That's much better," he said with relief in his voice. "I have one more thing I want to do." He pulled something else out of the bag. It was a doorbell.

"This is a doorbell with a camera with a rather good range. I put one up front already and since this door is on the side of the house, I wanted to get a second one. We will have another app to add but this is better for home use, and I don't have to run them to the router."

My mouth fell open. "You've thought of everything." He put the box down and came over to me, his hands like ice.

"My God you need to take a break." I grabbed his hands and pulled them to my face to blow warm air on them. "I made coffee, let me get you some."

I let go of his hands to get him a cup of coffee, but he grabbed my arm and pulled me back to him. His gaze was serious, and his grasp was tight. "Vivian, I'll be fine when I know you are safe. I hope this isn't all too much."

My heart swelled. "No, it makes me feel better knowing Aunt Rose will be safe here alone. I just can't believe you spent all this money and time on this." I leaned into him, and he bent down to kiss me, his lips as cold as his hands.

"Ok mister," I said, patting his chest, "you need to warm up, that was literally the coldest kiss I've ever had." I turned, grabbed a mug, and poured him some coffee.

He held it in his hands for a minute then turned it up to take a sip and let out a satisfied moan. *That sound.*

"You were right, this is right on time." He took another sip as I poured myself a mug and added a little creamer.

He opened the box and pulled out the pieces then went outside and shut the door. I could see him through the windowpanes on the top of the door and could hear the drill. He was so serious while he worked. His brow scrunched down over his eyes; lips pursed tightly amid the bushy beard. Such precision and focus, like he was operating. The sun's reflection bounced off the glass into his blue eyes but caused the green specks to really pop, almost making his eyes green.

I didn't realize it until he looked over and caught me, but I was leaning on the counter staring intently at him. He smiled when he noticed then looked back at what he was doing. I quickly stood up, grabbed my mug, then sat at the table. I could feel myself blushing but also full of tingles all over. I stared at him a bit and anytime he caught me, he always seemed as if he enjoyed it.

He came back in and held his hand out to me. "All done, hand me the phone and I will set these up." I grabbed the phone from my bag and handed it over. He did a few things then pulled a chair up next to me.

"Ok, this is the app for the house," he said pointing to the phone. "It'll have chimes anytime someone gets as close as the mailbox or the neighbor's yard on the side door. The one labeled 'front' is the front door, and the one labeled 'side' is the side or kitchen door. You just push here to see a live view, or you can swipe if it alerts you. That's it."

He handed the phone back, so I put it on the table and grabbed his hands, trying to warm them up by blowing warm air on them then put them on my face. They were so cold, but my face was still hot from my blushing. I was rubbing the outside of his hands to warm them up while his palms were to my cheeks, and I felt him pulling me to him. We both leaned toward each other, and our lips met, just lips nothing else, but it was strong and passionate. My usual shockwaves were running through me and the tension that had been looming over me all day was slowly dissipating. He still was holding my face and my hands were wrapped around wrists. We finally parted, just barely, but enough for me to take a deep breath.

"Was that better?" He asked.

"Better than what?" I could barely get out.

He grinned. "Was that better than the coldest kiss ever?" I nervously laughed but nodded my head. "Have you ever been to a pool hall?"

I balked at the question "No, unless playing pool at a frat house in college counts."

He stood up and reached his hand out to help me up. "I want to take you to do some 21 and up stuff. Still improvising my original plan. Grab your coat, but first, we need to take the car to my apartment."

Chapter 19

We pulled into his parking deck, and I wanted to take my bag up to his apartment and needed to check on Aunt Rose. He was going to order a car service to pick us up, so I went to the room and put my overnight bag down and pushed it under the bed a bit then sat down to call Aunt Rose.

"Dear, oh gosh, how are you? How was your birthday? Tell me everything!" Aunt Rose was so excited on the other line.

"Well, I don't have time to tell you everything, but it was really amazing. So, you get to leave tomorrow, right?" We caught up on the details of her checking out of the hospital and I reminded her that since I would be at the shop Jake was going to pick her up and take her home.

"Oh, I know. Too bad I won't be able to do myself up much," she said with a chuckle. "But I can take a cab. Why the big to-do about him picking me up?

"Well, it's been an eventful weekend. Aunt Rose, we changed the locks on the house just to be safe, but Jake will have a key for you tomorrow," I tried to say as nonchalantly as possible.

"Changed the locks, why? What happened? Viv, what's going on?"

She was getting upset. "Aunt Rose, everything is fine, just in light of recent stuff I wanted to be sure you were secure there by yourself while I was at the shop, that's all. Nothing to get worked up over."

I heard her let out a deep sigh through the phone. "Well, if you say so but it just seems odd, are you sure everything's okay?"

She was getting more suspicious the more I spoke, so I told her Jake, and I were about to go out, so I needed to go. After reminding her to call or text me when she had an idea when he needed to pick her up the next day, I hung up but felt horrible. But I didn't want to tell her what happened and upset her. She had been there for days alone, and I knew she wanted to be home. I wanted her home. *No sense in worrying until there is something to worry about.* Still, I hated not being honest with her, especially since it was her house and her shop.

I was still sitting on the edge of the bed holding my phone and Jake tapped on the door. "Everything okay? How's Aunt Rose?" I nodded my head and turned to smile at him. He walked over and knelt in front of me, looking up at me. "Doesn't seem so, what's up?"

I shook my head and held my breath, trying to hold in the tears I knew were bubbling up. His face went from calm and curious to concerned. He sat on the bed next to me and pulled me close to him. I grabbed the arms of his shirt and had my face in his chest. The tears flowed out of me like a pipe had burst. He sat quietly, holding and rocking me. I finally stopped blubbering and tried to catch my breath.

I made sure my outburst was over before I said anything to keep myself from losing it again. He was still holding me tight, but I knew he was waiting on an explanation.

"I just hate lying to her but don't want to scare her. And I'm scared. And I don't know of what or who or why I should be, but I am. And I hate that feeling. Why is this happening?"

He rocked me and his low and calm voice was soothing as he spoke, "I don't know, but I wish I did. I don't want you to feel this way." He pushed me away enough so that he could look at me.

"But I promise I will do everything in my power to keep you and your aunt safe."

I nodded my head, but I couldn't help but ask, "Why, why are you still with me? This is all just...crazy isn't even the word...it's not logical. It's like something out of a movie. I mean, you barely know me really and I--" but he put his finger up to my mouth to keep me from saying more.

"Vivian, I told you before, I believe fate led me here now, to you." He tucked my hair behind my ear then stroked my face, his eyes darker and intense.

"I do know you and I think you know me. And something is telling me I am meant to protect you, from anything. Not just crazy old men looking for gemstones, but anything that could ever harm you. Do you," he paused for a minute and his face drew in, "do you not feel like you're supposed to be with me?"

Every fiber of my being felt connected to him. I barely could hold myself together when he was near, much less when he touched me, kissed me, took me. He was literally the man of my dreams. The look on his face made my heart feel like it was tearing apart. I struggled with the right words to say, but I had to make him understand how I felt.

I stroked his face, brushing his beard softly with my thumb and looked into his unsure eyes.

"I do, Jake, but all of this seems so unbelievable, so it's hard to believe it isn't. I mean, why would someone like you want to be with someone like me?"

His face softened and he cupped my face in his hands.

"You mean someone beautiful, someone kind, someone courageous, someone who isn't afraid of their emotions, someone who pushes through tragedy and adversity and movie-like happenings?" I was starting to tremble from all the emotions coursing through me. He leaned in and gently kissed me, and I felt the trembling begin to fade away. A sigh escaped me once he pulled his lips from mine.

"I'm such a mess, maybe that's why I just can't believe it."

He pushed my hair behind my shoulder. "But you're my beautiful mess."

I wiped my face with my hands and finally was breathing normally. Suddenly it hit me that we had plans.

I started rambling fast. "Oh my God, were you coming in here to tell me the car was here? I forgot we were going out!"

He grabbed my hand and shook his head. "I hadn't ordered it yet. I didn't know how long you would be on the phone, and I didn't want to disturb you. I only came in because when I poked my head in you weren't on the phone. If you want, I can order one now, or, we can hang out here for a bit. I think I have some twenty-one and up beverages in there and we can watch adult films." He shook his head. "Wait, that sounds bad. Not 'adult' films, just films for adults." He shook his head even harder. "Never mind, we can watch *a* movie." He finally stopped trying to make it sound better and laughed at himself. I couldn't help but laugh at him. The laughter melted the tension out of my shoulders.

Once I stopped laughing, I finally told him, "If you don't care, staying in kind of sounds nice, and we can totally drink adult beverages and watch adult movies." We both paused before we laughed hysterically.

He stood and pulled me up close to him. We held each other tight for a while as he rubbed my back with his huge palms. My breathing had become steady. Even though things were confusing and scary, I felt safe and content there in his arms. I could have stayed that way forever. Finally, we both let go and he grabbed my hand and led me back to the living room.

He went to the kitchen and came back with a couple of beers as I sat down. "Not as fancy as yesterday but it's over twenty-one beverages." I grabbed one and he sat down next to me but reached one of his strong arms around me and pulled me right up next to him into my favorite nook under his arm. He grabbed the remote and turned on the television and searched through Netflix for movies. He found Die Hard and looked at me like he was waiting on approval.

"Do you want to watch this?" I asked him with a hint of sarcasm.

"Well, it's technically a Christmas movie and has plenty of adult things going on," he replied. I laughed and nodded. He did find a chick flick for me last night, even though I passed out.

We sat and watched that movie and two others while we continued to drink beer and eventually, he ordered a pizza. We laughed and both talked through the movies but not to each other, to the characters of the movies. Eventually he pulled out the leftover birthday cake and we both drunkenly stood in the kitchen and ate the cake from the box, giggling.

After all the drinking and eating my jeans were feeling tight so I excused myself to go change. I had brought some nice pajamas that were not super revealing but also didn't cover as much as the gingerbread ones he gave me. In fact, they were shorts with a camisole top. I lost my footing in the bedroom when I leaned down to pull my bag from under the bed.

"You alright?" Jake yelled from the living room.

I straightened up and stumbled to the door of the room. "All perfect. Just couldn't reach the bag. I'll be right out," I answered as I strolled to the bathroom.

After a few shuffles of my feet and steadying myself to get the shorts on, I stood in the bathroom mirror and turned a bit to see how they looked. I felt confident, it was quite flattering. Not great to keep warm but that was okay, I knew another way to get warm.

I finally left the bathroom and went back to sit with him. He looked me up and down as I walked past him to sit, but he didn't make a move or say anything. Snuggling in next to him, he wrapped his arm back around me, and we continued to watch the movie that had started playing.

I waited for him to give me a sign or make a move, but he didn't. Surely, he wanted me, and I definitely wanted him. I'd hoped the pajamas would have tipped him off. Time kept passing and I felt that we were both getting tired, so I decided I would make a move and started slowly running my hand up and down over his abdomen and chest. He put his beer down, but as my hand kept moving lower, he finally stopped me. At first, I thought it was a game, so I slowly started again but when I moved lower again, he stopped me again.

I looked up at him with a mischievous grin, but he looked down and shook his head. "Not tonight."

Blood rushed to my cheeks and knots started swirling in my stomach. I went to sit up straight, and the inside of my head felt like it was rolling around. He sat up and put his arm around me, but I sharply pushed it off. *He just blocked me so what was he doing now?*

I tried to stand to get away from him. I wasn't sure where I planned to go but I still tried and was very wobbly. He stood up casually and grabbed me by my shoulders to steady me. I awkwardly tried to push him away again but that just made the wobbly feeling worse. Suddenly he reached under my knees and easily picked me up. I wiggled a little, but it was worthless to try, plus the ground seemed really far away and was spinning. I quit fighting it but didn't put my arm around his neck or make it easy for him and turned my face away from him. *How could he push me away?* Why didn't he want me now after all the things he said earlier? I just didn't understand.

He walked me into the bedroom and moved the covers with one of his feet, which had to be difficult with my dead weight hanging in his arms. He gently put me in bed and pulled the covers up over my shoulder and leaned down to give me a kiss on the forehead. I moved my face, so he missed but he grinned at me, tight-lipped, then walked out of the room. He came back in a couple of minutes with a glass of water and put two pills on the nightstand.

"You may want to take these now, but if not, they'll be there in the morning." He walked back out of the room. I rolled over to see the time and it was only nearly ten, but I had to close one eye to see that. I had to set the alarm to make sure I got to the shop in the morning. Scooting over to his side of the bed, I attempted to set the alarm, but it wasn't like mine and it was dark. I reached up and turned his lamp on and was investigating the alarm clock when he came back in and sat on the edge of the bed.

"Can I help you with something?"

I rolled my eyes and said, "Nooo, I am perfectly capable of setting the alarm, I just couldn't see in the dark." I continued to try to set the alarm but with seeing double and not wanting to do the one-eyed trick with him there, it was proving to be difficult. I finally put it down and scooted back to my side of the bed.

"I'll wake up, I don't need the balarm," I slurred out, confident he didn't hear the "B" I added to alarm. I was still getting comfy and trying to get the spinning to stop when I heard buttons. I rolled over quickly but he had stood and left the room again already. I scooted back over and could see the little red dot indicating the alarm was on. *Well, if he needed it that's fine.*

Getting comfortable was a struggle. I had to prop the pillows up more, so my head wasn't spinning. Reaching over, I grabbed the two pills and water and took them. I drank most of the water before slamming the glass back down. I plopped back down and had to fix the pillows again, so my head was propped up. Everything was still spinning but it was bearable enough to keep my eyes closed and try to sleep. I just wanted to go to sleep so I could wake up and leave. *Unbelievable...he turned me down and left me in here alone.*

I lay there trying to breathe steadily and make the spins go away. Eventually, things went dark.

Chapter 20

Stars scattered across the dark night sky and the only light was the glow of the moon. I lay there staring up at the sparkling stars, just at the edge of the barn propped up on the pile of hay to be fed to the horses tomorrow.

The layers of petticoats and my apron pulled up over my arms kept me from freezing. Boots barely poked out from the long skirts spread out on the hay pile. Unsure if it was the cold or the hay pile, I kept squirming and moving my legs, unable to get comfortable. Scanning the area, I realized I didn't know where a lantern was and wasn't sure I should try to walk back to the main house without one. *Great, stuck here in the dark.*

The horses began stirring so I leaned up and looked around. At first, I didn't see or hear anything besides the huffing of the horses and their hooves stepping around their stalls. I turned to face toward the night sky again and a figure was standing over me. My eyes took a moment to adjust but I began to see his large frame. Then as he became clearer, he removed his overcoat and leaned down to put it over me before he sat down next to me. At first, I tried to avoid looking at him, but he was stroking my hair and my face.

I was angry but the more he touched me the more that feeling faded away, stroke by stroke. I finally rolled on my side and was just inches from him. It was dark but I could feel the hairs of his beard as they tickled my face. His hands gently ran over my neck, shoulders, and arms. I moved even closer to him and felt his warm breath on me. I finally reached my arm up to grab behind his neck...

The beeping from the alarm had been soft, and it took a few moments to peel my eyes open. I felt weight on the other side of the bed rolling. Jake had come to bed at some point, and he was turning off the alarm. He rolled back toward me, but didn't get too close, and softly rubbed my cold arm that had made it out of the covers.

"What time is it," I almost screeched out, my mouth and throat dry, head pounding.

"Seven, I wasn't sure how much time you'd need to get dressed. How's your head?"

I squinted my eyes, trying to adjust to the bright beams of sunlight peeking through the curtains.

"I need all the meds and all the water on the planet." I reached up and rubbed my head. "I think I overdid it last night."

He let out a small chuckle and scooted a little closer but still didn't grab me or pull me to him.

He let out a soft sigh. "So, are you still mad at me?"

I had been such an ass. Thinking back now I was getting embarrassed about how I had acted and the fact that I clearly don't know my limits.

"Was I terrible? What I remember, or think I remember, seems bad."

He stroked my hair and smiled. "You were fine, just a little too much to drink. And you don't like being told no." I rolled over and shoved my head in the pillow to hide it.

"It was hard to bring you in here that way and walk away," he said as he gently rubbed my back. "I hope you're not still mad, but it wouldn't have been right."

I rolled my head over a bit to peek at him with one eye. "Not that I want to rehash this but what would have been wrong? We did after having wine the day before."

He was still smiling and stroking my hair. "Having a little wine and drinking beer all day are not the same. Plus, you couldn't see or stand up straight last night, so it was best to let you be mad and go to sleep." I put my face back in the pillow, the mortification all coming back to me. He sat up and threw his legs over the bed and walked to the kitchen.

I sat up and at first my head didn't catch up with my movement, but once I was upright things were coming into focus better. I could hear things clattering so I quietly stood up and went to the bathroom.

Finding the toothbrush I used the day before, I brushed my teeth twice trying to get rid of the awful aftertaste of beer. I also took a huge gulp of mouthwash and swished it around long enough to burn the inside of my mouth. I also took a small gulp and swallowed it to help with the taste and what surely was the worst morning breath of all time. After I splashed some cold water on my face, I skulked back to the bedroom, and sat down on the bed. Jake came in with two coffee mugs and handed me one. That first sip was perfect and made my head feel slightly better. He sat down, sipping his own coffee as I downed half of mine then put the mug on the nightstand. I smiled and slinked down into the bed, taking a big stretch with my arms and legs, and arching my back a bit to get the creaks out from a strange night's sleep.

I was still pushing my arms well above my head and my face was scrunched up when I heard him put his mug down and then suddenly felt his hand running down my arm and he had moved in close to me.

"So, how are you feeling now?" He asked while softly running his hand over my arm, my neck, down my side, over the small part of my stomach exposed from the pajamas when I put my arms up over my head. Excitement was welling up inside of me and I suddenly felt a surge of unabashed lust and rolled quickly onto him.

I leaned down and kissed him hard as I pinned his arms up over his head. He could have easily overtaken me but let me have my way with him. I leaned down and kissed his neck, still holding him arms down. But as I continued to kiss him down to his chest and below, my arm's length couldn't stretch any further and I could feel him stroking my arms and my shoulders as I kneaded his huge pec muscles. I kept moving further down and he flinched and reached his hands under my arms in a move to stop me, but I just pulled away and kept going, using the opportunity to move my hands down in front of me to start easing his sweats down out of my way. I heard his breathing begin to labor and I glanced up to see his chest heaving up and down and we locked eyes for just a moment.

Still looking into his eyes, a deeper shade of blue but glistening from the light entering, I took him into my mouth, and he let out a deep moan. I felt powerful and sexier than I had in my entire life at that moment. Like I had taken control of him, and he was at my mercy. I made slow work of it, occasionally peeking up to see how it excited him. I had never done this with any man and wasn't even completely sure what I was doing. But it excited me, seeing him this way, how it made him writhe and moan, so I continued and was completely lost in the moment and found that I enjoyed it much more than I expected.

Suddenly, he leaned up and pulled me up from under my arms quickly and he made a fast move to roll us both and he was there over me, nose to nose, belly to belly, and then before I knew it hip to hip. The shift happened so fast, but I was ready and by the feral look in his eyes, so was he.

"Vivian, I need to be inside you now."

He worked quickly to pull my pajama bottoms down, grabbing a condom from the drawer and quickly sheathing. I pulled my top over my head as he did. His hand ran up my thigh and found the silky wetness waiting for him. He stroked his fingers from my channel to the swollen nub and made circles over it as he gently pressed.

"I'm ready for you, Jake," I whispered as he ran his tongue over my collarbone.

He entered quickly and I let out a moan, louder than I had before as the intense connection was made. He tucked one arm under me, our bodies practically melting into one another, and my legs were wrapped around him. He was looking down to meet my eyes with a searing heat radiating from his look as he thrusted slowly but deeply. The way his lips were barely parted as he watched me, made me crave them on mine. I was coming unraveled and tried to pull him down to me, but he pulled away, flashing a devilish grin.

I was desperate, so I whispered breathily to him, "Jake, please."

His grin turned intense, and he finally leaned down and took my mouth into his, tongues deep into each other's mouth. I began to grab him hard with my hands and my legs were getting tense around him. He knew I was close to my finale, so he pulled back from the kiss and watched me again as he quickly thrust deep into me several times before my body squeezed tightly around him and waves of energy began to flow as I let out an unmistakable moan of pleasure. He made a guttural grunting sound at the same time, both of us grasping tightly to each other.

We both were still but catching our breath and I was still having trouble seeing straight, only this time it wasn't from alcohol. He had tucked his face into the crevice above my shoulder, breathing hard and fast for a minute, but finally it began to slow as his warm breath tickled my neck. He lifted his head and put a hand to my face, caressing one side then tilted it to him and gave a long, slow, and deep kiss. As my adrenaline subsided and he pulled away to look into my eyes, I remembered what I had just done and began to feel self-conscious, and blood rushed to my cheeks.

"Are you okay?" He asked with sincere concern. The fact that he noticed only made it worse. I went to sit up so I could hide my face pretending to look for my pajama bottoms.

"Totally fine, I just need to get showered and ready," I said, hoping I didn't sound too obvious. He pulled me back down onto the bed holding me while searching my face.

His face was twisted, and his voice was urgent. "Vivian, did I do something wrong? Tell me. I didn't mean to. I'm sorry," he pleaded quickly. I had to fess up before he got really upset.

"You didn't do anything wrong, at all, that was all great. I just...I'm a little embarrassed." My admission made it worse, and my face was on fire. His brow furrowed as he continued to search my face for answers.

I was trying to get the nerve to say it and I felt my face scrunch as I asked, "Can you look the other way?" He tipped his face at me but then laid his head down on my chest.

"I just hadn't done, *that* thing, before. And afterwards, I don't know, when you looked at me it seemed weird." He was trying not to laugh but I could feel his body moving and he was covering his mouth trying to hold it in.

He finally gained his composure again, leaned up, and looked at me with an unbelievably dashing smile. "Believe me, Vivian, it wasn't weird. I *thoroughly* enjoyed it. But if you think it's weird then don't do it." He leaned and gave me an innocent peck on the lips. I let out a deep sigh and felt my cheeks heat up again.

I covered my face but for some reason blurted out, "I liked it."

He pulled my hand down off my face and his deep voice was comforting. "Vivian, you don't need to feel 'weird' about anything with me. I told you before you can do whatever you want to me, and I meant it. I want you to be comfortable with me, and you must know there isn't anything you can do that I would think is weird." Relief washed over me, so I reached up and pulled him down to kiss him.

We lay there together a few minutes holding each other, but I finally looked over at the clock.

"Okay, I definitely need to shower and get dressed now but maybe just a tad more coffee first." We both leaned up and he slid off the bed, found his pants on the floor, and pulled them up then grabbed my bottoms and held them out for me, so I slipped my feet in, and he scooted them up. He walked into the bathroom then I shuffled in after him. When I was done, I found him waiting in the kitchen. He handed me my mug after stirring in some creamer.

He spoke as I sipped the warm rich drink, "I figured we can grab something to eat on the way. I took the day off since I need to get your aunt later so if we run behind, I can drop you at the shop and go grab breakfast for us."

I was still sipping my coffee but was filled with a different warmth at his words

"I didn't know you would take the day, I just figured you could slip over and back."

He shrugged. "Well, I didn't want to be rushed and figured I could hang out there until you got home since she may need help."

I turned toward the windows overlooking the town so he couldn't see my eyes filling. I had been so worried about her being alone but would never have asked him to do that. I couldn't believe how easy this was with him.

I drank the rest of my coffee quickly and when I turned said, "hot," so the watery eyes didn't seem odd. I put the mug in the sink and then went to grab my bag so I could shower.

I walked into the bathroom and turned the water on but reached into my bag and pulled out my journal. I found a pen deep in the bottom of the bag and put the last dream in; even though it was short, and alcohol induced, I didn't want to miss any pieces. I stuck it back down in the bag, pulled out my toiletries, and hopped in the shower.

His shower was incredible. Lots of room and the shower head was huge but had great water pressure. Plus, the water was hot almost immediately. It was so easy to forget everything happening outside when I was at Jake's. It was like an escape from everything, and his shower was no different.

I was still washing when I heard tapping on the door. "Vivian, is everything okay?"

I had lost track of time. "Yep, just a lot of hair to wash, be right out." His water never went cold, so I didn't even realize how much time had passed. I finished up and found the towel hanging outside the shower to dry off. I stepped out, brushed my teeth again to combat the coffee breath, then attempted to tame my hair. I toweled off a bit more since it was still steamy in there before getting dressed.

I opened the door and Jake was there with a fresh cup of coffee. "Drink this while I shower, I'll be quick."

I took the cup and sat down at the kitchen table and gazed out the window. I didn't want to go out there, into the cold, into the real world. I wished I could stay there with him all day. I was almost done with my coffee and heard the bathroom door open and got a glimpse of Jake heading to his room. He didn't shut the door but from where I was sitting, I couldn't see him getting dressed. A part of me thought of getting up to go peek, but that could lead to some severe lateness in opening the shop.

We finally left his apartment and in the parking deck I began to walk to my car, and he grabbed my arm to stop me.

"Just ride with me," he almost pleaded to me. "I'll drop you off, go grab some food, then I'll come get your car later."

"But that's silly. I can just drive it now, then you don't have to keep going back and forth. It's just practical." I shrugged. No sense in so much work for him, especially since he was going to pick up Aunt Rose later.

He pulled me close to him, clutching my jacket in his fists.

The timber of his voice was low as he stared down into my eyes. "I'm not trying to be practical; I'm trying to be with you as much as I can." A ball of electricity churned in my belly at his words. He gently pulled at my jacket that he still was holding, so I let my feet follow his lead into his car.

Chapter 21

He parked almost in front of the shop and got out with me to check the door and it was still locked. I had looked at the live view of the shop on my phone on the way over and all seemed fine, so he got me inside and then left to go get us breakfast.

I turned the open sign on, even though it was a few minutes before opening, flipped all the lights on, then walked to the computer to get everything up and running for the day. I put my coat and bag down under the counter and moved the mouse to wake the screen. *Shit.* It was locked on the password screen. I was so out of sorts yesterday I never went back to check once he took prints from the keyboard. I knew someone had been here snooping around. *What did they think they would find on the register?*

Annoyed but thankful nobody was able to login, I reset the password on the computer then checked my cell. No text from Aunt Rose yet so I texted her that I was at the shop, all was fine, and to let us know when she could be busted out. I checked the ringer to be sure it was on so I could hear if she texted or called and then set it down.

As I put the phone down, I noticed the old book that needed to be cleaned up. I pulled it closer and pulled the cover open. Some incredibly old pictures, drawings, a few newspaper clippings. The idea of sorting that all out now seemed daunting, so I carefully closed it and pushed it back to the side. The bells jingled, and it was Jake with donuts and more coffee.

"At this rate I'll be up all night." I laughed as I took my

coffee.

"Well, maybe that's my plan," he said with a mischievous grin inside of his beard, "if you can control your volume level." Some coffee came out of my nose.

"What? What are you talking about?" I asked with offense. He leaned against the counter casually but took a moment to look me up and down. *I knew exactly what he meant from that look.*

"Well, if we're taking care of your aunt, in that old house with thin walls, you'll have to be quieter." My cheeks started to burn so I grabbed a donut and walked away, shaking my head at him. But he was right. We wouldn't be in the solitude of his apartment, probably all week. I know she won't mind if he's there, but we still had to be respectful.

He brought the bag over and held it out to me open. "Have another, it'll help soak up the booze and make you feel better." I cocked an eyebrow at him but reached in and took another one. The bells jingled and I looked up to see some of our usual ladies coming to peruse the shelves. I went to greet them and one commented that they hadn't seen Aunt Rose since the week before.

"She just took a little time off, finally, now that she has someone here to help," I said as cheerfully as possible. They both nodded in agreement that it was a good idea and kept browsing. I walked back to the counter and Jake was sitting there, blowing the hot liquid, and sipping his coffee on one of the stools. The way his lips pursed as he did made me jealous of the cup. Trying to not stare, I reached over and looked at my cell. Still no text from Aunt Rose.

"Did she call or text you?" I asked him. He had given her his card, maybe she was bypassing me.

He took his phone out. "Nope, nothing."

I shrugged it off, maybe the nurses were in there with her getting her ready to be discharged. The ladies came up to the counter with a few small things, so I rang them up and that began a steady stream of one or two customers for a while. I greeted them, answered questions, walked around with them, and before I knew it, lunchtime had come, and Aunt Rose hadn't messaged yet.

I tried to call her cell and it went to voicemail. I called the hospital and asked to be sent to her room. She didn't answer there so I hung up and called back and asked to speak to the nurse on the floor. It took several minutes for them to confirm I was next of kin and only told me she was still there and not discharged. I asked if there was any reason she couldn't answer the phone and they couldn't say.

I hung up and Jake could see I was upset. "What did they say? Is she okay?"

I shook my head. "I don't know, they wouldn't tell me anything except she's still there." Suddenly my thoughts were getting frantic. "Why did her phone go to voicemail? Why didn't she charge it? I...they wouldn't tell me anything. I need to go; I can't just sit here and--" I started to ramble and looked around for my bag.

Jake cut me off and stood. "You stay, I'll go. I'm sure it's fine. She'll be mad if you close up." He grabbed his coat then grabbed me and hugged me tight. I could feel my pulse slowing down as he held me.

"Keep your phone with you, I'll call as soon as I get there." Then he practically ran out the door.

I stood there feeling helpless, but he was right. If she were fine, she'd just be mad if I had closed the store and gone up there. And we already all agreed Jake would pick her up so it was reasonable that he would go. I took a few deep breaths and straightened up. *No sense in worrying until there was something to worry about.*

I walked around the store with my phone in my hand and some more people came in and browsed. It was difficult to carry on a good conversation, but I attempted some small talk. I tried to not keep looking at the phone, but I glanced down over and over, willing it to ring. It seemed like an eternity had passed since Jake left, but it had only been fifteen minutes. I was ringing up a customer when finally, the phone rang so I excused myself to the customer and took the call but kept ringing up the items.

"Jake, is she okay?"

He sounded like he ran there. He was heaving into the phone. "She's okay, she wasn't in the room earlier because the doctor ordered a test before she could be discharged, and she didn't realize she hadn't plugged in her cell phone, so it died."

A wave of relief washed over me. "So, is she coming home today?"

He was still catching his breath. "They said they couldn't say yet. They had to review the test and the doctor would have to sign off and she is motioning to give her the phone so here she is."

I could hear some muffled sounds and they were saying something to each other, then Aunt Rose came on.

"Dear, why did you send this man here in such a fuss. This poor thing could barely breathe when he got here. I'm fine, just normal hospital stuff."

I felt silly for being so worried. "Well, you could have texted me, I tried to call and text you and after a couple hours passed, I got worried."

She laughed. "You mean worried like I was last night when you didn't text good night like you said you would?"

She had me there. I didn't want to tell her I got pass-out drunk, and no excuse came to mind.

"I'm sorry. I was with Jake and lost track of time, but he made sure I got here on time. So, I guess just let me know when you guys leave." We chatted for a few minutes then she gave him the phone and he said he would wait there and let me know of any news as he found out. I hung up and someone came in not long after with items to drop off. I took some time to sort through and make an offer. They haggled a bit, but I had no patience and stuck to the original offer, and they eventually took it. I took it to the back where we had a table setup to clean up newly acquired items and price them before taking them up to the front.

I heard the doorbells jingle again, so I turned to go to the front. I yelled a greeting to the person before I had turned the corner but when I looked up, I stopped in my tracks.

"Can I help you?" I asked firmly.

"Just looking," the man in the hat said as he walked quickly to the same shelf I had shown him before.

Anger bubbled up inside me. He had been in my house. He broke into the shop. He was looking for something that was mine. I knew I had no proof of anything except a hunch and the coincidence that he had been asking for the stone. If I questioned him, he would know I knew something. The last time he asked I really hadn't known anything, so I seemed genuine when I answered him that I hadn't seen anything like what he was looking for. So many things I wanted to do or say to him flashed in my mind, but I had to keep my cool. I glanced at the counter where I sat my phone, wishing I had kept it with me.

He looked back at me after looking over the shelf. "Still no new gemstones?" I shook my head with a small shrug, not wanting to speak since I knew my voice would be shaky. My heart was racing as quickly as my thoughts. *Stay calm, Viv.*

"Where is the owner? Is she not here?" I shook my head again, still not speaking. He gave a small smile and tipped his hat then walked out.

Once I couldn't see him out of the window, I rushed to the counter and grabbed my phone. I was furiously typing a text to Jake but before I hit send, I stopped. He was with Aunt Rose. She didn't need to get upset and he would have to tell her something if he left in a hurry. The man was gone, and it was the middle of the day still. Surely, he wouldn't try anything crazy in broad daylight in the square. And he must have noticed the cameras. I put the phone back down and took steady breaths to calm myself.

A steady flow of customers came and went without any other purchases the rest of the afternoon. Then I realized it was almost five o'clock. I texted Jake to see if anyone came back to mention discharging Aunt Rose, but I got a text back from Aunt Rose. The doctor wanted to redo the test in the morning, so he was keeping her, and Jake was on the way back.

I called her immediately. "Why do they want to redo the test? Why didn't they already do this?"

A heavy sigh came through the phone. "Viv, it's typical hospital stuff and doctors get busy. They just said some numbers still are more elevated than they like but nothing to be concerned about, better safe than sorry." As she was talking some strange sound came from my phone, so I pulled it away from my ear and a notification for the home doorbell had popped up, but I wanted to finish the call.

"Okay Aunt Rose if you say so. I guess we'll see you tomorrow then, hopefully. I need to go, I think I see some customers walking in, but I love you." She told me she loved me, and we hung up.

I swiped the notification and the app opened. There was someone standing on the street in front of the house, looking down at a phone. I couldn't see their face clearly, but I could see the clothes and it looked just like the coat and hat of the mysterious little man. But he wasn't in the yard or at the house, just in front of it on the street. *But what was he doing there?*

He looked up briefly, then down at his phone again, then walked away out of the frame. My pulse and thoughts were racing again. It was him. I know it was him. The face was too far to clearly make out, but he had been in just a couple hours before and had the same hat and jacket as always. I closed the app but kept the phone in my hand as I sat staring out the front windows waiting for Jake to arrive.

I glanced up to see Jake walking in with food and drinks. I went to open the door for him and followed him to the counter.

He sat the bag and drink holder on the counter, and I must have looked frazzled because he didn't even take his coat off before he asked what was wrong.

"Didn't your aunt text you? She told me she'd take care of it and to get you food so here I am." I nodded my head and I felt tears welling up but instead of my normal breakdown, I was angry. My body shook, and tears welled because the emotions had to come out of me somehow, so they were exiting out of my eyeballs.

Shaky words slowly came out. "That man was here today, in the shop, then he was at my house."

"What, when? Are you okay?" He asked as he grabbed me and pulled me to him. I was still shaking, saying it out loud just made me angrier than before. I grabbed my phone and shakily pulled up the feed from the shop and handed it to him. He found the section when the man had come into the shop. As he watched I tried to explain the call with Aunt Rose and how the app notified me someone had been there, so he pulled that up and watched it as well. Both of course were hard to see and grainy on the phone, but you could make out the hat, coat, and some of the facial features.

Jake's face turned red as his face drew into a grimace.

"Well, I know it wasn't the plan but since Aunt Rose didn't get to go home anyway, I think we should stay at my place again tonight," he said in a deep, gravelly voice.

I nodded my head vacantly. "But I need clothes."

He nodded his head and started pulling food out of the bag. "First I eat, then I can go to your house and grab whatever you need." I nodded and grabbed my food as he passed it to me. I didn't realize I was hungry until I smelled the food.

We ate quickly and quietly, then he stood up and put his coat on. I tried to think of some things to grab and jotted down a list. I didn't want him to forget underwear and socks.

"I'll be back soon. I don't want to leave you here alone once it gets dark." He grabbed the list from me but wrapped his body around mine and pressed his face into my neck. It was so warm and safe in his arms I didn't want to let go. Eventually he kissed the top of my head and loosened his grasp around me, so I let him go. He flashed me a smile as he left, then I saw him pick up his pace.

Jake made it to the house quickly. He was in and out fast and right back to the shop. He told me he was sure everything was secure before he left, and my things were in the car. We sat behind the counter together waiting for closing time to arrive. Only a few people popped in and browsed briefly so the time was moving slowly.

I finally stood up and went to the back to see if I could clean up the new items dropped off earlier to pass the time.

As I was clanking the trinkets around, Jake called back to me from the front.

"Vivian, what is this?"

I wasn't sure what he meant since I was in the back, so I just called back to him, "What's what?"

I was still fiddling with the items when he came to the back holding a piece of paper that looked old and delicate and he looked like he had seen a ghost. He reached his hand out, so I took the paper.

It was a piece of dull yellow parchment, wider than long, and it had writing on it. The penmanship was difficult to read, the words faded. I held it up to the light and could make out most of it:

Contracts

Jackson Alexander Adams of this Parish of Cumberland, house of William and Jane Adams, and Vivian Elaine Acworth of the Parish of Devon, house of Henry and Elizabeth Acworth, have given their names to hereby proclaim intent to marry within 30 days but no sooner than three Sundays from this day, the 1st of November 1560.

The year was the same one from the scroll in the box, and there was my name. And Devon. And the other names, specifically Adams...

I looked toward him, my brows pulled together. "Where did you get this?"

He answered abruptly, "The book sitting on the counter, the one you said you needed to clean up. What is this, Vivian?"

I shook my head, unsure of his meaning.

His eyes narrowed and his arms were crossed. "I don't know what's going on, but I never told you my full name, so why is it on this piece of paper?"

I looked puzzled at him, "I don't understand, your name isn't Jake?"

He walked toward me and looked me in the eye, his hand poking at the parchment. "Vivian, this isn't funny, what is this? Are you trying to trick me or something?"

I stood up taller and smacked his hand away. "First of all, you need to calm down and stop acting accusatory. Second, this isn't mine. Third, is your name *Jackson*?"

A sigh escaped him, and the tension melted from his shoulders, but he rested his hands on his hips. "If this isn't yours then what is it and why are our names on it?"

I shoved past him and walked to the front and saw where he had left the book open. I flipped a few pages, but this time really looked at the items in there. There were scattered pictures, newspaper clippings, handwritten notes, all different years, some going back to the 1500's but some as recent as the 1900's. Jake had slowly started walking back up front and over to the counter but was keeping his space. I frantically flipped through the pages, like I knew I was looking for something. *But what*?

Suddenly, something caught my eye, and I turned the page back to the one I had just flipped. There was a drawing, or maybe it was a painting. It was not exceptionally large and was cracked a bit, so I was careful not to pick it up. But I was mesmerized as I traced my fingers lightly over the edge. There was a girl in a dress of blue, green, and gold with large luxurious skirts and curly locks of dark hair piled up on her head. She was standing next to a man in a long dark colored coat with white pants, or were those tights, and dark shoes. He had dirty blonde hair, but it was pulled or brushed back. Her hand was resting on top of his, and I could make out the faintest of thin gold bands on her ring finger. I shook my head and took a step back away from the counter, my chest tightening with each breath.

Jake was still standing on the other side of the counter, but his stern look was dissolving into a softer, concerned look. "What is it, Vivian?"

I heard him but couldn't look away. He slowly walked around the counter and stood next to me but leaned over to see what it was I was looking at. When he did, he first leaned in closer then whipped his head toward me, with what I imagine was the same look I had on my face.

"Vivian, where did this come from?" He asked calmly, his voice low and smooth but his eyes questioning.

I shook my head at first but finally found enough breath to respond. "I honestly don't know. Aunt Rose took this lot in a few weeks ago and I sorted most of it and just kept putting this book off." I finally looked up at him. "I don't know how there is a picture of us in this."

He put his hand on my back. "I'm sorry," he said genuinely. "I just opened this because it was sitting here and then saw my name. I dunno, it bothered me that you were keeping more from me."

I stepped away from him. "Kept *more* from you, like what? The only thing I kept from you, for a few hours, was why I didn't keep our date Friday night and it was because I promised my aunt."

He seemed as if he was looking right through me but spoke softly. "You only told me that because I went to check on you and stumbled onto it. And you never told me anything about it, just showed me what it was. And I think there are other things you're keeping from me. Am I wrong?"

I sat for a minute and considered all he said...and he was right. I didn't explain what the scroll said, what happened when I held the stone, and didn't tell him about my dreams even though he mentioned he had some about me.

"Okay, there may be some truth to that, but it's not because I don't want to tell you, I just didn't want to scare you away or for you to think I am losing my mind." He cocked his head and lifted his palms like he was waiting for me to spill everything then. I looked down at the time on the computer.

"It's almost time to close. Let's get out of here first and I promise, if you really want to know, I will tell you everything. But you may not want me to stay after that." He pulled me to him, and our faces were just inches from each other, so close I could smell his lip balm. The tension was palpable and had my whole body fluttering.

"Vivian, have I gone anywhere yet? When will you believe me? I am not going anywhere. I just want you to trust me." We were about to lean into each other, but my cell phone dinged. I looked over and it was Aunt Rose just checking in to say she was charging her phone and about to try to sleep. I texted her back saying I love her and hoped to see her at home tomorrow.

I turned back to Jake. "Let's get ready to go. I need to put that stuff in the back away really quick then we can go." He nodded his head and grabbed his coat then grabbed my things from under the counter. I went and moved the items off the table and to the shelves then walked back up to shut down the register. Jake put my coat on, handed me my bag, and we started to walk to the front to turn the lights off and lock up. He turned back to grab the book.

"We probably shouldn't leave this laying around. Plus, I want to look this over some more, don't you?" He asked. I gave an acknowledging nod and then we left the shop, making sure the door was locked.

Chapter 22

Once we made it to his place, he put my things in the bedroom, and I took the book to the kitchen table. I sat down and at first just looked at it without opening it. He brought me some ice water, but he didn't sit down. He went back to the fridge and pulled it out. He then pulled up the fake flap of wall and I heard digital beeps. He pulled the bookbag out and put it on the counter and then pushed the fridge back to its normal spot. He brought the bag over to the table and pulled the box out then gently pushed it across to me.

"So, here we are. Start wherever you like," he said very calmly but with a hint of demand. I stood up and went to get my journal from my bag. If I was going to tell him everything, I may as well make sure it really was everything. I walked back into the kitchen and sat down.

"Well, I need to start from the beginning so that would be here." I pushed the journal to him.

"What's this?" He asked while he put his hand on the journal but didn't open it.

"After my parent's accident, I started having dreams, almost every night. At first, I just thought my mind was trying to give me subliminal messages or something. And yes, I was seeing a therapist so she sort of planted that seed. But they kept happening and didn't really line up with what she said, but she had suggested I keep track of them and my sleep in a journal. I haven't been great about my sleep, but I have documented every dream I've had in there." I tilted my head toward the journal, and he opened the cover and found the first entry. He read silently and intently.

He looked back up at me. "So how do you think this ties into everything?"

I shrugged then continued. "Well, as you can see in the early entries the man in the dreams was a mystery. I couldn't see his face, but I could make out his build, hair, and some facial features sometimes, but he felt familiar to me, like I knew him. Anyway, that went on for months but then I ran into you. It was hard to explain," I had to pause to muster the courage to tell him, "But when you touched me, I felt like you had touched me before, like I knew you already. But we had just met. Fast forward a bit, eventually, in a dream like the others, a face finally came to me." He was watching me with all his attention, leaning in like he was watching a thriller on television.

"So, the face...whose was it, Vivian?"

My mouth felt dry, so I took a sip of water. I pulled in a deep breath and looked straight at him, heart racing. "It was you."

He sat up but instead of seeming confused he almost seemed relieved, and a small smile spread on his lips.

"Vivian, remember how I told you I had some dreams about you? Well, that was true, but I didn't keep track of them," he said as he pointed to the journal. "Still, I know I had some before we actually met. And thinking back, I guess I really couldn't make out the face at first, but I know that once I met you, suddenly it was you in the dreams." My heart was racing faster. *Did he have the same dreams I had?* "I think that's part of the reason I knew we were drawn together for a reason. And the first time I touched you at the donut shop, I knew I had to find you again. I wasn't immediately sure why, but it was intense. A need. So, I made sure I did." He stuck his hand out for me, so I put my hand into his across the table. "So, tell me the rest," he said as he gently squeezed my hand.

I told him all of it. I recounted the day I researched the gemstone and saw one identical to the one in my dream, how Aunt Rose told me the story of how she came to have it and where she hid it, that she swore me to secrecy, or I would have told him. I finally got to the point where I opened the box.

"I had taken it to my room and for some reason locked myself in. I guess I was shocked I even found it. I think I thought Aunt Rose was delirious and I just tried to find it to appease her. But I did find it. So, I put it on the bed and pulled out the scroll first." I stopped and pulled the box closer to me and then opened it to grab the satchel out with the scroll inside. I gently opened it and pulled the scroll out and passed it to Jake. He read it and seemed to be absorbing the info, his brows pinched together and lips in a tight straight line. He finally handed it back to me, so I rolled it up and carefully put it back in the satchel. "The gemstone, well, we may need to go to the room for this." He seemed confused but stood up and put his hand out for me, so I took his hand, grabbed the box, and walked to his bedroom.

I kicked my shoes off then sat on the bed and put the box in the middle then motioned for him to sit across from me.

"When I pulled it out last time, something strange happened, and it sort of scared me, so I dropped it. That's why I suggested we come in here." I opened the box and picked up the bag with the stone inside. "Hold your hands out in front of you," I told him. He put his hands out in front of him, so I opened the tie and held the bag over his hands and let it drop. He looked at it for a moment then I closed his hands over it. When I did, he closed his eyes, his brows pulled together, his jaw clenched, and his muscles went tense. After just a few seconds he dropped it and his eyes were open again.

"What the hell was that?"

I shook my head. "I don't know, what happened?"

He shook his head and shoulders like he was shaking off something. "I was seeing places from my dreams, and you, but it didn't seem like dreams. It was real, or at least it felt real. What was that?"

I grabbed his hand. "I don't know but that's what happened to me. And like you said, it seemed real, it was from my dreams, but it felt like I knew those places and had been there, lived there even. Hard to explain."

He leaned over to me and grabbed my face with his hands. "Vivian, I wish you had just told me. You shouldn't carry so much on your own. But I'm here, and I'm not going anywhere, ever. I promise." He pulled me closer, his warm lips meeting mine, and tears formed in my eyes.

He felt the tears and pulled back, wiping them away. "Why the tears?"

I swallowed hard. "I'm just glad you know now, and you didn't ask me to leave."

He laughed gently. "I told you that wouldn't happen, and I meant it." He tucked some of my hair behind my ear. "But, what about that book?"

We both straightened up. "I really don't know any more than you do." I nodded my head to the side toward the kitchen and he and I got up off the bed and went back to look at the book.

The paper he found was in the back with the picture of us. We turned page after page together. Nothing of help to us, but certainly plenty to confuse us more. There were clippings with our names, but the dates were all over the place. Some like the older one he found at the shop from the UK, the Restoration period in the UK, some from what seemed to be around the time of the American Revolution, and some around prohibition in the US. There was parchment paper with dates and names, some letters from Jackson to Vivian, clippings of newspapers with Jackson listed as a Captain and mention of his wife, a picture of a club, and some clippings showing the club being shut down after being caught selling alcohol, more drawings. There were other clippings and letters inside that didn't seem to have anything to do with us, or Jackson and Vivian. Pictures of homes and other people with little to no info written or printed. It was hard to figure out if those were there on purpose and had something to do with the rest, or they just got added randomly over time.

Before we knew it, it was already almost eleven. We had been sitting there a while reading over all the letters and clippings, trying to piece them together somehow. He stretched his back and I leaned away from the table and realized how heavy my eyes felt once I wasn't staring at random pieces of paper.

"We need to put the gemstone back in the box and put it away," I said as I finally took a big stretch. He stood to go to the bedroom, but I called out quickly, "Wait, we need potholders or something." He stopped and turned with a strange face but walked back into the kitchen as I stood up and pulled some out of a drawer.

We both walked to the room, and it was sitting there on the bed where we left it. It sparkled as the light hit it. We both walked over and just looked at it for a moment.

"What do you think would happen if we held it again?" he asked.

I shrugged because I wasn't sure. "I don't know, I did what you did that one time then put it back in the bag with silicone potholders. I was scared to touch it again."

He carefully sat on the bed. "What if we tried again now, together, since we know what to expect?" I stood there for a moment in hesitation, biting my lip. I wasn't sure I wanted to, or to expect the same thing. He reached his hand out to me to urge me to sit. I slowly walked to the other side of the bed and climbed up with my legs crossed. He turned to face me, and the gemstone sat there on the bed between us.

We both looked at it for a moment and finally he spoke up. "So, do you want to go first? Technically, I think it's yours."

I shook my head as I was still unsure that I wanted to do it at all. "Maybe you should try."

He sat up straight and rolled his shoulders a bit like he was about to work out and needed to loosen up. He slowly reached his hand out but right when he was about to touch it, he stopped short then pulled his hand back.

He looked back up at me. "What do you think would happen if we both grabbed it?" My muscles went tense. I already was reluctant to try again at all, much less with an added twist. "Vivian, I'm here with you. I think we should do it together. Do you trust me?" I nodded my head slowly because I did, but he didn't know what would happen anymore than I did.

"I'm not scared of you, I'm scared of it," I said.

He leaned over enough to grab my hands and brought both up to his lips and kissed them softly. "Whatever happens, we're together." I nodded a little more quickly this time in agreement. He gradually moved our hands down toward the stone until we both were just inches from it. We both looked at each other and took a deep breath in and blew it out, then he lowered our hands the rest of the way, all four hands covering the deep pink hues and no more light was hitting it to reflect off the facets.

Suddenly, my eyes were closed but instead of lots of flashes through different dreams, this time, it was one scene. I was in the dress, the one with the blue, green, and gold with my hair piled up neatly on my head. I was standing in front of two incredibly old, tall, wooden doors and it was dimly lit where

I was standing, only one candle on either side of the doors in wall sconces burning. The doors opened, and I began walking into what appeared to be a small chapel. It was bright inside with large stained-glass windows on the walls on either side and behind the altar. More candles were lit on stands around the room. There were not many rows of pews, but they were beautiful and carefully crafted with heavy cherry oak. Only the first three rows had anyone sitting in them and in total it was only maybe fifteen people.

There was a priest straight ahead of me in a long white robe holding a bible and a censer. And there to his left, or my right, was Jake, or Jackson I suppose, in his long navy-blue jacket and dress shirt underneath. Once I saw him, I only saw him. My heart was racing.

I continued to walk toward them both at a steady and slow pace, hands together at my waist and my shoulders back, chin up, trying to take slow steady breaths to keep my heart from jumping out of my chest. Finally, I was there next to him, and we turned, face to face. I could sense the priest was speaking to us and we were listening, but I couldn't make out what he was saying. We seemed to understand as we were nodding while still gazing deep into each other's eyes, the green specks in his glimmering from the light coming in over my shoulder from the stained-glass.

It was as if everything was in slow motion and there was some kind of sound buffer. I could hear speaking, but nothing was clear. We both were saying something while still looking at each other, but I still couldn't make it out. Then someone stepped to the front and placed something onto the bible the priest was holding, and we both looked over. He rocked the censer over what turned out to be two gold bands and he was speaking, but I still couldn't make out what was being said. The priest then reached his arm out that was holding the bible toward Jake, and he grabbed one of the bands and reached out to me, so I instinctively put my hand out. He slid the band onto my finger, then kissed that hand. The priest then reached the bible toward me, and I reached for the band still sitting upon it and turned back to Jake, sliding the band onto his finger before he took my hand into his.

The priest carefully tied a blue scarf around the wrists of our joined hands, not tight, but our wrists were bound together. We held the other's arm as the priest then rocked the censer over our wrists while reciting something. Then, the priest must have completed the ceremony and instructed us to kiss because we both smiled and leaned toward each other and had a slow, but somewhat innocent kiss.

We turned back toward the pews and faced the door, and I could see faces of those sitting. I scanned them all as we started to make our way slowly back to the door and there he was. It was the man who kept coming in asking about the gemstone and then made a visit to our house.

He was with a woman. He was dressed as the other men in the long coat, and he was sitting so I didn't see his pants or tights and the woman was dressed in a beautiful velvet black cloak and I couldn't see what else she had on. She had light red hair and fair skin with light eyes, but I wasn't close enough to make out the exact shade. But both of their faces were stern, not cheerful and smiling like the others. As we began to pass the pew they sat in, I felt my pulse begin to race very quickly and my breathing was labored.

Suddenly I was back in Jake's room, sitting across from him as he grabbed my shoulders.

"Vivian, are you ok, breathe, take a deep breath and blow it out," he said as he gently shook my shoulders and was close to my face with a deeply concerned look.

"Did you see it? Were you there? That felt so real?" I asked him frantically, grabbing at his arms.

"I don't know, I was somewhere, with you. We had on the clothes from the older picture, and well, I think we were getting married. All was fine but when we walked out, you had turned and stopped and I couldn't get your attention and you seemed to be upset, so I let go. When I came back you were breathing hard and your pulse was racing so I pulled your hands off," he replied, still checking my face for signs that I was fine.

"Because it was him, he was there, in the chapel," I said, still frantic.

Jake still had my shoulders and was trying to comfort me and calm me down. "We are here now, just you and me. Now slow down, who was there? Who upset you?" I stopped and took a few deep breaths and blew them out intentionally, trying to settle myself so I could make sense of it to him.

"The man that is looking for the gemstone, the one that has been to the shop several times and then to our house today, he was there, but you know, in that time. But it was definitely him. It just spooked me. It all felt real, you were so real. So, when I saw him, I don't know, it didn't make any sense. How was he there, Jake?" I asked, fighting the pressure that was building behind my eyes.

"I'm not sure, but it's just us here now," he said with his soothing, low voice as he pulled me to him. He held me for a few minutes, stroking my back. Finally, we pulled apart.

"I think that's enough for tonight," he said. "Let's put this away now." He took the potholders and picked up the stone, so I grabbed the bag and pulled it up over the stone then tied it and set it back into the box. He shut the box and walked it back to the kitchen.

I could hear the zippers on the bookbag then the sounds of the fridge moving. I was still sitting there on the bed when I looked over and saw the time, nearly midnight already. I made myself slink off the bed and grabbed the bag Jake had grabbed for me today and took it to the bathroom.

He packed me some fresh pajamas, but they were not as cute as the ones I had brought the day before, and much more modest with pants and a t-shirt. Begrudgingly, I put them on anyway and then looked through the bag to see what else he got, he did well. The other bag from the night before was still with me, so I was all set. I brushed my teeth quickly while I was there then decided to leave the bag in the bathroom since I would change after a shower in the morning. Jake had turned the lights off in the kitchen and living room and was in bed.

I walked in and he had brought me a water and my journal and left them on my bedside table. I climbed into bed and scooted in close to him. He turned his alarm on and his lamp off making the room dark and quiet, then he pulled me in even closer and kissed my head.

"Try to get some rest, I'm here and you're safe. We will keep sorting this all out as we can. But for now, sleep," he said. I finally closed my eyes and was being lulled to sleep by the steady rising and falling of his warm chest that I rested my head on.

Chapter 23

The dark and narrow hall was dimly lit with candles along the way. My full and plain skirts dragged along the stone floor, and I pulled my shawl closer in at my chest to keep the chill at bay. Coming toa large wooden door, I pushed it open to find the fire had been made for me, giving me enough light to navigate my room. I removed my shawl and placed it on the mount. There were lights out the window and movement below. I pushed the shutters just enough to peek through, trying to keep the cold out. Soldiers roughly pushed men through the muddy streets. I didn't want to be seen looking out, so I gently closed the shutters and made sure to secure them, so they didn't come open in the night.

I began untying my bodice to prepare for bed when I heard a creak from the floor behind me. I quickly turned, panicked that someone was there, but I was relieved to see him and couldn't help but go to him. The sight of him in his uniform warmed me quickly. Before I could ask how long he had been there he grabbed me, kissing me hard. It was a kiss reserved for a soldier's return from war, and it sent tingles from my lips to my toes. I hadn't gathered my wits from the kiss when he quickly pulled off my bodice. I knew I should protest, but my body wanted him as much as my soul. I began to unbutton his dress coat and finally pulled the arms down, then I quickly began to pull his shirt up over his head. I ran my hands across his large, heaving chest then up around his neck to pull his mouth back down to mine. I could feel his arms reaching around me and untying my skirts. As they fell to the floor, I could feel him pulling my shift up higher, his hands caressing my skin as he did, cupping my ass and picking me up as he grabbed both sides with his large, rugged hands.

He walked us to the bed and gently laid me down, standing to begin to untie his britches. I lay there, watching him, breathing in deeply and letting out my breaths just as deeply. I was desperate for his weight over me. His muscles were tight and flexing with every little move he made, and his shoulders rose and fell with each labored breath he took. He began to drop his pants...

The alarm buzzed loudly. I was still laying on Jake, but he moved slightly to hit the snooze button, forcing me out of the comfy crevice.

He gently rolled toward me and kissed my forehead. "Good morning. Sleep well?"

I slept very well and had the best dream until the alarm went off. "It was good, yes. But coffee?" He chuckled and rolled out of bed, turning the alarm off as he stood up, then walked to the kitchen. I took the opportunity to go to the bathroom and brush my teeth.

I walked into the kitchen to find him standing in his sweatpants and no shirt waiting by the coffee pot. The sight sent a warm rush between my thighs. I went up beside him and put my arm around his back, only after getting a good look at the lean muscles running on either side of his spine and the many smaller but defined ones around his shoulders. The coffee pot was still percolating and dripping but he pulled the carafe away and poured the steaming liquid into the mugs on the counter. He wrapped a long arm around me as I stood next to him, but he made a turn like he needed to reach for something then he suddenly was behind me, both arms wrapped around me.

I could hear him smell my hair, then he moved his head down to my neck and took a deep breath in with his lips close against the skin under my ear. Blood was rushing to my face and between my legs. He slowly began to run his hands over me, first just across my abdomen then up my sides, but finally one found a breast and was gently running his fingers over it, my nipples already hard and sensitive. Each stroke sent shooting waves of heat all over me. He began kissing my neck, but lightly and just enough to make me feel like I could lose my footing. As one hand was stroking a breast, I felt the other begin to run lower, teasing at the elastic waistband and I felt a rush of fluid and heat collecting. As electricity shot through me, my breathing became shallow and quick. I grasped onto his arm and tried to reach behind me to feel him, but he squeezed closer to me, leaving no space between us. As he molded to me from behind with his hard shaft against my back, his hand reached down and for a moment I couldn't take a breath. He stopped briefly, only returning to his work when I finally let my breath out and took another in. His top hand moved to the other breast as the lower continued stroking me below. My legs were getting weaker and weaker, and I let out a small moan that sounded more like a squeak. I had a feeling of electricity flowing through me again and I could have just let him finish me off, but I didn't just want to be finished, I wanted him so badly.

I finally grabbed his arms with force, so he knew I wanted to get his attention and all his motion stopped, like he was unsure if he had done something wrong. I took the opportunity to turn to him quickly and he was looking down at me, confused. I quickly reached down and grabbed him, stroking firmly up and down, and leaned to kiss his chest, then nibbled at a nipple softly. He let out a low rumble and it only made the electrical bursts fire more quickly.

I could feel his hands at first just on my shoulders as I worked. His eyes closed and he turned his face to the ceiling before leaning down to press his lips to mine. He slowly began rubbing my back, lifting my shirt up, so I released him to let it go up over my head. He wrapped his arms around my bare back, and we kissed, hard, like the kiss from the dream. Like he was a soldier returning after a time away from home. I began working my pants down and they fell once over my ass. I worked to step out of them without breaking the intense kissing. I pressed my body against his, then he spread his huge palms over my ass and picked me up, placing me on the counter.

He entered quickly but stopped as his shaft was completely engulfed and held me for a moment, both of us just enjoying the feeling of the other. His face and lips were so close only a piece of paper would have fit between us, but he didn't lean all the way, just hovered there, breathing me in. I could feel the heat from him, and the waves of electricity were rushing through me hard and fast. He slowly began moving his hips, still just hovering close to my lips. I was taking slow breaths to his rhythmic movement. I leaned closer to kiss him, but he grabbed my hair and pulled my head back away from his face and was watching me with a primal look, like he could eat me alive.

After a few seconds I let out a small moan, begging for him to give me his mouth. "Jake, kiss me."

He finally pulled me closer and leaned down to smash his lips to mine as his tongue entered my mouth, still holding my hair with one hand and the small of my back with the other. The kissing alone was enough to drive me crazy, but he began pushing into me even deeper and a little faster, pulling me to him as he moved to me. I could feel the ripple of pleasure pulsating around him, and my legs tightened as he let out a soft but deep moan.

Everything had gone fuzzy again for a moment and I didn't realize I was holding my breath until he leaned his down to my neck and whispered, "breathe," into my ear. I let out my breath, suddenly breathing heavily but trying to breathe in my nose and out through my mouth. We were holding on to each other tight, me still on the counter, while we caught our breath.

He slowly pulled himself from me while he grabbed my

face with both hands and kissed me deeply. As he pulled away my eyes slowly opened to find him grinning down at me as he reached for the mug.

"I may need to warm that up for you," he said as he poured a small amount of the rich coffee into the mug.

I grinned and took a sip. "You have a bad habit of letting my coffee get cold."

He reached down and grabbed my pajamas, helping me get them back on, but I had to jump off the counter to get them up over my hips. As I did, I pulled him close to me and rubbed my hands over his back and then down over his ass. He wrapped his warm arms around me like a cocoon, and I could have stayed in that cocoon forever.

I leaned up to kiss him again then finally let him go so he could pull his own pants back on and I hurried to the bathroom. He strolled past me as I went back to the kitchen and grabbed my mug.

I looked over and was thankful for the cold outside that made the windows dewy with condensation, preventing any good view of what just happened in the open kitchen area. Jake came back to the kitchen and topped off my mug to warm it again before warming his own and putting the carafe on the warmer. He stood behind me again, but this time with an arm just wrapped around me, the other holding his coffee mug.

"I wish I could just stay here all day," I said out loud, not meaning to.

"Well, maybe soon. But for now, you have to go to work." He kissed the top of my head. "And I have to check in to work today but I'll still go get your aunt when she's ready to go."

Hopefully, she would be able to come home today. I felt a tinge of sorrow that he wouldn't be able to hang out with me again; we had been together for days. My head dipped as I began to wallow in pity for myself.

"Hey, head up, I just said check in. I'll be back at the shop before you realize I was gone."

I lifted my head and turned to him with a grin. "Okay, I can live with that." I leaned against him again. "I'm going to hop in the shower," I said before I leaned in for a short kiss. I took my coffee with me to the bedroom and took a few more sips and put it on the nightstand.

Once in the bathroom I turned the shower on, then got all my items from my bag and put them on the side of the shower. I still couldn't get over how fast his water got hot compared to home. I hopped in and washed but made sure not to get caught losing track of time again. After combing my hair and dressing quickly so I could get more coffee, I went and got my mug as well as my journal and he was there ready to pour me some more. He put the carafe down and walked to the bathroom and I heard the shower turn on.

I took my coffee and went and plopped down on the couch. I looked around and found a pen in the side table drawer, so I wrote down my latest dream. As I finished my mind went to what happened after and I could feel the blood rushing to my face.

I hadn't even heard the shower turn off, but the bathroom door opened, and Jake was walking to his room with just his towel on. I peeked over my shoulder briefly but turned back to the journal. I started flipping through the pages again, looking for any sign. The events of the last few days were filling my mind, especially yesterday. I took my journal and coffee to the kitchen table where the book was still laying and sat down. I was thumbing through the book when Jake walked over to me.

"Whatcha doin'?" He asked, moving my hair off my shoulder.

"I don't know, just trying to see if anything from here jumps out at me here," I said, holding up my journal. I looked slowly through pages again, but nothing seemed to be familiar except the picture of the two of us, or what looked like us. "I want to keep looking at this, but I don't think it's a good idea to have it with me at the shop. That man keeps popping in and so far, he hasn't mentioned a book but if he saw anything...I just don't want him poking around further."

Jake nodded his head in agreement. "We can probably fit it in the safe if you want." I nodded my head and closed the book realizing while I wasn't rushed, now wasn't a good time to be looking since I had to leave soon. Jake stood and moved the fridge, opened the safe, then came back to carefully pick up the book and he locked it away with the gemstone.

I stood and went to grab my bags and toss my things back in, but he came to the bathroom.

"Do you need those at home?"

I shook my head. "No, I have regular size stuff at home, but I just figured I would clean up my stuff."

He leaned over and grabbed the couple of items I had bagged already and put them back in the shower. "That way you don't have to have a bag every time." I stood with a blank stare holding my empty bag. I don't know why I was so shocked he wanted me to leave my things, but I was. After my shock wore off, I grabbed my dirty clothes and shoved them inside then got the other bag from his room. He started getting ready to leave for the day, so I put my shoes on and grabbed my coat.

My phone dinged as soon as I was putting it on, so I grabbed it and looked down. Aunt Rose was letting me know she was told she will be discharged today around lunchtime; all tests are good now. She just had to wait for the doctor to sign off, but he wouldn't be there until lunchtime.

"Jake, they told Aunt Rose she can leave around lunchtime. Is that okay?"

He looked at me funny and walked to his chest of drawers and started to grab some items. "Of course, I can't pick the time, they do. I got it. Can I shove these in one of those bags?" He was holding some sweatpants, socks, a t-shirt, and I'm fairly sure I saw a pair of undies rolled up. I reached out and grabbed them and put them in my bag as he pulled jeans from his closet and handed them over.

"If she's going home today, I know you'll want to be with her, and I want to be with you, so." I smiled and zipped up the bag and looked around to be sure I had gotten everything.

"What about the stuff in the safe? Do we just leave it here?"

He shrugged. "Well, we have a long day ahead so are we going to need it? It's safe in there and we know where it all is." I nodded as that made perfect sense, but I felt like we should have it close. I fought the urge to say anything, though, since his reasoning was logical. It was safe, literally in a safe, and we would be distracted today and maybe the next few days. He grabbed the bags, and we left the warmth and seclusion of his apartment and headed to the elevator which led to the real world.

Chapter 24

"Why don't you just ride with me again?" He asked as he walked to the parking area.

I thought about it for a second. "Well, as much as I want to be with you, I think maybe I should take the car home later. Plus, that way you won't have to leave the house later to come get me."

He looked disappointed but he walked me to the car and got me inside. "I'll take the bags; I can take them in when I take your aunt home. Text me when you get there." Then he leaned into the car and gave me a long kiss, one that almost made me forget all my responsibilities and tell him to take me back upstairs. He finally leaned out of the car then shut the door and watched me drive away.

It took so little time to get to the square that the car's heater hadn't even warmed up all the way. I was earlier than normal and there was still plenty of parking near the shop. Pulling into one of the spaces almost right in front of the shop, I looked over at the door before I got out of the car but didn't notice any obvious issues and it looked to be still locked. I left the semi-warmth of the car and ran to the door to unlock it and locked it back behind me since it was still a few minutes before opening time.

It was quiet and cool in the shop as I turned on the lights and the computer, so I went to the thermostat and turned it up just a couple of degrees. It had gotten much colder overnight, and the door and huge windows were not forgiving when it came to the cooler temps. I went to the counter and logged into the register and checked the site. Thankful that there was nothing new, I walked around to make sure everything was straightened up.

Missing Jake made the time seem to pass like cold molasses being poured. I walked to the front to look out and was kicking myself for not stopping to get some coffee and a donut before I came in. I was considering if I had time to run over when my phone dinged. I walked to the counter quickly to check in case it was Aunt Rose, but it was Jake. I hadn't texted him when I got in. I texted him back that I was fine, and all was normal at the shop. He replied he would be by soon with breakfast and coffee. *Mind-reader.* I saw the time on the phone, and it was just five minutes until opening so I went to the front and turned on the sign and unlocked the door.

It was quiet for what seemed like an eternity, but I happened to look up from the computer to see Jake walking up to the door. He came to the counter and put the coffees and bag down, unzipped his coat, and took it off before pulling me to him and wrapping his arms all the way around me, melding me into him.

"I missed you," he said low and quiet into my ear. My heart was racing just from hearing his voice and feeling him so close against me. He pulled away and gave me a quick kiss then reached for one of the coffees and handed it to me. I reached inside the bag and grabbed something, not a donut.

"I had to pass the market on the way, so I grabbed a few pastries," he said, seeing the questioning look on my face.

"Fancy, but a nice change," I said, grinning as I took a bite out of the cheese Danish. "I thought you had to work today," I said between bites and sips of decadent coffee.

"I went by there first and checked in, then I left. I'm an investigator, I don't often sit at a desk, so I won't be missed."

I nodded my head and gave him a sideways look. "So, you're milking the company time?" We both let out a small chuckle and he shrugged. Finally, some customers started strolling in. I jumped up and went to greet them and we chatted a little.

There was a slow but steady stream of customers for a while, so the time began to pass faster. Jake sat patiently at the counter as I spoke to customers and checked people out. Finally, the phone dinged, and it was Aunt Rose. They told her it would be within the hour, and she wouldn't be discharged without a ride.

"Jake, Aunt Rose can leave soon, and her ride has to be there," I told him, holding the phone out so he could see.

He jumped up and grabbed his coat and pulled me over for an innocent peck. "I'll keep you posted. I guess I will see you at your house later." He smiled as I nodded and then headed out the door. It was getting harder to watch him leave. I just wanted to be near him constantly. But at least I knew Aunt Rose was in good hands.

It was closer to lunchtime now, so the flow of traffic was increasing but most people were just browsing all the shops, going in and out to get out of the cold but still walk around. Just a little past noon I got a text from Jake that she was all ready to go, they just were getting a wheelchair for her even though she insisted she didn't need one. Aunt Rose was certainly stubborn. I told him hopefully she would behave for a while and to let me know once they were home and settled.

I continued walking around the store and talking with people as they browsed through the shelves. When I found a bit of a lull, I went to sit and started to wonder what I would do for lunch since I couldn't leave, when a young man walked in with a bag and a fountain drink.

"I'm looking for Vivian Acworth," he said, reading the name like it was a joke.

"That's me, can I help you?" He passed the bag and drink to me and said have a good day then turned to leave. "Wait, I didn't order this," I called out to him.

He stopped at the door and said someone called it in, "A man called and paid then said to deliver it at twelve thirty. Have a great day ma'am." *Jake.* I wasn't complaining and it smelled delicious.

I pulled out the food and it was a sandwich, soup, and a bread bowl for the soup. I left the soup in the plastic container and opened the sandwich and began to eat when my phone dinged. It was Jake making sure I got a delivery, but he didn't say of what.

I sent a picture back to him of the meal then a message, "How do you do that?" He didn't reply, as expected. I continued eating my lunch but once I was full, wrapped it up and put it in the fridge. I grabbed my cell and went to the back of the store to begin organizing the new lot that had been brought in the day before.

Finally, a little after one, my phone dinged, and it was Jake letting me know they were in the car about to go home. I clutched my phone to my chest as I let out a relieved sigh. Aunt Rose had been gone a week now and I was so glad she was able to be home. I texted him back I'd be there later and let her know everything at the shop is fine.

Such a weight had been lifted now that she was going home and seemed to be fine after her surgery. But then I thought about the strange man, the gemstone, and of course now the book. And her in that dream. It had been so odd, but it was she and I, and Jake, and the gemstone was involved. But what did it mean? And sure, we had surveillance cameras everywhere now, but was she safe? Jake couldn't be with her every day, and she absolutely didn't want to close the shop. My head was spinning with all the possible bad scenarios, and I was too distracted to continue to work on the items.

I stood up and walked to the front of the store to look out the window. I could feel the cold seeping in through them. For such a cold day the square was still quite busy with people shopping and popping in and out of restaurants. All seemed completely normal. I was almost in a trance staring aimlessly out at the town when the phone made a chiming sound, so I looked down and swiped the app of the doorbell. They were pulling into the house. I sat and watched as he jumped quickly out of the driver's side and went to help Aunt Rose out of the car and helped her to the door. They were laughing and smiling, she looked much better than the last time I saw her a few days ago. Jake waved and then pointed at the doorbell, so Aunt Rose waved at it as well. Then they were inside and out of sight. I went back to staring aimlessly out at the town for a minute but then saw a couple of ladies walking towards the door, so I stepped back and turned to greet them. The after-lunch rush was finally picking up.

Customers and browsers were in the rest of the day and before I knew it, closing time was near. I texted Jake to see if I should stop for dinner or if they needed anything else, but he quickly replied dinner was on the way and to hurry but be safe. I walked around the shop straightening up the shelves and dusting as I went. Then I put on my coat, grabbed my leftover lunch and bag, turned off the computer, and walked to the front to turn off the lights and lock up. I took a quick scan around before I left the shop to be sure there weren't any strange men in a hat and long coat lurking around, but the coast was clear. I pulled the door and locked it, then gave it a push to be sure it was secured before turning and getting into the car.

Tossing my things in the passenger seat, I cranked the

car, freezing while I waited for the engine to warm. I pulled my phone out to see what the actual temperature was and to check for tomorrow's weather. Something caught the corner of my eye, so I looked up then around and didn't see anything strange, but a few couples were still walking around and some of the other shop owners were rushing to their cars. Must have been one of them. I looked down again and the current temperature was only twenty-five. It wasn't even Christmas yet and already below freezing in Georgia. Normally it didn't get much below freezing until January or February. The house would be cold. It was old and the furnace was as well. We had some small space heaters for the bedrooms because upstairs could get frigid with the furnace grate being on the main level and away from the stairs. Hopefully, I could find them once I got home. The vents in the car finally were pushing out air that wasn't cold, but not exactly warm, so I went ahead and buckled in and left for home.

Chapter 25

I pulled into the driveway and several lights were on. I could hear faint talking as I approached the door. I walked in through the kitchen and put my things down and followed the sounds into the parlor. Aunt Rose was sitting on the sofa with her legs stretched out, a handmade quilt draped over her, and Jake in the wingback chair.

"Oh honey, you're home, come here to me!" Aunt Rose practically squealed with her arms outstretched to me. I leaned down and gave her a huge squeeze and she rocked me a little. She pulled her knees up to her and motioned for me to sit on the sofa with her.

"So, how are you feeling? How's it been being home?" I asked her.

"Oh, we've had loads of fun today! Jake is quite the caretaker, being kind to such an old woman," she said as she gave him a big wink.

"The pleasure has been mine, ma'am. Aunt Rose told me all sorts of childhood stories about you, and maybe showed me some questionable pictures," he said with a huge grin. I playfully hit her foot for talking about me in my absence and showing incriminating childhood photos. Then my phone made the chimes sound again but out the window we could see a driver get out of a car with a bag of what appeared to be food. Jake jumped up out of his chair and went to the door. He brought it back into the parlor and sat the bag on the coffee table and started pulling out containers. It was Vincent's. He handed one to my aunt with a plastic fork and a napkin, then handed me one with a plastic fork and a napkin before rushing off to the kitchen behind us.

"Wow, he's really something, Viv. He's a keeper. And this is delicious," she murmured as she stuffed a heaping amount of pasta into her mouth. Jake returned with two glasses of water and placed them on the table, then hurried back to the kitchen again.

He finally returned with another glass of water then grabbed his own container of food and sat down. "Is it okay to eat right here?" Aunt Rose chuckled and motioned with her arm as she nodded her head for him to eat, unable to speak as her mouth was full.

"Vivian, I put that bag of food on the table in the fridge in case you wanted it tomorrow," Jake said between bites.

I looked at him and smiled since I had a mouthful of pasta, but all I could think was, "Is this guy for real?"

I tried to watch him without staring. He was sitting casually with my aunt and I, eating pasta that he probably paid for, after picking her up from the hospital and still making sure I had lunch. It had only been a few weeks since our first encounter, but everything felt so perfect and easy with him. I couldn't help but think...usually if something seemed too good to be true, it was. There just had to be something about him I didn't know, something else he was hiding. I tried to shake the feeling and enjoy the meal, and the fact that Aunt Rose was home.

"Whew, I am stuffed. I could probably eat off that meal for three days. Jake, that was so kind of you to get that for us," Aunt Rose said as she put the lid back on the container and put it on the table.

She was getting situated again under her blanket, so I asked, "Well, you didn't really say before, how are you feeling?"

Her shoulders lifted in a shrug; mostly straight grey hair plunged over them. "I feel great, just tired but that's because I've been at the hospital for a week. Do you know how hard it is to sleep there? So many beeps, nurses in and out of your room at all hours, the blood pressure cuff always randomly squeezing your arm. It's a wonder people can get better there with all that going on!"

I rubbed her foot a bit. "Well, you're home now and can get a good night's sleep in your own bed and no beeping sounds. And I won't come into your room, promise." We all seemed to take deep breaths together and let them out at the same time. I had been holding my food container on the arm of the sofa with one hand, so Jake reached out and took it, putting the lid back on since there was some left.

"I feel like a pig, I finished mine but both of you had plenty left," he said as he started grabbing things to carry to the kitchen.

"Well, you're a big handsome man, you need your sustenance," Aunt Rose said plainly. I squeezed her foot and gave her a side look but also glanced at Jake and I thought I saw some pink in his cheeks, but he quickly exited with the food to the kitchen.

"Aunt Rose, what is wrong with you?" I asked, laughing as I did.

"Just making a statement. Was I wrong?" She asked, sarcastically.

I rolled my eyes and could hear Jake in the kitchen still, even though he should be done by now. "I think you scared him off," I told her.

She looked over at the clock on the wall. "Well, it's late for this old lady anyway. I am ready to get some sleep in my own bed." I stood to help her up, but she batted my hand away. "I will tell you like I told Jake; I am absolutely fine. I may even go back to the shop this week. So, you just stay here and let him know I won't harass him anymore, not tonight anyway." She put the quilt over the back of the sofa and headed up the stairs.

Jake came back with two plates with cheesecake. "Where did she go?"

"She said she was heading to bed and wouldn't harass you anymore, for tonight anyway."

"Well, I had one for her and figured we could share one. I also made some decaf," he said as he put one plate down and walked back to the kitchen. Maybe he hadn't been embarrassed by her; he was just making coffee and dessert.

He came back with two mugs and one fork and sat down next to me. I grabbed one of the mugs and took a sip. It was nice to have a hot drink because the house was cool. We sat quietly and he fed me bites of cheesecake in between his bites of cheesecake. He put the fork down when we had finished it and wrapped his arm around my shoulder.

"I missed you today," he finally said, gazing into my eyes. Warmth spread through me, and my heart and stomach were fluttering.

"I missed you, too," I forced out, trying not to sound like a fool. He leaned to me and placed his lips on mine, tasting of coffee and cheesecake. I was about to suggest we go to my room but then it hit me. "Oh, I need to go find our space heaters, I bet her room is freezing!"

I had started to stand but he gently pulled me down. "She already mentioned that, and I found them earlier. But if you want, I can go up and turn yours on so it's not freezing when we go up." I nodded and he immediately stood and went quickly but quietly up the stairs. It was still fairly early, but I was already getting tired. The last few days were catching up to me and I think the relief of Aunt Rose coming home expelled some of the adrenaline that had been keeping me moving. I sat, sipping my coffee, and soon he returned next me to the sofa.

"So, Aunt Rose seems to be smitten with you. I appreciate everything you've done for her today," I said quietly to him.

"Well, she was an easy patient, and if I'm being honest, I really did it for you," he said as he tucked my hair behind my ear then pushed it off my shoulder. His fingers dragging over my neck as he did sent goosebumps over my arms.

"So, back to work tomorrow then," I said, not sure if I was asking or telling him.

"Well, in the morning I can go check in before you leave and then come back. I may have to pop in and out of here, but I'll try to mostly be here. I can slack off a decent amount, but I need to at least pretend to be productive." I leaned over close to him, and he tightened his arm around me. My face dug into his chest, so I breathed him in, the crisp, citrusy, but manly scent. I loved that smell, not because of the smell, but because it was *his* smell. Feeling his warmth and inhaling his scent helped melt the day away.

I sat still there long enough for my eyes to start getting very heavy, so I popped up. "Let's go up, it should be warming up now." We both stood and he took the plate to the kitchen, and I followed to put my mug away. He made sure the door was locked in the kitchen then went back to the front to check that one while I waited at the foot of the stairs. We then quietly walked up, trying not to disturb Aunt Rose.

We walked into my room, and I gently closed the door. It was warm but not hot. Jake was sitting on the edge of the bed, so I walked over to him, and he pulled me to him, hugging me close with his head at my chest. I put one arm around his shoulders and ran my other hand through his soft hair. We stayed that way for several minutes, just holding each other in the quiet of the night. Finally, he began rubbing my back and pulled away enough to look up at me.

"Vivian, what do you think those visions were? We seem to have similar dreams, and last night when we both held the stone, I think we saw the same thing. When I told you what I saw you agreed but said you saw that man. So, what could it be? How can that be?" I stared down at him trying to think of a reasonable explanation, but I didn't have one. I had been journaling my dreams for months and couldn't make sense of them, especially now that I saw his face.

"I really don't know, Jake. I wish I did. I thought my dreams were just dreams for a long time, but then you ended up being the man in them. If I show you the journal again, will you read some of the recent ones and tell me if they seem familiar?" He nodded his head and pointed to the corner of the room where he left my bags, so I went and dug the journal out. I walked back, kicked my shoes off, and climbed onto the bed and he turned to face me.

I handed it to him, and he opened it, but then he pushed his shoes off and scooted up next to me with his back to the headboard. "No light over there."

I sat and watched as he flipped through the journal, finding the most recent entries. I looked over and turned back a few more so he wasn't just looking at the last week or so. He began reading as I sat staring at him, waiting for some kind of reaction.

His brows were furrowed down like he was in deep concentration and occasionally he would tilt his head, but I couldn't tell if it was in recognition or just because it was interesting. He didn't speak but continued to read and turn the pages. He finally read one and pulled in a sharp breath then looked over at me. "Vivian, this one here, I remember more than you have here. It started before yours. I was riding to you because I found out someone was coming for you and the witch. I had to get to you and get you out of there before they found you both. But this, you noted at the bottom here. You said it looked like your aunt, the woman with you."

Witch?

I had to ask. "Why would you assume she was a witch?"

He barely blinked. "In my dream, I overheard a conversation, but I didn't see who it was. It sounded like two, maybe three people talking to each other, it was hard to tell. But one of them said the woman they were seeking was in the woods outside of the town with the witch, then the other said they better hurry before it's too late. I don't know how I knew where to go, but I tethered the horses and took off. I must have known a shortcut because I wasn't on a trail but was riding through the woods in the dark. I remember an overwhelming sense of urgency and fear. I saw the fire, so I got off the horse and drew my sword and walked around the area, but it was just the two of you. The others hadn't found you yet. Then I started to call for you and you looked over, but then I woke up." I looked straight ahead for a minute, trying to process what he just said.

I finally turned to look at him again. "What about the others, Jake? Did any other dreams seem familiar?"

He nodded. "Yes, but sort of like this one, my perspective is a little different and they start differently. They seem to end up the same. So now the bigger question is, how are we having the same dreams?" My breathing was becoming difficult, and my heart was racing. My lips and fingers started tingling. I tried to take some deep and regular breaths to calm myself, but the more I fought it the worse it became. It was another anxiety attack and Jake was about to witness it. He could sense something was happening because he put the journal down and reached for my hand. My fingers were tense so I couldn't reciprocate.

Concern coursed through his words. "Vivian, what's

happening? What can I do?"

I shook my head, afraid that if I spoke, I would start crying. Plus, my lips were so tense and tingly I didn't know that I could make out any words. Pulling my hand away I scooted to the edge of the bed and as much as I didn't want to, threw my legs over the side, and leaned my head down between my legs. His weight moved behind me and he began rubbing my back softly and slowly. I stayed that way for what seemed like hours, but I know it was likely just a couple of minutes.

When I regained feeling in my lips and fingers, I slowly began to sit up. As I did, I felt him scoot up behind me, his legs on either side of me and his arms wrapped around me tightly. I reached up and held his arms with my hands and squeezed tight. I was breathing more steadily now. We sat that way for several minutes not saying a word. He must have been waiting for my heart rate to slow down because when it was normal again, he finally spoke to suggest we get ready for bed. Comfy clothes and cuddling with him sounded great even though my mind was still reeling from what he had just told me.

When I eventually started to stand, he released his hold and stood up as well. I went to find something warm to change into while he pulled his sweats from his bag and changed into them before excusing himself to the bathroom. He came back in and closed the door and climbed into bed where I was waiting. I set the alarm then turned the lamp off and snuggled up close to him.

It was quiet with the light humming sound of the space heater. Even though I was tired, I was still wide awake. He gently stroked my back with the arm that was around me as I settled into him.

I finally muttered, "Sorry."

I could feel him tilt his head toward me, "What are you sorry about?"

He seemed genuinely confused so I replied, "Sorry about my little attack. I have them sometimes, not a lot. But they came on after my parent's accident."

He shifted under me and pushed up a little and he softly grabbed my chin to make me look up toward him. "Vivian, you have nothing to be sorry for. Don't ever apologize for that. This is all crazy and unbelievable. I'd be worried if you didn't have some sort of reaction to it. So, don't be sorry. And whatever it all is, we will figure it out together," he said.

I nodded in agreement. He got situated down on the pillow again and I snuggled back up to him, drawing the covers up over his chest and right under my nose. He pulled me close and held me tight. I relaxed my head on his chest and felt the rhythmic movement of his breathing in and out, raising his chest up and down, lulling me to sleep.

Chapter 26

I walked into my dressing room to get ready for the show. The lamp was already on. My dress hung on the wall, its sequins glimmering from the light, sparkling like diamonds. I put my bag down in the red side chair in the corner of the room. When I turned to sit at the vanity, I saw something that hadn't been there the night before. It was a box. A rectangular cherry-wood box with carvings. It seemed familiar. Even though I had just come in alone and the room had no real hiding places, I scanned the room looking for someone, or maybe a sign that someone had been in there. My dressing room was off limits to the others and nobody who was employed by the club would enter without my invitation.

I turned the switch to light up the mirror bulbs. I slowly took a seat on the bench in front of the vanity and ran my hands over the box. I wanted to see what was inside but wasn't sure what I would find. I slowly cracked the box open and tried to take a peek. I didn't hear any ticking or smell anything strange, so I finished opening the lid. There was a silk bag tied with ribbon and a small little pouch also tied with ribbon. I picked up the smaller bag, untied it, and saw some sort of paper inside. I pulled it out and unrolled it then...

Beep, Beep, Beep...I quickly rolled over to slam the alarm clock and plopped back onto the pillow. A warm arm pulled me close, spooning me. It was so comfortable and warm; I could lay there forever. A small glimmer of light peeked through the curtains. I was afraid I'd fall back asleep if I lay there too long, so I started to pull away to leave the bed, but Jake pulled me in tighter.

"I need to move, or I may fall back asleep," I whispered, not knowing if my aunt was awake yet.

"I think I can make sure you stay awake," he whispered back into my ear. Then he began moving his hands over my abdomen lightly, first side to side across my belly, but then he began moving upward under my shirt and finally found one of my breasts. He kneaded it softly, occasionally running his fingers lightly over my erect nipple. My breathing grew heavy, but I was very aware that my aunt was in the house.

"We have to be quiet," I whispered breathily. I started to turn toward him, but he stopped me.

"Just stay where you are," he whispered into my ear. As he did, I felt his warm hand begin moving down my abdomen and then slip under my pajama pants. First his hand cupped over my mound, over the thin cotton panties, massaging it. Then quickly, his hand moved under the material and his fingers were gliding back and forth, sending all the blood from my body down between my legs. I felt his other arm push under me and reach around, grabbing my breast. My senses were on overload, and I was trying to keep my noise level down and not cry out. He occasionally thrust his fingers inside but then would return to gliding back and forth over the wet and swollen area. My breathing was becoming quicker and shallower as I began to get closer to my release. He inserted two fingers again, still stroking the top with his thumb. He was plunging them in and out at a steady rate and suddenly my whole body was tense with waves of pleasure, my insides clamping around his fingers along with the waves shooting through me. I saw static behind my closed eyes, and he must have known I was about to let out a sound because the hand that was under me caressing my breast suddenly was over my mouth. As my body released the tension, I let out a chuckle as his hand was still over my mouth. He finally let me roll onto my back and was staring down at me, smoldering over me. I was working to catch my breath but went to reach for him and he pulled away.

"Later," he said softly. "I just wanted to be sure you were awake." He then leaned down and kissed me, holding my head with his hand. When he pulled away, I looked over at the clock.

"I may be awake, but now I feel like mush. And I need to get up," I said and dramatically rolled off the bed, then stood up. I took a big stretch and he stood up and wrapped his arms around me and stared down at me for a moment, then pulled me even closer. His chest was warm, and I could still smell his cologne. I wanted to climb back into bed and lay with him, inhaling that scent and feeling his warmth. But we both had to work, and Aunt Rose was home.

He pulled away, pulled his shirt on, then motioned that he was going to the bathroom. I stepped over to the bed and grabbed my journal to jot down the dream I had before the alarm interrupted. I finished up the entry and put the journal away as he came back with two coffee mugs and handed one to me.

"Aunt Rose is up, and breakfast is ready. She said to come back down and bring you with me," he said with a grin. I took a sip of the hot coffee and then headed downstairs. We walked into the kitchen and Aunt Rose had made French Toast and sausage.

I sat down and looked around in awe. "I haven't been to the grocery store. How did you whip this up?"

She laughed. "Dear child, I keep all sorts of things in the freezer in the cellar. Now eat up so you can get dressed. I want to go to the shop today. I am going to get dressed while you eat!" I had already stuffed a large bite of French Toast in my mouth, so I was unable to protest what Aunt Rose had announced. Jake was grinning as he ate his breakfast.

I finally swallowed and asked him, "What are you

grinning about?"

He took a large gulp of coffee then replied, "I think she's going to the shop today, and you aren't going to stop her." I kept eating and didn't say anything else because he was right. She had made up her mind and I wasn't going to change it. She seemed well enough to be out and about, and she could ride with me in the morning and drive home when she was ready. I finally finished a few minutes after Jake, and he quickly grabbed my plate and put it in the dishwasher. I began cleaning up the rest of the food and poured some more coffee for us both. Aunt Rose came back downstairs and poured the last bit of coffee. I told her I was going to go get ready and would be back down in a bit and we could go together, and she shooed me away as she sat at the table to drink her coffee. Jake and I went back up the stairs and into my room. I checked my closet for something warm to wear and he put his shoes on and started to grab his bag.

"I'm going to run home and shower and let you two catch up. I'll come by the shop in a bit." He pulled me in and gave me a lingering kiss, then he hopped down the stairs. I could hear him putting his coat on and telling Aunt Rose he would be by later to check on her. Once I was dressed, I headed back down to the kitchen and found Aunt Rose still sipping her coffee.

"Let me just grab my coat and I'll go warm up the car for us," I said as I grabbed the car keys. After cranking the car and putting the heat to full blast, I hustled back inside into the warmth of the kitchen. I walked over to Aunt Rose and put my hand on her shoulder. "Are you sure you want to go to the shop? It's fine to take some time off and rest."

She shook her head quickly. "Honey, I need to get out. I have been stuck in a bed for days!"

I nodded knowing nothing I said could change her mind. She stood and went to grab her coat, then we left together as I made sure the house was locked.

On the ride over, Aunt Rose finally asked, "So, cameras by the doors at home. What happened last week?"

Staring straight ahead, I shifted in my seat but stayed silent.

"Viv, hello? I know you didn't just do all that because you were bored. So, what happened?"

I found a parking spot by the shop and pulled in, jumping from the car to help her out, but she had already exited on her own. She pulled her keys to the shop from her pocket and opened the door. At first, she walked in like normal and put her things behind the counter. As she leaned up, I watched her face furrow as she saw one of the cameras. She straightened up and looked around, discovering the other two. I was frozen by the front door.

"Viv, honey, now I am worried. What is all of this?" She asked.

I took in a deep breath, not moving from the nearest exit. "Well, when you were in the hospital, that man came back and broke in. At least we think he did. So, we put cameras up."

Aunt Rose put her hand to her chest and as her jaw fell down as her eyes blinked rapidly. "And you didn't tell me? Vivian, this is mine. This is *my* shop. Why did you keep this from me?"

Aunt Rose glared at me, waiting on a response. When I didn't speak or move, she started to move toward me.

Before she made it to the front I finally spoke. "I didn't want to upset you."

She stopped. Her face twisted; anger melted into disappointment.

"I'm sorry, Aunt Rose. You're my only family now and I

was already worried about you. I didn't think you needed to know yet," I stammered out, trying not to cry.

Aunt Rose slowly walked to me.

As the tears filled my eyes, I threw my palms into the air. "I'm sorry. I'm so scared and doing and saying all the wrong things. I should have told you." I felt so ashamed for not telling her and couldn't hold the tears back any longer. My shoulders were bouncing with each heaving breath I took.

"Honey, it's ok. It'll be ok. I just wish you would have told me. Calm down," she said softly to me as she closed the space between us and pulled me into her embrace. She held me close as I sobbed into her shoulder.

Several minutes went by before I stopped crying and caught my breath. She pulled away from me, smiling with a nod. I nodded in turn, so she let me go and started walking around the shop. I took my coat off and walked to the counter to put my things down.

"So, we have cameras and holiday lights. Festive," she said.

A nervous laugh escaped me. "Well, Jake helped with both."

Aunt Rose nodded then walked back to the counter.

"So, do you plan to tell me what else happened while I was gone that led to the special ops here and at the house?"

I looked at her for a minute thinking about all the things that happened in the last week, but finally decided on what she may need to know.

"Well, that man lurking around made me nervous and you being home alone after the surgery did, too. So, I asked Jake about somehow securing the house. Then, the shop was broken into, so we called the police, and they were no immediate help. Since he was installing surveillance at the house, I asked if he could here as well. Nothing was taken, but he, or whoever it was, was definitely looking for something." I shook my fingers through my curls and sighed. "Then, the man came back here when I was here alone, and he went by our house. I don't know for sure it was him because I couldn't make out his face on the app, but he was wearing the same hat and coat. He creeps me out bad, Aunt Rose. He's looking for the gemstone, I just know it."

Aunt Rose was listening intently and biting her lip, an action I don't ever recall her doing. "He is definitely looking for the stone. We have to keep it away from him, Viv. Where is it?"

I looked away. "It's at Jake's in a safe. But how do you know I'm right?"

Aunt Rose slowly started pacing around in front of the counter. "Vivian, listen, when I told you about the stone, I didn't tell you everything. But we just wanted to protect you."

I wasn't sure how to react, but I blurted out, "What do you mean?" That came out more sharply than I meant.

Aunt Rose kept pacing. It was her turning away from me this time.

I walked around the counter and positioned myself in front of her. "What do you mean? What didn't you tell me?"

Aunt Rose seemed to struggle to find words as she wrung her hands. I stood there waiting for her to say something, *anything*, when the bells on the door jingled. Two regular customers walked in and when they saw Aunt Rose immediately broke into squeals and shuffled quickly over to her, talking over each other with lots of questions and hugging. I stepped back behind the counter, full of confusion and hurt. She was keeping something from me. *Something else.* But she was saved by the bell. I certainly couldn't ask her about it again with people in the shop.

Word got out that Aunt Rose was at the shop and there

was a steady stream of customers and visitors all day. They all asked where she had been, though she never did say she was in the hospital, just that she took a little break but was happy to be back. She stayed busy entertaining the visitors, so I was busy at the register. Jake came by, but since it was so busy, he only stayed long enough to drop off some food and coffee for us and said he would be back later in the day.

Finally, around five, Aunt Rose came to tell me she was feeling very tired and needed to get home to rest. There were still customers in the store so I couldn't say anything about the unfinished conversation, and she knew it.

I gave her the keys to the car as I said, "I'll be home right after closing."

She gave me a half smile and leaned in to give me a quick hug before turning to leave.

Several people came in after she had gone asking about her so I told them she would be back in the morning. They were all disappointed they missed her. I knew everyone knew her, but until today I didn't realize how much everyone loved her.

I was trying to be grateful that she was home, and we were surrounded with friends in this town, but what she said was still nagging at me. Dwelling on it wasn't possible since we had been busy all day, but it began slowing down as it got darker outside. I finally got a break from customers, so I snacked on what Jake had brought earlier then walked around the shop to tidy up. Everyone that came in today made a purchase, so the shelves were a mess.

I was near the back of the store when the bells jingled. I looked up and my heart fluttered at the sight of Jake. We both took long strides towards each other, and he wrapped his arms around me tightly, the cold still clinging to his coat. I heard him inhaling the scent of my hair as he dug his face into my wild curls. He pulled back enough to lean down and give me a kiss that made me forget where I was or anything that had happened that day.

"I missed you so much today," he said as he finally removed his lips from mine, still just an inch from them.

I leaned up, kissing him again before replying. "I missed you, too." He let me go and we walked back to where I had been tidying up.

"I didn't see the car out front. Why don't I grab us some dinner and I'll come back and drive you home?"

He was about to turn to leave without a response from me, so I quickly grabbed his arm. "Jake, I may need a bit with Aunt Rose alone tonight. She was trying to tell me something earlier, but we were interrupted. It seemed important, but she hesitated, then customers just started coming. Is that okay?" He forced a small grin, but I could see disappointment swimming in his eyes. He nodded but his head was low and grabbed my hands in his, running his thumbs over them lightly.

He sighed but smiled. "If you need to be with her, I understand. But how about I still go grab food and drive you home?" I nodded in agreement and pulled him closer, pulling his face to mine for a slow kiss. He broke away and smiled again before he turned to leave. I still had a few minutes before closing so I finished straightening the last shelf and went to check the trash. I was logging off the computer and getting ready to close it all down when I saw his car pull up outside. He came back in, but I was already wearing my coat and ready to leave so he opened the door for me and watched as I locked up. He opened the car door for me, and I was about to step past him to get in, but he grabbed my arm and swung me back to him, grabbed the back of my neck with the other hand, and pulled me in hard and fast. The kiss was reminiscent of the one we shared the night I found the gemstone. I forgot where we were. I forgot it was freezing. I forgot about the gemstone. I forgot about everything except for him. It was like the first time we touched. Shock waves were traveling all over me and the world around us didn't exist, it was just the two of us. He slowed and I could feel him beginning to pull away, but I grabbed his coat and pulled him back to me for another few seconds.

Finally, he broke free but leaned his forehead to mine. "We need to get you home so you can sort things out with your aunt." I remembered. She and I needed to talk. I begrudgingly got into the car, and he shut the door for me before he got in and took off.

Chapter 27

We arrived at my house quickly. Jake held my hand on the short drive over and seemed reluctant to let go once we arrived. He lifted it to his lips, kissing it before finally letting go, got out, and ran to open my door. I took those few seconds to gather my wits and not blurt out to take me to his place.

I started toward the door as he grabbed some bags from the back. I winced as I noticed his overnight bag in the backseat; he had planned to stay. I stood with my hand on the door and my mind was racing with thoughts. Should I just invite him to stay and worry about the conversation with Aunt Rose later? Should I have him come in and just go upstairs? No, now I was just being greedy and selfish. I wanted to know what she had to tell me but didn't want Jake to go home but instead send him to my room like a child. I needed to talk to her with no distractions and no interruptions. As he approached with the food, I pulled the door open for him to go inside and followed him in.

The light in the parlor was on and Aunt Rose called to me, so I told her I'd be right there. We pulled food from the bags; it was Pho. There were several containers, two with broth, a package of noodles, two smaller containers with what looked like uncooked beef, and then a package with basil leaves, jalapeno slices, sprouts, and limes.

"When I picked this up, they told me we may want to heat up the broth again, then add the noodles, then the meat, then the extras. He said it was important to do it in that order," Jake said plainly. I put the broth into the microwave and turned it on for a minute then I motioned to him I was going to the parlor. I went to Aunt Rose and hugged her from behind the sofa.

"Jake got us some Pho noodles, we just have to finish putting it together and I'll bring it to you," I told her.

She shook her head. "No dear, I will have soup at the table. I don't want to make a mess for you to clean up." Aunt Rose stood and headed to the kitchen, so I followed behind her.

She walked to Jake and grabbed his arm. "Thank you for bringing Viv home, and for the food."

She sat down so I made her some water and sat it down.

After she took a sip she asked, "Jake, are you staying again tonight?" He looked at me, clearly unsure how to respond.

"No, Aunt Rose, he's going home tonight but will be back soon, I'm sure."

I saw a look of fear flash in her eyes, but she played it off quickly. "Oh, well I do hope to see you again soon. So nice to see Viv happy again. She hasn't been herself in months."

There was an awkward silence only broken by the shuffling of containers as we prepared the soup. Jake carried a container to Aunt Rose, and I grabbed the package with the extras and put it on the table for her to add her own how she liked it.

"Jake, did you not get soup?" Aunt Rose slurped out between spoonful's as I sat down with my own bowl.

"No ma'am, I plan to grab something on the way home, but you mentioned you loved this yesterday and soup is good when it's cold out." He inhaled a deep breath and rubbed his palms together as he exhaled dramatically. "I guess I'm actually gonna take off."

I put my glass down and told him I would walk him out. He gave Aunt Rose a soft squeeze on her shoulder and smiled before he turned to leave, and I followed him out. It was freezing out, but I had left my coat inside.

"You need to get back inside and eat before you freeze and the soup gets cold," Jake said as he rubbed my arms briskly to keep me warm. I wrapped my arms around him under his jacket and his big arms went around me blocking the cold from my back. The side of my face was warm against his chest, and I was breathing in his scent. I didn't want to let him go but I knew I had to confront Aunt Rose. She wouldn't talk with company over.

"I know I told you I needed to talk to her tonight alone, but I don't want you to go," I finally said. He leaned his head down and kissed the top of mine and squeezed me a little tighter.

"Don't worry. I'm just down the street and a phone call away. And I'll come to the shop in the morning. Go do what you need to do." He kissed me again softly and slowly. He finally pulled away and got into his car and I stood and watched as he pulled away.

I turned and went back inside, shivering from the cold. I locked the door behind me and sat down, rubbing my arms trying to warm up. Aunt Rose was quietly eating her soup. I sipped my water and started to pick up my spoon but briefly hovered my hand over it before I laid my hand flat on the table. I looked over at Aunt Rose and she didn't look up at me, but I knew she could feel I was staring at her. I watched her for a moment. Her long silver hair had been neatly brushed but cascaded over her shoulders. Her face was tired. Part of me wanted to let her eat and go rest in peace. But she had something to tell me, and I wanted to know. I moved the hand closest to her and gently grabbed her wrist to stop her spoon from going into her mouth. She didn't protest but continued looking down.

"Aunt Rose, you have something to tell me and now you're avoiding it. You won't even look at me. I need to know." She slowly put her spoon down into the soup container and sat quietly again for a moment, looking down at her lap.

Still staring into her soup bowl, she finally spoke. "Viv, listen. I need you to know that I didn't tell you all of what I am about to tell you to protect you. And because your parents made me promise." She was smoothing out the napkin in her lap over and over as she spoke. I had pulled my hand away, watching and listening intently. She had a long pause, so I cleared my throat hoping to speed up the process. She shifted in her chair a little but still didn't speak.

I was getting anxious, and the numbing sensation began to invade my fingertips, so I insisted. "Aunt Rose, tell me. What is it?" She reached her hand over and placed it over mine and scooted her chair closer to mine. I took deep, steady breaths through my nose and blew lightly off my lips, willing the numbness to subside.

"Vivian, I may have not told you the whole truth when I told you about the stone. Your parents made me promise not to until I found a way to fix this if that ever happened. But I had hoped to before your birthday. I just couldn't." I didn't understand, but I continued to listen. She went on. "Your parents knew about the gemstone before they took possession of it. They had been searching for it. They had been searching for a long time. And they knew what it was. We wanted to reverse it before anything happened, but I couldn't. We all tried but failed. They knew their time was growing short, so they made me promise to keep trying and to protect you until I had figured it out. And I promise I…" her voice was quivering and trailing off. Tears formed in her crystal blue eyes and her grasp on my hand was tightening.

I was becoming even more confused; she wasn't making any sense. But she was so upset I had to give her a minute. I reached over with my other hand and grabbed her water to encourage her to take a sip. She took a large gulp of water and put the glass back on the table.

She grabbed my other hand and continued. "Viv, you were cursed." I pulled my hands away from her and cocked my head to the side.

"Cursed? What do you mean? Like a lady in a pointy hat murmured words of my demise into a cauldron? C'mon Aunt Rose, you're gonna have to do better than that." Her face was serious, and her eyes were set. I stood up and walked to the counter, leaning against it to face her, running both palms down my face trying to stifle a laugh. "Seriously, that's not real. Even if it were, why would anyone want to curse me. I mean, do you hear yourself?"

Aunt Rose straightened in her chair. "What I'm about to say will make this even more difficult for you to understand, but you wanted to know. Frankly, you need to know." She held her fingers to her lips for a moment. You weren't cursed in this lifetime. You were cursed a long time ago. Over 400 years to be more specific."

I shook my head trying hard not to laugh. "So, you mean to tell me I've been cursed for 400 years? Ok, I'll play along. What does the gemstone have to do with it? Is it cursed, too?" The sarcasm dripped off of my last question.

The look on Aunt Rose's face was becoming less worried and more irritated. "Vivian, do you mean to tell me you haven't put any of this together? You didn't open the box? Your dreams? Any of it?" She threw her hands up in the air like I was the unbelievable one. But when she mentioned my dreams, something clicked.

I went and sat back down next to her. "What about my dreams? Did you know? Did you know what they meant? But never said anything?" Aunt Rose sat still with her lips tight. Her eyes darted around so I asked, "So, you knew all this time about the dreams when I told you about them. I was confused and you never said anything. You let me just constantly wonder." I stood and walked back to the counter. "Ok, so Mom and Dad knew about the stone. How does that play into this? Why were they looking for it?" Aunt Rose was still taking forever to gather her words, so I blurted out, "Tell me!"

She stood up with a grimace. "*You* were cursed, the gemstone was a protection for you. It would bring your protector to you and keep you safe. But if we could break the curse it wouldn't matter. But...if they get the stone, the curse will never be broken and you could lose your protection and your protector, forever." *My protector*?

"Are you my protector? Protector from what?" I walked to her and grabbed her shoulders. "Stop talking in code and just say it, Aunt Rose. Protector from what? Who is *they*? Tell me!"

She batted my hands down and stepped back. "I will tell you, but you must calm yourself. And you must listen."

I wanted to know what she was trying to say, and my head was spinning so I sat down at the table again, trying to keep my cool long enough for her to explain. She continued to stand.

"In another life, you fell in love and that man loved you. He brought you a gift, a gemstone, as a symbol of that love. Someone else thought the gemstone was theirs. And that someone had a sorceress that he loved. She was angered by the story her love told her as she was to get the stone, so she cursed you and your family. In that life, I was there with you and tried to reverse what she had done, but her magic was too strong. I was, however, able to enchant the gemstone to allow time to find a way to undo her spell. If the spell wasn't broken the enchantment would last as well, but only if she never got her hands on it. If the sorceress ever got it, she could break the enchantment then only her curse would remain. There was just no way to enchant the stone without a sacrifice and that was the price. That her curse would never die on its own." The dream at the fire. *It was her.*

"But how did my parents know about the stone? I've never seen them in my dreams. You said they searched for it."

Aunt Rose finally sat back down. "I started having the dreams when you were young. It took them a while to believe me, but a book was sent to them, and we don't know from where. But you were in it, only it wasn't *you*. It was someone that looked a lot like you, you were just a girl at the time, but the face was unmistakable. They read it over and over and started researching some of the info in it and everything started to piece together. They made it their mission to find it to protect you. In the meantime, they researched practitioners to help break the spell. Everyone said they couldn't undo the magic of two others. So, it was up to me to figure it out. I never dabbled in that stuff, not in this life anyway, so I was lost. There were always rumors simply because I'm an old hippie soul with quirky outfits and an antique shop. But if I did it then, I figured I could try. So, for years I've tried to learn all I can, and I've tried everything I could find to break the curse. No matter what I tried, I just couldn't. I found someone to help me, but they even said what we are dealing with is old magic not seen in centuries. But they couldn't explain how the curse was still so strong."

I felt my brows drawing together but I tried to control the scowl I felt trying to spread over my face. "How did you know the curse was still strong? Until Mom and Dad died nothing bad ever happened."

She stared down at her hands. "Oh dear, we shielded you from so much. There were so many things you never knew about, and maybe sometime we can talk about them. Now isn't the time for that. But, after my dreams, and especially the book showing up out of nowhere, well, we started to wonder."

I shook my head hard. "But if you found the stone then why did Mom and Dad die? Didn't that protect us?"

She gently shook her head. "I wish it were that simple.

Apparently, I wasn't as good as the other woman back then. We think it at least protects you, but she cursed your whole family. I live with this guilt every day. I've tried everything I have found to break the curse, but nothing worked obviously," she said as she put her hands up in defeat. "But at least the gemstone is safe which means you are." The stone was safe at Jake's. *Jake.*

"Aunt Rose, do you think Jake is my protector?"

She turned her face toward me quickly and her tone was certain. "He's the one. I knew when I saw him. But I couldn't say anything. I had seen him in town not long before he had come to see you and I thought it was him but wasn't close enough to be sure. But when you started having the dreams, I knew he would come to you soon."

My head was swirling, and my chest became tight. "So, he's just under a spell, then? He doesn't really want to be with me?"

She grabbed my hands tightly and leaned toward me. "Vivian, the enchantment was to bring your soulmate to you and keep him close. He is not *just* under a spell; he is your destiny. He was your soulmate before any curse was cast and he has found you in every lifetime to not only keep you safe, but because you belong together."

I still couldn't shake the feeling that if all she said was true, something other than me was keeping him close. How could I know it wasn't the gemstone?

Aunt Rose shook my hands to snap me out of my trance. "Viv, he was the one who gave the stone to you to begin with because he loved you so much. He is here for *you*, not some curse."

I nodded even though I wasn't fully convinced, but I had another question. "Why did they make you promise not to tell me? Wouldn't it help for me to know all of this?"

She took a sip of water first then said, "Well, kids don't

come with manuals and there certainly isn't anything about this in the mom groups. They did what they thought was best and asked me to keep it secret. And they put too much trust in me." Aunt Rose's lip began to quiver, tears filling her eyes again.

An exacerbated sigh escaped me. "Aunt Rose, this isn't your fault. It's insane they put this on you. This is all insane but it's not our fault, none of us. Like you said, it's not like there's a book somewhere with instructions on how to handle all of this." I reached my hand across to her. "I just wish you had trusted me enough to tell me before. I knew Mom and Dad kept things from me, but I figured it was normal parent-stuff. I thought you and I had no secrets."

A single tear rolled down Aunt Rose's cheek. "I should have trusted you. I should have told you. And I'm sorry. So sorry."

I leaned toward her, and our arms wrapped around one another, squeezing tightly. Neither of us let go for minutes as we let the embrace absorb all the outed secrets, hurt, and realizations.

Finally, she pulled away. "The stone is safe, right? You said Jake has it locked away."

I nodded and swallowed at the mention of Jake. "Yes, it's in his safe at his apartment. But what do we do now? You said you tried everything. I don't want some curse hanging over my head my whole life, and the next one. We can keep it locked up, but I want to break the curse."

Aunt Rose grabbed my hands once again, her eyes wide and alert. "We will keep looking and keep trying. I will never give up, Viv. I promised your parents and I am promising you now. I will never give up." She drew me back in and I heard a small sniffle as I fought off tears of my own. I pulled away and wiped my face with my hands to clear the few that escaped anyway.

Aunt Rose stood up and blew out a tired sigh. "Honey, I

love you and know this has been a strange day, but this old woman is tired."

"It's late and you've had a long day. You need to rest. It wouldn't hurt for me to try to get some, too. I love you. I'll lock up." I watched her head toward the stairs then found myself staring at the table for several minutes.

My mind was going crazy with all the information it just received but my body was tired, so I decided to attempt to rest. I went to check the doors to be sure they were all locked before turning the lights out and heading up to my own room.

I changed and climbed into bed, but just lay there a while. I still had so many questions, ones that Aunt Rose probably couldn't answer. Does the enchantment only mean I'm protected? Does it mean bad things will still happen to me? And to my loved ones? Who sent the book to my parents? And if it's the same one, when did they get rid of it and why? Did they purposefully give it to someone to ensure I got it if something happened to them? Why not just give it to Aunt Rose as well? Or did they lose it? How did my parents track down the gemstone? How did I know if Jake wasn't simply enchanted? I know what Aunt Rose said...*but how did she know?*

The questions kept coming over and over, more and more. The thought of Jake not really wanting me made new tears well up in my eyes. Letting them quietly run down for several minutes, the warm liquid turned cold as it rolled down the side of my face. I was able to keep myself from sobbing, probably because I was exhausted from the day. Glancing over, I wished for music, but my radio was out of reach, and I couldn't make myself lean over to turn it on, so I just lay in silence. Finally, my eyes couldn't stay open anymore and I drifted off.

Chapter 28

It was cold as I walked down the narrow corridor. I was carrying a chamberstick to light the way since there was an absence of windows. It also felt like nighttime, but I couldn't be sure since there were no windows to indicate sunlight or moonlight. I finally arrived at a large wooden door and gently tapped it. After a few moments and no sounds or movements, I twisted the handle, gave a small push, and scooted inside quickly then shut the door back behind me. I turned to see him kneeling in front of a long wooden table under a large window that only showed darkness with a small spattering of twinkling lights in the night sky. The room glowed from the large fire. I placed the chamberstick on the desk that was just left of the door then slowly walked to him. He hadn't moved a muscle since I came in until I placed my hand on his shoulder. Both shoulders had been rolled forward, his head down and one arm grasping onto the table as if he were trying to leverage it to stand, but he hadn't moved. When he felt my hand, however, his head lifted slightly, and his other hand came up across his chest and covered mine. I knelt beside him and leaned to look at him, but he just looked away. I tried to get him to look at me by putting my hand under his chin and directing it to me, but he just pulled back and continued to look the other way. In the glowing light of the fire, his stubble shadowed his jawline. His hair was pulled back at the nape of his neck, but loose tendrils had fallen around his face. I stood, looking to the table, and there sat the stone on an ornate pillow. He still didn't move so I turned to leave, but as I did, I heard him say, "I'm sorry." I turned back to look at him...

The beeping of my alarm startled me. I rolled to turn it off then plopped back on the bed. My eyes felt like glue, so I scoured them with my fingertips. When I finally peeled them open, they burned from the faint light coming in from the crack in the curtains and the cool air in the room. I sat up, blinking wildly to try to get the sting to go away. Once I could focus my eyes, I sat staring at the foot of the bed for a few minutes. I had slept all night but was mentally exhausted and my eyes still burned.

My journal was there on the nightstand, waiting to be picked up. I didn't even want to write anything down, but I begrudgingly reached for the journal and the pen. I sat there, the covers over my legs, and wrote out the details of the dream. The last part--*I'm Sorry*--was written a few lines down with a question mark.

What did that mean? Why was he being so distant? What was he sorry about? I stared at the words for a moment then slammed the journal shut and tossed it on the nightstand. I threw back the blankets and crawled out of bed. Once I pulled my door open, the rich aroma of freshly brewed coffee wafted upstairs. After a quick stop in the bathroom, I headed downstairs.

Aunt Rose was sitting at the table, dressed, sipping from a mug. She went to stand when she saw me, but I brushed her away and poured myself some coffee. I took a few sips before finally sitting down at the table. There was an awkward silence as we sat drinking our morning coffee.

Finally, Aunt Rose spoke up. "How did you sleep, dear?"

All I could muster halfway into my coffee was a nod. Her drawn together face studied mine.

I reached over and put my hand over hers. "Really Aunt Rose, I'm ok. Just a lot of processing."

She nodded, probably more in acceptance that I didn't want to talk about it than agreeing with me.

"I'm going to head over to the shop early and try to get acclimated. Yesterday was such a whirlwind I didn't even get to look around or barely sit," Aunt Rose exclaimed as she stood and put her mug in the sink. I was sipping my coffee as she asked, "Are you ok to get there? It's cold out."

I nodded my head and smiled at her. A little cool, fresh air may help clear my head. Aunt Rose put her coat on then leaned down to give me a side hug and kiss on the forehead before heading out.

I stood and refilled my cup before going to get ready for the day. After I grabbed clothes from my room, I headed to the bathroom. Staring into the mirror, I cringed at my red and puffy eyes. Luggage could fit in those bags. I lightly ran my hand over my cheek and could feel the sheet of salty dried tears I had let run down my face last night. I even had some flyaways stuck to the side of my face. *No wonder Aunt Rose looked so concerned.*

I turned around to turn the water on and let the shower run to get hot. Turning back to the mirror, I stared at my puffy reflection until the steam finally covered the mirror. I took a big gulp of the coffee before undressing and climbing into the shower. I washed slowly, letting the hot water run over me, trying to somehow wash away what I was feeling.

How could I free myself of this curse? Aunt Rose made it sound like she tried for years unsuccessfully. And Jake. Was he just drawn to me because of all this? Maybe what we felt wasn't real. But to me, it seemed real. I could feel it in my muscles every time he touched me, in my bones every time he looked at me, in my soul every time we were together. *But was that part of the curse, too?*

I slowly washed my face, doing it last, then let the water wash over me. I stood with my face in the water until it finally ran cool before turning the shower off. The mirror was completely fogged, but my face didn't feel as rough, and my hair was clean and not sticking to me. I rubbed some serum through my hair before drying it briefly, scrunching it as I did to keep some of the curls, and then finished my morning routine and got dressed.

I walked back downstairs to refill my mug. I saw a flash in the corner of my eye and turned to see Jake pulling into the driveway. Suddenly my thoughts were racing almost as fast as my heart.

Do I tell him what Aunt Rose said? Doesn't he have the right to know? But what if he admits it's not been real? Maybe it will all make sense to him, and he won't want to be with me anymore. But if I don't say anything, isn't that selfish? And I'd always wonder. But is now the time?

I watched, panicked, as he exited the car and took long strides toward the kitchen door. I took a breath and forced a smile as I opened the door. It had barely closed as he wrapped his arms around me, the cold from outside still clinging to him.

"I saw Aunt Rose and she told me you were still here. I'll take you when you're ready. It's freezing out today," he said before he let me go. He leaned down to kiss me and I kissed him back, but he pulled away and looked down at me with a furrowed brow. "Are you alright? You seem tense," he said.

I never was good at hiding my emotions. I grabbed his hand from my neck and rubbed my face into it, trying to remember how it felt. Then I leaned into him to remember his smell, his warmth. He put his arms around me, but gently.

"Vivian?"

I pulled away. "Jake, you may want to sit down. I need to tell you something."

He didn't sit. "What's the matter? Did something happen? Are you ok?"

I grabbed his hand and squeezed it so he would stop asking questions. His face was riddled with worry. I looked down as I tried to find the right words to explain what Aunt Rose had told me.

He put his fingers under my chin to tilt my face back up. I took my time staring at his face, into those blue eyes trying to remember each little green speck, the way his bottom lip poked out a bit when he was serious. His eyes were searching my face for answers.

I looked away, unable to see his eyes as I said it. "Aunt Rose did have something important to tell me last night. She said, well shit I'll just say it...she said I was cursed...400 years ago. And I think you were, too." I turned my eyes back to him just enough to see if his expression changed and it had, and his hand was no longer under my chin.

His brows squished together as his lips turned down. "What do you mean, cursed? How?"

I shrugged as I began to pace the kitchen. "Well, from what she told me, you gave me the gemstone, back then, but someone else wanted it for his wife or girlfriend or whoever she was. She turned out to be a sorceress, so she got pissed and cursed me. So, Aunt Rose, back then," I said as I swept my hand through the air, "tried to counter it but had to put a spell on the gemstone which seems to have put a spell on you. And I can't believe I just said all of that because saying it out loud just sounds ludicrous."

I wasn't crying but blood heated my face and pressure built up behind my eyes. I took a few breaths and said nothing for a moment to gather myself. Jake's lips pinched closed as his head slowly shook side to side. I wanted to take it all back but couldn't, so I crossed my arms across my chest, holding opposite shoulders trying to become invisible. But, even so, the silence was deafening, so I cleared my throat to break it.

His eyes were fixed to the floor as he finally asked, "Let me get this straight. *I*," he said as he put a palm to his chest, "400 years ago, gave *you* the stone that is sitting in my safe and somehow, *we* both got cursed?"

I nodded my head just barely, but enough to signify he was following. Even if I could think of something, anything, to say, I knew I wouldn't be able to contain the tears if I spoke.

He rubbed his hands slowly down his face as he exhaled a loud breath, still not looking at me. "Vivian, I...I gotta go, I'm sorry."

He turned quickly and out of the kitchen fast as lightning. Without moving, I glanced out the window and saw his car peeling from the driveway. Once I couldn't see his car anymore, I couldn't contain it any longer. The tears finally began to flow.

It was as I suspected. It hadn't been real. The feeling was false. Fabricated by the spell cast by my aunt all those years ago. I stood in the kitchen against the counter, shaking and laboring to breathe through the tears. My knees began to feel unsteady, so I slid down the cabinets and sat with my knees pulled to my chest as I sobbed uncontrollably.

I knew this was a possibility, but so badly didn't want it to be true. Everything felt real to me. But maybe it wasn't. Maybe I only thought it felt real. Still, the raw emotions I felt as he left abruptly were definitely real. I sat for several minutes trying to get myself under control. I was barely sucking in air through my heaves and my vision became blurry. I pushed my legs out in front of me and lifted my arms over my head, desperately sucking in oxygen to make the dizziness dissipate.

When I could take a good breath again and the tears started to slow, I walked upstairs to splash water on my face. I stood in front of the mirror holding a wet washcloth over my eyes for a few minutes to get the puffiness to go away. I re-wet it several times to keep it cold. While it was still obvious, I had been crying, it did help a little. The air was frigid outside so I could always say my eyes got red from the walk to the shop.

I grabbed my cell from my nightstand then went back downstairs and grabbed my coat. I went to check the front door to be sure it was locked then left from the kitchen, making sure that door was locked as well.

I put my gloves on once in the driveway then put the hood from my coat up to cover my head. The brisk air made my breath visible as I exhaled. Even still, I stood in the driveway for a moment, closed my eyes, and took a deep breath of the cold fresh air through my nose and blew it out of my mouth to try to release the tension I was still feeling in my chest. It didn't help, so I started down the driveway to the sidewalk.

I felt numb, but not from the cold. An emptiness washed over me as I walked; much how I felt immediately after my parent's accident. It wasn't anger or sadness, it was like feeling nothing. Maybe it was my way of ignoring what just happened. Or what happened in the last month. Even the last week had been filled with such high-running emotions that now, faced with another loss, I felt as if I used up all the emotion I had. I tried replaying things in my head, but I couldn't. The thoughts just weren't coming. My mind had gone blank besides focusing on the steps I was taking on the sidewalk.

My body, not my mind, was guiding me to walk the way to the shop. I could sense there were people out and cars driving past, but it all sounded as if they were outside of a bubble I was trapped in. My eyes were burning from the driving cold and wind, but I continued to walk at a steady pace. As tears from the cold air ran down my face, I didn't wipe them.

I made it a block from the square and even though my thoughts were blank, I managed to push the walk button and wait at the corner. The street was residential, but the houses sat far back from the road surrounded by lots of trees for privacy since they were so close to the square. Looking up and across, I could see the sidewalk in front of the shop. I glanced at the sign to see how many seconds were left until I could cross the street. When the number nine flashed on the screen, I felt an arm around my waist and before I could make a sound, a cloth was slammed to my face covering my nose and mouth. I looked up again to see the number seven turn into a blur of orange.

Chapter 29

My head pounded, my breathing shallow. My vision seemed unable to focus, but I rapidly blinked hoping my eyes would adjust. Slowly things started to become clear. I was on a small cot and there was a candle burning on a table nearby. The small room felt damp, certainly very dark with no windows. The walls were grey, maybe concrete or stone. I wore a dingy white shift, and my feet were bare. I sat up on the cot slowly, as every movement sent shooting pains into my head. I looked around and didn't see any shoes or other clothes, beneath me one wool blanket. I pulled it up around my shoulders to shield the cold.

I noticed the door across the room, so I slowly stood, still grasping the blanket, and took slow unsteady steps toward the door. There was no latch, just a handle. I reached out to open it, but it wouldn't move. It must have been locked from the outside. I turned and looked over the room again, but there was nothing besides the cot, the table, and the candle in a small holder.

Panic rose within me, and my fingertips began to tingle. My eyes darted around the room looking for anything I may have missed. I heard footsteps approaching, so I stepped back away from the door. It slowly opened and there was light flooding in, but I could see two figures standing there, one seemed to be a man and the other a smaller figure, maybe a woman. They both started to approach, I tightened the blanket in my fist, ready to scream...

The sound of a door slamming startled me awake. My head was pounding in real life now. I heard footsteps and tried to open my eyes. When I did, everything was blurry. I raised my hand to my head. In that instant I realized I wasn't restrained, but getting abducted off the corner wasn't good, restrained or not. I had to figure out where I was. I had a fairly good idea who and why. I felt like I was in a soft recliner sitting almost upright, but my head was supported. I could tell the lights were on and someone was with me, even though the footsteps stopped. I smelled faint hints of nail polish remover and wondered if that was from whatever was put over my face. I blinked furiously to get my eyes to adjust but they were horribly dry. Slowly the room came into focus. As I took stock of myself, I realized my jacket wasn't on. *Shit.* My phone was in the pocket.

Things around me continued to become clearer, so I scanned the room. And not surprisingly, the little man stood just a few yards away from me. *This would be a time to start worrying if ever there was one.*

He didn't have his coat or hat on, just dark blue dress slacks, a white button-up dress shirt, and a brown tie. He was watching as I struggled to regain my sight and get oriented. He walked to a table and poured water from a pitcher into a glass then walked toward me with it. I stared at him as he held the glass out to me. He was a small man, bigger than me but still not impressive in size. I looked at the glass. *Could I break that over his head?* As a wave of dizziness filled my head again, I knew I wouldn't be able to put up a good fight right now. Instead, I glared at him as he stood holding the glass out to me.

"This will help with the wooziness, just drink it," he said.

I shook my head but didn't say a word, regretting the action as the room spun. He shrugged then walked out of the room. I scanned where I was, but I was still slow moving and he was back before I could get out of the chair to investigate the window. He was carrying a bottle of water.

He saw me glance at the window and smirked. "You don't want to go out that window. Not that you can open it anyway.

Plus, we're out in the country and you don't know where we are. So, take this water, it's still sealed, then we can talk a bit." He put his arm out toward me with the water bottle. My mouth was so dry I could barely stand the feel of my own tongue against my teeth, so I begrudgingly took it from him.

I tested the lid, and it was still sealed, so I opened it and drank some. I took several small sips without, occasionally glancing at him. He pulled a wooden chair across the room but still left a few feet between us, flipping it around to sit like he was a cop in some cheesy movie.

"Vivian, do you know why you're here?" he asked.

I glared at him without saying a word. I may be the hostage here, but I'll be damned if I made this easy for him.

He drew in a deep breath then continued. "I knew your aunt had something of mine, but I didn't know where. But when I realized you were with her, I knew she would make sure you got it by your birthday. That just passed, right? Happy belated birthday."

I kept staring at him, imagining squirting the water in his face and running through the door. As I lifted the bottle, I realized I was still feeling weak. *That won't work, Viv.*

When I didn't move or respond he continued. "You see, that isn't really yours. Your parents stole it. And I need it back. If you cooperate, this will be simple, and nobody gets hurt. If you don't, well, I can't make any promises." He shrugged and held his palms up.

I tightened my grip on the arms of the chair and spoke through clenched teeth. "I don't know what you want but if you touch my aunt, you'll be sorry."

He chuckled a little. "She speaks!" He shouted, sarcasm dripping off the words. "But will I? It seems as if I have the upper hand here."

I gritted my teeth for a moment. "We have cameras everywhere; you *will* be caught. And once they realize I'm not home or at the shop, they'll call the police." He tipped his head up a bit with a grin across his face, then pulled my phone from his pocket.

He pushed a button and then faced it toward me. "You see there, those cameras were somehow disabled early this morning. Sorry about that," he said with a cocky grin. He then turned the phone screen back to him and opened the other app to show me it was also disabled.

"Well, the police will still be looking for me soon. And they already have a description of you from when you broke into her shop."

He sat looking for a moment, a small grin pulling at his lips. He looked down at the phone again, touched something and then turned the phone back to me. There was a text to my aunt that I was going to take a walk and wouldn't be in until later. She replied that it was fine. She thought I sent it. My pulse started to race but I fought to keep my breathing steady. I didn't want this asshole to see me nervous.

"I noticed Jake left your house in a rush this morning. He seemed upset. I honestly hadn't planned to do this, but with him running from you and your aunt not around, it seemed like a good time to take advantage of the circumstances."

I shot daggers from my eyes at him. He had been watching the house. Just far enough the cameras didn't pick him up, but close enough to follow me when I left.

He leaned forward and a smile crept across his face. "I don't think the police will be looking for a while. Your aunt won't think much about it until later. Even so, I have the phone and can text her back. So, let's get back to the real matter. Where is it, Vivian?"

I replied through a clenched jaw, "I told you, I don't know what you're talking about."

He tapped his thumbs on the back of the chair then looked down at his watch, keeping his cool but clearly agitated. "I asked about it before. And I know you looked up what we searched for on your site."

I caught something he hadn't mentioned before. "We? Who's your friend?"

He stared for a moment, still with a pleasant look on his face. "Maybe later. For now, we are talking about *you* and what you have of mine. So, where is the stone, Vivian?"

I sat still and silent, still working hard to keep my breathing from tipping him off to the storm of fear and anger inside me.

He let out a sigh then stood, moving the chair back to the table it came from. "Okay, I'll give you a few minutes to think about this." He walked out of the room and shut the door. I waited until I no longer heard footsteps, then put my feet on the ground and stood. I had to stand in place briefly to get my bearings. *What the hell had he put on that cloth?*

Once my brain caught up to my body, I walked to the window and pulled the curtains to the side. There were no clasps and I looked out. It was extremely high off the ground, a straight fall down. I felt the edges of the window anyway but there was no way to open it. I turned and looked around for any kind of possible weapon.

It was a sitting room or living area with the chair, a small table with a chess game on top with two chairs, one he had pulled over, there was an older sofa with a side table next to it but no drawers on it and nothing but a small arrangement of fake flowers in the center. I figured the door was locked, but it was still worth trying. I walked over and as expected, couldn't open it. I continued looking around the room for a few minutes but besides a few books, there was nothing that would help me. I didn't have my phone or coat and had no clue where I was. I looked out the window once more trying to see if any landmarks were nearby, but all I saw were trees.

Feeling defeated, I sat back in the recliner and sipped more water. All the movement had exacerbated the side effects of whatever he had used to sedate me. I had no idea where I was, no good weapons, no plan, and no way out, so I sat and waited. If I could stall until later in the day, eventually Aunt Rose would catch on that something was wrong, even if he did text pretending to be me. I sat still for a while and the sedation still was not fully worn off, so I felt myself nodding off.

I was startled awake at the sound of the door opening.

"Sorry to disturb your nap, but we need to get a move on. Do you have something to tell me now," he asked.

I shook my head with a smirk on my face and my chin turned up like a bratty child.

He tilted his chin down as he shook his head, his lips tight. "I didn't want it to come to this, but I guess I need to show you something," he said as he pulled a different phone out of his pocket. He tapped a few times then turned it to me. It was a selfie of a woman outside of the shop. I could see Aunt Rose inside tending to customers through the window. "You see there, this," he said as he pointed to the screen, "is the other half of *we*. She's been hanging around the square this morning waiting for an update from me. If you don't want to cooperate, she'll go inside. And I'm not sure if you know who she is, but I can assure you that you *don't* want her to go inside with your aunt. So, let's try this again, what do you have to tell me?"

My pulse was racing again as I looked at the photo, and it was nearly impossible to keep my breathing under control now. *It was her*. The fair, red-headed woman that was with him in my dream at the wedding. She had to be the same one. Which, if any of this was real, meant she may be a sorceress. *The sorceress.*

Even though I tried to control it, my chest was heaving with each breath. "I told you I don't know anything, leave her out of this."

He put his phone back in his pocket and sat back down. "See, I know that's not true just as well as you do. And you telling us to leave her out of it does nothing. We have the upper hand. But, if you just take me to it, everyone goes free, and you'll never see us again. So, where is it?"

I knew he was probably lying, but if I risked it then that woman may hurt Aunt Rose, or worse. My mind still wasn't moving fast enough to process a good way out of this.

"I know you must be a smart girl, so you know that if you delay long enough your aunt will get suspicious and call the police. So, here's the deal...If you don't tell me where it is in the next hour, I'll text my other half and she'll do as she pleases with your aunt. And without your cooperation, I'll have no use for you. With you both out of the way, I'm sure we can find it." He stood up and started to walk out.

I didn't know what else to do and my gut was telling me he was serious, so I blurted out, "Wait, I know where it is, just don't hurt her."

He stopped and turned with a huge smile on his face. "Now see, that wasn't so hard." He stepped closer. "Okay, where is it?" I had drunk all my water and my mouth and throat suddenly felt dry as cotton.

"Jake has it."

His face looked confused. "You mean the same Jake that left in a hurry this morning?"

I nodded my head. "It's in his apartment. He was keeping

it safe."

He stood with a hand on one hip and was rubbing his chin with the other. He paced a moment.

He stopped and turned to me. "Did you have a fight this morning?" he asked.

I shrugged because honestly, I didn't know how to label what had happened. "Not exactly, but I guess he got upset and left."

The man grunted. "Well, that can pose a problem. I know he won't give it to me, but will he give it to you if you're on the outs?"

I shrugged again. I wasn't sure. Maybe he didn't want to speak to me or see me. But even if this man hadn't kidnapped me, the gemstone was mine. *I should be able to ask for my things, shouldn't I?*

The man sat again rubbing his chin. "Do you not realize who he is?" That question and the sincerity in his voice put me off.

"What do you mean?" I asked as I continued to glare at him.

"I can't imagine what could have made him run off. If you don't mind, what did you talk about this morning?" He asked.

"Not that it's your business but since you seem to know most of it anyway, I told him about the curse. I guess he didn't like being under a spell and he left."

The man laughed a good belly laugh. "Wow, you don't know much at all do you? What a shame. I almost feel sorry for you." He shook his head, still laughing under his breath. He glanced at me, and his face softened. "*He's* not under a spell. Just you. What made you think that?"

"My aunt explained what happened with your 'friend' then how she tried to save me from it."

He laughed a little again, but not as loud as the last time. "Oh, you poor girl, that man was never under spell. But he *was* the reason you were cursed, so maybe this is for the best?"

What he said hit me like a ton of bricks. Jake didn't leave because of the curse...he left because it was his fault.

I needed to see him. I needed to speak to him. But I was stuck in the middle of nowhere with some psycho planning to do terrible things to my aunt, and likely to me, if I didn't give him the gemstone. Aunt Rose had told me that I absolutely couldn't lose it to him. I didn't know what to do besides try to get it for him, though. I would have to worry about the repercussions later. Right now, I just needed to keep her safe and hopefully get myself out of harm's way. If we left, I had a better chance of escaping or somehow alerting Aunt Rose what was happening.

"We can't get into his complex without him opening the gate. I need to call him."

The man shook his head. "No, we'll get him to meet us somewhere else and bring it to us. And I'll handle it." He pulled my phone out and was tapping away. He waited a few minutes then my phone dinged. "Great, he'll meet us in an hour. We need to get going. And remember, one message to my lady and your aunt is done, so let's just walk nicely to the car and get in, okay?"

I nodded my head as my heart pounded and we walked out of the room.

I followed him downstairs, and we headed toward the door. I hoped to see anything familiar as I peeked out the windows on the other side of the house but still nothing but trees lined outside.

He grabbed my coat from the rack and handed it to me, so

I put it on, not moving my eyes from him. He opened the door and there was a car inside of a garage. He motioned for me to go ahead so I walked to the passenger side and got in. Once he was in and we both had our seatbelts on, he cranked the car and pushed a button to raise the garage door then pushed it again once we pulled out to close it.

Chapter 30

As I focused to keep my breathing under control, I tried to gather details of the outside of the house and pay attention to the ride back. I tried to notice any detail I could and to remember turns, but my brain was still feeling foggy, and my erratic breathing wasn't helping it clear. My childhood home wasn't terribly far from Aunt Rose's but the quickest way to get there was the highway. I wasn't familiar with the country road we were on.

I was taking in everything I could, trying to make a note of how to get back to that house when he spoke up, "You can keep tabs all you want. I wasn't kidding. Once we get the stone, you'll never see us again. We won't be back at that house, and I won't be in this car. But I applaud your efforts."

I rolled my eyes and turned back to the window. Even if he was right, I needed to know for myself where I had been. And down the road it may be useful. He just wanted me to be uncomfortable. We drove a long time with no landmarks around, just a lot of two-lane roads and trees.

The silence was unnerving, so I broke it. "So, what's your big plan? Do you really think he's going to just hand it to me with you standing there?"

The man tipped his head to the side with a silly grin. "No, I won't be with you. He'll give it to you if you're alone. And I know you won't try anything funny because of your aunt. When we get closer, I'll tell you the specifics."

He had already shot down any ideas I could come up with

to get away as soon as he reminded me that woman was slinking around the shop. I sucked in a deep breath and blew it out with puffed cheeks.

"So, you're going to take the stone and go live happily ever after with your lady friend? You don't think the police will catch up to you?" I asked with a raised eyebrow.

"Vivian, I thought we had a deal? But if you want to try to call the police that's fine. But don't leave out the part where your family stole that stone and your aunt has been practicing witchcraft in her cellar," he said plainly as he kept his eyes on the road.

"You don't know what she does," I snapped. "And even if she did, there's no crime against it, this is the twenty-first century not medieval times. So, who cares? And you have no proof that the stone was yours or *you* would have gone to the police," I said then turned to look out the window.

"We'll have to agree to disagree. But, while it may not be a crime to practice witchcraft, it sure could ruin someone's reputation, being a small southern town and all," he calmly replied.

Several minutes went by silent again then finally I had to ask something I had wondered since I started piecing everything together. "Why did you kill my parents?"

He seemed surprised at this question, but he did answer. "Well, you know what they say, there's three sides to every story. They can't tell theirs; I could tell you mine, but you won't believe me, and then there is how the outside would see it. But I will say I *didn't* kill them even though that won't change anything."

I glared back at him. "You're right, I don't believe you."

He shrugged and drove on.

"Do you know what will happen to me? When I give you

the stone?" I needed to know.

"Do you always ask this many questions?" He chuckled. He glanced at me sideways quickly then turned back to the road, shifting in his seat. "No, I don't know exactly what will happen to you. I do believe that our hex will be lifted and that's why we need it back."

My head flinched in a double-take.

"Yeah, your aunt didn't tell you about that, did she? Her little protection spell for you put a curse on Aideen."

I looked away for a moment but then spoke again, "Well, I'm not sure I feel sorry for her. She apparently ruined *several* of my lives. And if it weren't for her, my parents would be alive."

He kept his eyes on the road. "She may have acted out of anger, but your boyfriend is the one who started this all, so if you want to be mad, be mad at him."

"Ha! So, you're saying since he gave me the gemstone that she wanted, it's really all his fault. You're right. It's totally fine she cursed me because she didn't get her gemstone; she was just righting a wrong. I will gladly hand over the stone so *she* can make it better for *her*."

He chuckled again but before he could say anything else, I did. "This conversation is over. When we get close enough just tell me what I'm supposed to do so I can get you both out of my life...this one anyway." He nodded his head and kept driving.

After a while of riding, he finally cleared his throat, "I'm going to park up ahead and you'll get out and walk down the sidewalk. The car will be out of sight, but I'll be able to see, and you only have a few minutes. He said he'll be in front of the church by the old oak tree. Just get it from him and come back."

I rolled my eyes. "You don't think he's going to have anything to say or questions? How can you expect me to do this quickly without raising suspicion?"

He nodded. "It's difficult, yes, but I have faith you can do it. The walk will take two minutes and I will give you six minutes to chat, then two minutes back. Once you pass it along, you can go."

I was getting frustrated with his basic answers. "How do I know that woman won't harm my aunt? How do I know you'll keep your word?"

He tipped his head to the side and put his palms up. "You don't, you just have to hope I'm telling the truth. But the other option is you know for sure she will. So, what do you say, can we make a deal?"

I felt sick to my stomach. *What was I thinking?* I should have done so many things differently. But I couldn't turn back now. I had no phone and the interaction I was about to have with Jake would probably drive him away again.

I was familiar with the area we were driving into, but it was still a few miles from the square and, of course, nobody would likely be in the church this time of day in the middle of the week. If this man didn't communicate with the woman again in the timeframe he provided to her, she would go after Aunt Rose. Once he was gone, if he did in fact go quietly, it would be a while before I could find a phone to use to even call to check on her, much less save her. But like he said, I knew for sure what would happen if I didn't cooperate. She was all I had left, so I had to take the chance to save her.

"Fine. Deal." I would've spat the words at him, but my mouth had gone bone dry again. We drove another couple of minutes before he finally pulled off to the sidewalk to park.

"Okay, remember, two minutes down, six to get it, two back. Once you give it to me, I'll call Aideen and then drive away. I'm sure you can find your way back to the square."

I knew the answer but had still had to ask, "What about

my phone?"

He smiled and said, "Report it lost or stolen when you get home, and they'll replace it. But I'll toss it eventually. I can't very well give it to you when I drive off, you understand." He waved his hand through the air. I glared at him one more time with tight lips then finally decided it was time to get out of the car.

The frigid air smacked me in the face as soon as I opened the door. I walked briskly mostly to keep my nerves from paralyzing me. I reached into my pockets and found my keys but no gloves. Rage filled me. That jerk took my gloves, and it was freezing outside. All he had to do was put them back in the pockets. I put my hood up and shoved my hands back into my pockets and picked up the pace.

I looked up and glanced around for Jake. I saw him leaning against the tree across from the church. I had to cross the street to get to the tree so when I came to the intersection I looked around and didn't see anyone or any cars, so I walked diagonally across. As I began approaching Jake it occurred to me, I had no phone and no watch. Panic rose within me because I needed to get the gemstone and get back in approximately eight minutes if he was right about the timing of the walk, but I had no way to time myself. *He really was a jerk.* He had to know he had my only timekeeper in his pocket. I decided I'd keep it short and simple and just try to get away with the gemstone as fast as I could.

Jake saw me coming so he pushed off the tree, facing me. He had the backpack in his hands, holding it in front of him with both hands. Even far away, I could see the tension in his jaw. I stopped a few feet away from him. I stood for a moment looking at my feet, not sure what to do or say. Normally when I saw him, he rushed to embrace me or kiss me, but now we both stood there like statues. I knew time was ticking so I had to muster up something.

Finally, I choked out, "I appreciate you bringing this. I

thought it was best I didn't go to your apartment. So, I guess I'll just take it and go."

I reached my hand out and he took a few steps toward me. "Vivian, I know. And it's gonna be okay."

"What do you mean, I just need it back. And you don't owe me anything, I get it."

I reached my hand out again and he started to slowly pass it to me, but he looked at me, his blue eyes searing into mine. "I know you didn't ask for this. I know you didn't ask to meet me here. So, it's okay. You don't have to be afraid."

He had figured this out.

I started to shake at the idea that I didn't have to pretend. "But they'll hurt Aunt Rose, Jake. Just give me the bag and we can talk later. You can even wait for me here but just give it to me, please." Tears formed in my eyes, and it seemed like I was looking through a kaleidoscope. I was trying hard to fight them back and stay calm so I could just finish this. I reached my shaky hand out again, this time leaning more to grab it from him.

He stepped closer again. "Vivian, listen to me, Johnny's in your aunt's shop right now. The gemstone isn't in the bag. You need to quickly take this back, give it to them, then move away as fast as you can. Once you're out of sight I'll let Johnny know and he'll sneak her out of the back of the shop, and I'll be following whoever brought you out here. You run to the market and your aunt will be in the café there."

I was trying hard to not sob but the tears were still squeezing from the corner of my eyes and my breath jumped in my chest. "Jake I'm really scared and if I don't hurry, he's going to know something's wrong and he'll tell that woman. Johnny and Aunt Rose won't be able to get away."

Jake nodded and gave me the bag but grabbed my arm as he let go of the strap. His face was inches from mine.

"I told you I won't let anything happen to either of you and I meant it. I love you, Vivian, now go." My breathing stopped. He never said that before and now he was professing his love, *after he ran out this morning*? This jolted me so hard I stopped crying for a moment.

I was still stunned and frozen, but Jake pushed me. "Go, and remember, run that way towards the square and go to the market." He motioned with one hand while pressing my shoulder with the other. "I'll find you soon."

With a nod, I turned to cross the street back to the sidewalk. I started running back to the car, wiping my face as I went. The shock of what he said left and the fear was rushing back along with the tears that burned as they ran down my freezing cheeks. I had no idea how much time had passed and only hoped the car was still there. When Jake said he loved me, it seemed as if time stopped altogether. Relief filled me once I saw the car and the man was still inside with it running.

I walked to the passenger side door and opened it, waving the bag but holding it close to me. "Here it is, now call her."

He took his phone out and started to dial. My heart was pounding in my chest and despite the cold, my hands were sweating. My only option was to trust what Jake said. I knew he would open the bag soon. I had to make a run for it now. He was looking down at the phone, so I tossed the bag into the backseat and then sprinted between the old buildings down the alley, hoping it was the right way.

I hadn't been through all the streets in this area and got turned around easily in alleyways. He yelled after me briefly, but he was in a predicament as well and knew he had to get out of there and couldn't leave the bag or car just sitting there. The car wouldn't fit down the old, crowded street I was running down. Knowing this, I kept running as fast as my legs would take me. The freezing air was beating on my face, forcing tears out of the corners of my eyes, and hurting my lungs, but I kept going. My hood wouldn't stay up, so my ears went numb. I couldn't stop or look back, I had to keep going. My hands were purple as they pumped up and down beside me. I couldn't feel my fingertips, but I couldn't focus on that, I had to keep going.

After running what felt like a marathon, I finally saw the outskirts of the square and the market was just a street over. The sight gave me a second wind and I ran faster, struggling to get a good breath in. The air was so cold, making my chest burn. It must have been the afternoon because the restaurants weren't full, and the sidewalks only had a few people going in and out of shops.

I finally arrived at the market and slowed my pace but went to the corner and leaned out of the way to throw up. Between not being able to breath and running so hard for so long I had made myself sick. I heard a few women make some snarky remarks about how I must have overdone brunch that day. I leaned back up and glanced around making sure I didn't see the man or the redhead. Still struggling to catch my breath, I wanted to get inside away from roaming eyes, so I walked through the front into the market.

The café was off to the side with quaint little round tables scattered around. I was still breathing heavily but trying not to be obvious, so I walked slowly, breathing through my nose so it wouldn't be as loud. The adrenaline was waning, and my body was starting to ache.

I got to the edge of the café and only two tables were occupied, one was Aunt Rose. Tears filled my eyes as I approached her, and a lump filled my throat. *She was okay.* When she saw me, she stood up. She smiled, but as I got closer her brows pinched together and his lips turned down at the edges. As I made it to her, she put her arms out and I yanked her close to me, digging my face into her shoulder. She held me just as tight as I held her. I was crying but her coat muffled the sounds, and she petted my head, shushing quietly into my ear.

I calmed down enough to pull away and look at her. "You're okay? Nobody hurt you?"

She nodded her head and smiled, still grasping my shoulders. "A nice young man came by and chatted for a few minutes. Jake texted me that if he told me to go with him that I needed to just go. A while ago, the boy got a message and told me he was leaving and to meet him at the back of the shop. So, I snuck out the back. What the hell is happening?"

I hugged her again and let out a sigh. "Too much to tell you here, but in a nutshell those people tried to get the gemstone today. But we're okay and that's what matters right now." I grabbed her again, hugging her tight, but started to have thoughts creep into my head. We weren't safe at our house now. We probably weren't safe at the shop. I don't even know if it was safe to drive our car. For now, all we had was this café, and eventually it wouldn't be safe, either. She pulled away and told me to sit and she'd grab me a drink.

I sat and watched as she walked to the counter and ordered, my eyes periodically darting around to be sure those people hadn't found us. The employee quickly handed her a cup and smiled at her.

She brought the cup back and passed it to me as she sat. "That nice young man told them to give me whatever I wanted. Your cheeks are beet red; you need something warm."

I sipped from the cup, and it was sweet, flavored coffee with more creamer than anything and it was delicious, not to mention hot. As I was getting halfway down the cup, I looked up and saw a man walking toward us and my pulse sped up, but Aunt Rose smiled at him. He was tall but lanky with long black hair pulled into a ponytail at his neck neatly. He had dark-colored eyes, but they were bright and inviting and he had a very olive complexion with prominent features.

"Hey, you made it. I'm Johnny, you must be Vivian. Jake wanted me to let you know he's on the way." He reached his hand out, so I shook it. "Whoa, your hands are freezing. Wrap them around your coffee cup, it'll help warm them up. But you ladies just sit here. Jake will be here soon." He then nodded as southern gentlemen did as an exit gesture and walked away.

"That is the nice young man who whisked me away. Think he's into cougars?" Aunt Rose asked, and I wasn't sure if she was joking. I laughed and let out a sigh of relief.

Only a few minutes passed when I looked over and saw Jake walking toward us. When he saw me, he picked up his pace. My aunt and I both stood as he approached. He grabbed Aunt Rose's hands and asked if she was alright.

"Oh, yes, dear, your friend was lovely," she said with a smirk on her face. I felt a small blush rising to my cheeks because of her remarks. He chuckled at her and squeezed her hands before letting them go.

He then turned to me and grabbed one of my hands and electricity shot up to my chest, but the knots were back in my stomach.

"We need to go lock up the shop then grab some clothes from your house. You two can't be there right now." He slowly released my hand after looking down at it.

I nodded in agreement, and I saw Aunt Rose open her mouth, ready to protest, but I shook my head at her, and she backed down. Jake walked us out to his car and quickly drove to the shop. All of us got out and went inside. Someone had turned the sign off.

"A regular probably came in and did this once they realized nobody was here. I just need to make a sign and then we can go," Aunt Rose said shakily. She fumbled around for paper and a pen. Jake walked around nervously checking to be sure nobody was there now. He also found the line in the back had been cut to the video feed. Aunt Rose taped a sign on the door from the inside then we all left after making sure the door was locked.

We arrived at our house, locking the door behind us. Jake sent us both upstairs and said he would watch the doors. I went to my room and found my old duffle bag big enough for a few outfits and started tossing things in, including my journal. I grabbed a few things from the bathroom and yelled to Aunt Rose that I got her toothbrush and bath stuff. I was finishing up in the bathroom and Aunt Rose poked her head in to say she was packed up. We both walked downstairs and headed to the kitchen.

We were about to rush out the front door when Aunt Rose stopped. "Wait, I need something from the cellar, I'll be right back." Jake and I stood there awkwardly while we waited on her. I could hear her get to the bottom step and then her footsteps became faint.

I didn't know what to say or do. Last time Jake and I stood in the kitchen he had gotten upset and left. But then he said he loved me this afternoon. Maybe he said that to make me feel better about what was happening. But as I stood there, I could feel energy radiating from him, I just couldn't tell if it was good or bad.

I was trying to gain the courage to say something, anything, but then I heard Aunt Rose coming back up the stairs. She was carrying a tote bag made up of old cloth pieces stitched together and it was zipped.

"I'm ready now," she exclaimed.

Jake opened the door and then locked it on his way out. We tossed our things into the back with Aunt Rose and headed out.

It was still daylight out and we headed toward the highway. The car was quiet, and I still wasn't sure if I should speak.

"So, where are we going?" Aunt Rose asked.

I gasped like I couldn't believe she asked, but honestly, I was glad she had. I wanted to know as well, and it broke the silence in the car.

In true Jake fashion he smiled at her in the rearview and answered, "We're headed to the coast. We have a family house out there and leave it to your attorney father to have it untraceable. We'll be safe there until we sort this out."

Aunt Rose nodded, considering, then asked, "Can we get some food before we really hit the road? I'm famished. I didn't eat then got rushed away. All this excitement has me starving."

Jake nodded his head and once we got closer to the highway, he pulled into a fast-food drive-thru and ordered some food for us.

We immediately left and got on the highway going south. I was hungrier than I realized and quickly scarfed down my chicken sandwich and fries. Aunt Rose finished not long after I did. Jake took bites occasionally while also navigating us safely down HWY 75. It was getting close to rush hour and traffic was picking up, but he eventually got us into the HOV lane, and we moved at a slow but steady pace.

I put my trash in the bag and took another sip from my drink. When I put my cup but in the cupholder, Jake reached over and grabbed my hand. There it was...the electricity running through me again. I looked over and he smiled, untying the knots in my stomach. I heard Aunt Rose in the back shifting around to get comfortable to have a nap. With Jake's touch and a full belly, I felt safe and content. I leaned my head on the corner of the seat and the door and let my eyes close.

Chapter 31

I was wearing a heavy and beautiful gown with a huge petticoat. It was a cream color with pink embroidered flowers scattered all over the skirt and a pink bodice. But it was stained at the bottom and felt like I was carrying bricks. My hair had been piled up on my head but was coming loose around my face. My cheeks were pink, and my eyes were red.

I was running fast down a dirt road between a line of trees. It was dark with only a hint of glow from the moon passing through the trees to light the way. I felt someone behind me, but I never looked back, I just kept running. My heart was racing, and I was struggling to breathe. Sweat was pouring down my face, but I felt cold.

There were footsteps behind me, and they were catching up to me fast. I tried to run faster, but the dress was so heavy and the boots I had on were pinching my feet. Someone's hand grazed my dress, so I tried to run faster. I felt a tug; they had finally caught up to me. I began to lose my footing...

Jake shook me gently on my shoulder. I opened my eyes and scooted up in my seat, looking out the window. It was dark out but there were beautiful holiday lights on every streetlamp.

I kept looking around and nothing was familiar. "Where are we?"

He put his hand back on the wheel as he was getting ready to turn. "Well right now we are driving through Savannah but heading to my dad's house on Wilmington Island. It's not much further and I thought you may want to see the city. They always do it up for the holidays."

It was beautiful. The roads were cobblestone, and the buildings were all weathered and aged but still just as beautiful as they must have been when they went up. Huge live oak trees lined the side streets with Spanish Moss draping over either side of the road, creating a magical tunnel to drive through.

I hadn't traveled much even though my parents did constantly. They had always traveled for work so it wasn't like I could tag along. I hadn't lived far from here but just never came.

He turned again and was slowing as he pointed with one hand. "See that bench, that's the one from Forrest Gump." I had seen that movie so many times and was awestruck that one of my favorite actors of all time had been sitting there.

We then drove past a large, pink house with giant white columns surrounding the door, but it seemed busy, so I turned and asked, "What's that?"

Jake smiled and said, "The Olde Pink House."

"Yeah, what is it?"

He laughed a little but replied kindly, "It's called The Olde Pink House. It's a famous restaurant. I'll take you soon." I felt dense, but what a simple name for such an extraordinary building. There were many other breathtaking structures and homes as we drove through. It was obvious he was taking the scenic route for me to see. It was spectacular and sparkling with all the lights. "Alright, I promise to bring you back soon, but let's get to the island and let you both rest," he said as he squeezed my hand.

I nodded in agreement. I was still unsure where we stood but he kept grabbing my hand. *How could this be so comforting and maddening at the same time?*

Even though I napped for several hours, I was still

tired. Between last night's cry, this morning's drugging and kidnapping, the tense meeting in the park for the gemstone, then the brisk five-mile run, I could probably sleep for three days and still not be myself.

Jake stopped on the outside of town at a fast-food place and got some more food. "The house has been empty for months so we need something, but we'll get real groceries tomorrow."

He handed me the food but said it was just a short drive to the house and I wasn't starving so I didn't sneak any bites. Aunt Rose was still snoozing in the backseat.

We finally drove over a bridge and were plunged into darkness with fewer streetlights and buildings. Only a short drive more and we were turning onto an old dirt road lined with more huge live oaks. The darkness surrounding us, and the glow of the headlights made it look like a scene from a scary movie.

As I glanced around, I had an episode of deja vu. It was an unsettling feeling, but I was exhausted. The ride wasn't so smooth anymore on the dirt road and I could hear Aunt Rose shuffling in the back seat. I turned and smiled at her.

"Are we there yet?" She asked. I rolled my eyes but smiled at her.

"Yes ma'am, this is it. The house sits off the main road," Jake told her.

Suddenly we were pulling up to a huge house. It was straight out of a movie.

It was a grand white home with giant white columns the height of the house across the whole front porch. Green shutters surrounded large windows throughout the front and in the center were tall, green French Doors with etched glass windows on either side, which you arrived at by climbing a short but ornate white stone staircase that started wide at the bottom and became slightly narrower at the top. Evergreen shrubs lined the porch across both sides meeting at the stairs. Once Jake turned the headlights off it was eerily dark. He climbed out and opened our doors then grabbed our bags once we stepped out.

He handed me a flashlight. "Steer the way. And I'll need you to shine that on the door once we get up there or we'll be sitting out here all night." We walked up to the house, and I slowly went up the steps. It was even larger when you got up to it. I must have stopped completely because Jake started calling for me. I jerked my head and trotted up the rest of the stairs, shining the light on the doorknob for him. The key was sticky, but he finally jiggled it and got it opened.

It was dark, cool, and silent inside except for the flashlight and the noise we were making shuffling around. Jake walked a few steps away and suddenly there were lights on. A large staircase appeared in front of me and rooms to either side of it. At first glance both looked like a parlor or sitting area.

Aunt Rose was not shy and started to wander. "Viv, you've got to see this!"

I walked to the room on the left and it had a desk once you turned the corner, and a huge bookshelf lined the back wall. There were leather wingback chairs in front of the desk as well as in various corners of the room. Very upscale furnishings, mostly Mahogany.

Jake came up behind us. "Dad's study. The living room is across the way."

We started to walk toward the other room but once we were back near the stairs and the front door he pointed behind the stairs. "Down that way is the kitchen and dining room and the bedrooms are upstairs."

Aunt Rose had an important question. "Dear, where are all the bathrooms? I'm an old lady." Jake chuckled and led her down past the staircase then walked back to the foyer.

"There are more bathrooms upstairs if you need to go."

I shook my head, I could wait a few minutes and wanted to look around. I went to the living room and walked around. Older furniture but all very well kept. A large area rug in the middle of the floor. Quaint little side tables next to the burgundy sofa and between two cream colored Queen Ann chairs lined with a deep red trim. A large stone fireplace was off to the side. I heard Aunt Rose come out of the bathroom, but I heard footsteps go opposite of where I was, so I went to find her.

I turned the corner and walked down the hall and followed the light. There was a large, bright kitchen with an island in the middle. Aunt Rose opened the built-in stainless-steel fridge and as Jake said, it was empty. Not even a box of baking soda. Aunt Rose kept looking around, opening cabinets.

"Coffee! At least we can have coffee!" She practically yelled. I walked over and grabbed the container down. It was sealed, so hopefully it was still good. And next to it was powdered creamer. *I had creamer.* I turned and walked across the hall and found the light switch.

There was a long, Mahogany table with at least twenty chairs. On the wall was a large matching buffet table and everything was elegantly detailed. Beautiful silver candleholders with long, white tapers. Ornate silver serving dishes laid out. Plants in all corners, likely fake since nobody has been here to water them.

Aunt Rose walked in and said, "Wow! Look at this!" Then she went over to the plant closest to us, "Viv, these are real."

I walked over and felt the leaves then touched the top of the soil. "It's moist."

I was starting to get nervous, and Jake walked in. "There you are. I went to check all the doors and couldn't find you."

I immediately told him, "These are moist, someone has been here recently."

He nodded. "Yeah, we have a cleaning crew that still comes once or twice a week to make sure everything is in working order, flush the toilets to keep the plumbing moving, that sort of thing."

That made sense. Of course, there was a cleaning crew. This house was too big for one person to clean.

"You both need to rest. Let's eat then I'll show you upstairs to the bedrooms," he said as he placed the food on the table. We all sat at the end of the table close together. We ate quietly. It had been such a strange day that ended with an unexpected road trip.

We finished up and Jake quickly stood and grabbed up the trash and took it to the kitchen. Aunt Rose and I stood, waiting in the hall after turning the dining room light off. He came around the corner and told us to follow him up.

At the foot of the stairs, he flipped a switch to light them and the landing at the top up. He then went to turn the lights off to the area where we stood then he motioned for us. He first took a turn to the right and walked a few doors down then waved to Aunt Rose to enter a room after he reached in and turned the light on. She walked in and I looked in behind them. Her bags were on the bed. It was another elegantly decorated room. The bed was large, probably a queen, with tall bedposts and dainty white chenille blankets and shams. Still all dark wood furniture. There was a large dresser and a nightstand on either side of the bed with an antique gold lamp on each one. There was also a small table with a chair near one of the windows.

"I hope this suits you. There's a bathroom right outside your door." He motioned to the bathroom to my right.

"This is wonderful dear and thank you for bringing my

things up. I'm sure you know I have loads of questions, but I need some rest. We can all catch up tomorrow," she said as she held onto his arms like a mini embrace. He leaned down and kissed her on the cheek. I walked in and hugged her and assured her we would sort it all out tomorrow and to get some rest.

As we walked out, she shut the door, the light still glowing under the door. I followed Jake down an exceptionally long hall, so long that he had to turn off the stair light and turn on another leading us the rest of the way. He finally stepped to the side of a door and put his arm out to signal me to go inside. I reached inside the door and found the light switch. Once the lights turned on, I was again awestruck.

This room was like the other but much larger and the bed must have been a king size, but still had the tall bedposts. It also had chenille blankets and shams, but these were a soft shade of pink. Another large dresser. There was a table just a bit larger than the one in the other room and a Queen Ann chair on either side. There was a cream-colored bench at the end of the bed where my duffle bag sat. I saw two separate doors inside, so I went to open them. One turned out to be a walk-in closet and the other led to a bathroom with a huge, clawed tub and old pedestal sink. There was a shower head at the knobs of the tub that appeared to detach or lift depending on what you pleased. Shiny white tiles lined the floor. It was like standing inside a magazine.

I was so taken aback of the beauty and grandeur of the home that I almost forgot what happened today, until I turned and saw Jake standing there watching me. His jaw was clenched as I could see from the muscle protruding by his ears. He had his hands behind his back.

I wasn't sure what to say or do so I stood there trying to come up with something sensical to say but he broke the silence first. "I can sleep in the room next to this, if you like."

I didn't like that idea at all but wasn't sure what he was

feeling. "Is that what you want to do?"

His head dropped briefly, then it began to shake. "No, but I wasn't sure you wanted me in here with you after, well..."

I wasn't sure if he meant when he ran out this morning or when he said he loved me.

"Jake, listen," I started to say, but then he cut in.

"Vivian, let me speak first. I need to apologize. I shouldn't have taken off that way this morning. I just wasn't sure how to take that info and acted like a coward. You didn't deserve that."

I walked to him and placed my hands on his chest.

He continued without looking up at me. "If I hadn't left that way, none of this would have happened. I could never forgive myself if something happened to you and I let you down." His lip was quivering, and his eyes were getting red but no tears. I was looking up at him, but he wouldn't make eye contact with me.

"I...when you told me what your aunt told you it all hit me. This is all *my* fault. Maybe not now, but if me back then hadn't given you that gemstone to begin with none of this would have happened." He began to get louder, and he pumped his hand with every phrase. "It's my fault you're cursed, it's my fault your parents are dead, it's my fault there are strange people after you now. I just don't know how to carry that guilt, and I'm so sorry." His voice switched to absolute. He finally looked into my eyes. "But I do know one thing, I love you, Vivian. And if you don't love me, that's okay. I'll still never let anything happen to you." His lip was quivering the whole time he spoke and the more he said, tears filled my eyes as the words cut into my heart.

My voice was shaky, but I couldn't stay quiet any longer. I reached my hand to his face. "Jake, I love you. And I don't blame you for this. I thought you left because you didn't feel that way about me, knowing about the curse."

He put his hand under my chin to make sure I was looking back into his darkened eyes. "Vivian no, I know what I feel for you is real. I don't care about any stone or curse. I knew the moment I saw you; it was you." He leaned down slowly like he wasn't sure I would allow him, but when I leaned my head up and closed my eyes, he kissed me, and we wrapped our arms around each other. Tears were flowing down my face and my whole body felt supercharged.

Jake stopped for a moment and wiped the tears off my face then had his arms back around me but pressed his forehead to mine and breathily said, "Vivian, I need you, I want you, so badly it feels like my heart is breaking."

I whispered to him, "Then take me."

He pressed his lips to mine, and we kissed hard, like we hadn't seen each other in years. He held me tight, but we did a little dance toward the door, never breaking our kiss, and he kicked it closed then reached over to turn the light off. We continued our dance toward the bed. There was a sliver of light shining in still from the bathroom. As we continued slowly making our way to the bed, he pulled my hair away from my neck and started kissing me there, making my legs quiver.

We finally made it to the bed but didn't immediately sit or lay down. We began kissing again and were running our hands all over each other, his skin warm and muscles taught under my touch, his big hands exploring every inch of my skin. I pulled his shirt up over his head and tossed it to the side then ran my hands over his chest and planted kisses on it before he pulled my shirt up over my head. We both reached down to unbutton each other's jeans and push them down over each other's hips and shimmied our legs out. I tugged at the band of his boxer-briefs, and he pushed them off. He reached down and pulled my underwear down as I unclasped my bra, all the while intensely kissing.

Once we had successfully disrobed each other, he reached under me and lifted me up before gently laying me down on the bed. Once he had, he quickly slipped a hand down between my legs while still holding me from behind with the other. I let out a small sound as I felt his large fingers sliding up and down the wet folds and he began gently biting my nipple, occasionally letting his tongue roll over it. He pushed a finger inside and I let out another small sound before he found my lips again and thrusted his tongue deep in my mouth. All my senses were already exploding and all I could do was succumb to him.

I reached my arms around his back then ran my hands down over his ass, pulling him up and closer. His weight blanketed me, and my skin tingled against his. I could feel his hard shaft between my legs; he wasn't inside yet, but instead stroking himself up and down the slickness he created. I pulled him to me harder, desperate for our bodies to fully connect, and finally he let himself enter. He pushed in hard but once his hips had melted to my core, he stopped and lingered. I could feel myself tense around him as our bodies were still, but we were kissing even harder.

I felt like I was going to fall apart if he didn't move, so I lightly said his name, hoping he would give in to me. "Jake."

Slowly, his hips began to move. One hand cupped my breast and the other slid under my waist. I wrapped my legs around him and moved with him. We had a slow, steady rhythm, allowing us to completely feel the pleasure of each other. I ran my hands up his back, over his chest, and finally grabbed his face. We stared into each other's eyes as we continued for a couple of minutes. Eventually, I pulled him down to me and we began kissing. As the kissing became more intense, so did the thrusts. Suddenly, I was on the verge.

My breathing was labored, and I reached my hands down his back and pulled him in close. He could tell I was ready, so he shifted my hips under me and made deep thrusts inside. My body went tense, my legs were holding him tight, the waves of pleasure were flowing through my whole body, and I finally let out a moan at the same time he did. Static filled my eyes as my body pulsated around him.

Once he stopped, he gently lay over me, careful to not crush me with his weight, but skin to skin. I ran my fingers through his hair, and he wrapped his arms around me. We lay there for a while when I finally started to shift, but he wrapped his arms tighter around me.

I chuckled softly, but he quietly said, "I don't want to let go. Ever." So, I lay there under him a while longer with his warm weight hanging over me. I didn't want him to let go, either. As our blood stopped rushing quickly through us, we both began to feel the cold. I still didn't want him to let go, but we may freeze if he didn't.

"Jake, is the heat on? It's suddenly really cold," I said lightly.

He rubbed his face between my breasts, his beard rough against my skin, then looked up at me. "I suppose I need to go fix that. You don't go anywhere." He jumped up and threw his boxer-briefs on and quietly opened the door and walked down the hall. I ran to the bathroom quickly and then darted back to bed but pulled the covers down and climbed under. The sheets were like ice, but I knew if we lay there a few minutes our body heat would eventually warm the bed. He came walking lightly back into the room and shut the door. It was dark besides a small glow from the moon outside since I had turned the bathroom light off when I was done.

He still found his way back to bed and climbed in then reached over and pulled me right up against him. I was laying with my face practically dug into his chest, letting him engulf me with his arms and I had tucked a leg between his. I was breathing his citrusy scent in and had one hand against his chest. The room was quiet, but I could hear the house settling and the old plumbing. It was such a stark contrast to how the day began.

"So," I couldn't help but ask, "how did you know I was in trouble earlier?"

He shifted a little. "You wouldn't have sent me the text I got. To be sure I replied that I loved you, but the text I got back said I love you, too, so I knew it wasn't you."

I thought for a second. "I hope your dad pays you well for your investigator skills."

He laughed. "Well, he did, but for now I took a little break."

I leaned up a little to see him, my eyes finally having adjusted to the dark. "What do you mean a break?"

He looked over and ran a hand under my jaw, caressing my cheek with his thumb. "Well, it won't be safe back at home for now. And I believe we may be able to find some help in Savannah. It's known for being haunted, but there's a lot of mystical things and people there, too. Maybe we can find a way to fix all of this. And I know it's safe here."

I thought for a second. "But Aunt Rose's shop, the house, we can't just abandon that. And you know she won't allow it."

He took a deep breath then said, "Well, I thought of that on the way to the market. So, when we got to your house Aunt Rose gave me her shop key and left it for Johnny. He said he could keep an eye on it, and I considered finding someone to run it, but it wouldn't be safe for anyone there now. I explained this to her, and she agreed, reluctantly."

"So, you figured this all out then. But if you don't have a job, how will you possibly take care of us?" I asked jokingly.

"Don't worry, I got it. I'm just glad I finally have you under the same roof; just wish you didn't have to get kidnapped to do it."

I laughed then lay back down on him and got comfortable in my little nook under his arm.

We lay quietly for a few minutes, then he spoke again, "Vivian, I promise, no matter how long it takes, I'll keep you safe and we will figure this out. I love you, now, then, and forever." I leaned up to kiss him.

"I love you, Jake. It's us forever." Then I lay back in my nook and we drifted off to sleep to prepare for the journey that lay ahead...

The End...For Now.

Acknowledgement

This story was by far the most difficult for me. I had a lot of help along the way in this labor of love.

First, even though this is a little out of her typical Contemporary Romance genre, I must give a huge shout out to Author Melinda Harris. She spent so much time allowing me to pick her brain, ask her lots of questions, and has provided cheers and encouragement to me on this wild journey into publishing. Her support has been moving to say the least. Buy all of her books! That's the best I can do to ever attempt to repay her for what she did for me. She was the first author that made me believe I could do this.

To my best friend, Tammy Bassett, what would I have done without her unwavering support and love? She is very biased, but she has blindly followed whatever I decide on and lends me her ear adn her shoulder anytime I need it. I love you to bits and pieces and you deserve to have your name in print!

To my readers, you all give me life! It was scary to put out my work, but your love, support, reviews, and messages make me want to write more words than my fingers can put out! I will strive to continue to provide good stories you can enjoy as long as you'll have me! You keep me in tears constantly, but I woudn't have it any other way! I sincerely love and appreciate each and every one of you! I hope you truly believe that!

Kate Prada and WL Brooks...I don't know what I'd do without you both and all the snickers! Love you both so much!

Mom and Dad, thank you for supporting me even though my content isn't suitable for everyone! You always told me I could be whatever I wanted, and you only make it easier by supporting me regardless of what that is!

I'd be remiss to not thank Author Rebecca Hefner. Her support and kindness will be treasured forever. You should also buy all of her books because they are amazing!

To those who helped me polish this madness...Jenn Thedford, Jenyfer Patton, Melinda Harris, Kate Prada, and those who wished to remain anonymous, I couldn't have done it without you! Seriously, it was a dumpster fire!

Lastly, to my love, in this life and any other, thank you for pushing me to follow my dreams. You are my rock and I couldn't do this life, or any other, without you.

About The Author

April D. Berry

April Berry is a romance author born and
raised in Georgia. She still resides there
with her husband, son, and daughter.
When she's not creating fun stories with
happy endings, she loves to bake, read, and
sneak off to her favorite winery with her
friends! She also loves snuggles with her
various fur babies and binge watching
series! Follow her here: https://linktr.ee/aprildberry

Books By This Author

Served: The Club Series Book 1

She tosses men away, he's a hothead that grew tired of trying. When he swoops in to rescue her, will they find each other?

26 year old Lucy loved her fun radio job, her cool apartment, her best friend, and a revolving door of men. She had big dreams to have her songs played on the radio, so she had no time for a serious relationship. She really just needed a warm body from time to time and had no problem dropping the men she always found herself involved with. Her favorite hangout always had music execs but they came for the bands who played. When she landed the lead singer gig for the house band at the club, she was one step closer to realizing her dream of becoming a professional songwriter.

Burly bartender Jason had the hots for Lucy, but she was too busy entertaining losers to notice him, even though he worked at the club she frequented. He gave up on her a while ago but couldn't help look. It was probably for the best, he had already been through a lot and didn't want to be another notch for her. But her curls and curves were not helping him move on.

But when Lucy found herself in a dangerous situation and Jason came to her aid, would she change her tune? Was there something there all along? Or would it turn out to be a huge mistake?

TW: SA, 18+

Stroked: The Club Series Book 2

Can a stroke of fate change two lives forever?

Amy thought she had it all. An amazing best friend, her dream job, and a never-ending supply of beautiful one-night-stands. No complications, no drama, and no questioning of her hard limits. Was she living her best life? Hell yeah, she was...until her best friend blindsided Amy by getting engaged and moving out. Then an exotic stranger leaves her awestruck, sending all her rules right out the window.

Working in a male-dominated field made giving up a personal life and hiding her true self under the guise of finding success easy for Valentina. She focused on getting her clients on to the scene, and not being seen. Her calculated meet ups and secret rendezvous allowed her to stay under the radar of her traditional parents. But when a chance encounter turns into something much more, will she be able to keep up the act?

When pasts are revealed and secrets are threatened, can their impenetrable walls be torn down, or will they find themselves unable to break through?

References of: Past SA, Car Accident, Adult Language, Adult Situations

Love, Again

Can there be love after loss...with a movie star?

Kate always had a sweet southern heart and lived the ultimate cliché of a happily ever after when she married her high school sweetheart and started a family where she grew up. But after tragedy left her widowed, she became a shell of a person, only holding it together for her son.

When Action Film Star, Boyd Love, returns to their shared hometown after more than ten years away, Kate is surprised to see him and can't believe he asked her to catch up while he's in town. After he learns she's single, he drops a long-kept secret on her, opening a door she thought was forever closed.

But can a small-town widow and an A-List celebrity make it work? Or will their opposite lifestyles, and the miles between them, be too big of a barrier?

**For mature eyes only
**Military Loss

Write Next Door

Can two perpetually single people find love?

Layla was determined to live her dream of being a famous author.Forty-two, happily single, and childless by choice, she was making a huge push to finally add an extra title to her name. Committed only to her work and to herself, she hardly had time for her beloved friends, let alone men.

After years on stage, Henry was enjoying his new career path as a voice over actor. He also enjoyed the ladies but his time acting jaded him on the idea of a relationship. But at forty-four, the revolving door of women was getting old.

When Layla gets an idea to have a hot man act out some short scenes from a book to help boost sales on social media, she turns to her friendly, and handsome, neighbor, Henry. He and Layla had a simple, fun, and strictly platonic relationship since she moved in three years ago, so he was more than willing to help.

Plus, he was an actor so it made perfect sense she would ask him.

But when the time comes, acting out a scene from a romance book stirs them both. Layla wondered, was he just that good an actor? Had Henry imagined something that wasn't there? They were friends, and neighbors, and so much could go wrong.

But what if it went right?

What if love was right next door?

before you go...

Reviews are so helpful for authors! Even if you can't leave a written review, the star ratings, which are anonymous, help us as well!

Also, grab a free romantic short from me at this link AND stay connected with me for upcoming releases and announcements!

https://dl.bookfunnel.com/fq0elyq1b4

THANK YOU SO MUCH!

Made in the USA
Middletown, DE
03 September 2024

60262150R00163